Forbidden,
Hidden,
Betrayed

Kayla Danoli

Copyright

Disclaimer

This novel is a work of fiction. All characters and events are the product of the imagination of the author. While some of the characters might remind you of people you know, they are fictitious and any resemblance to anyone living or dead is purely coincidental. Although some locations also may seem real and familiar, most places referred to in this work constitute a collage of places the author has known. But they are fictitious, and any resemblance to an existing location is coincidental.

Ravenshead Estate Family Tree

Introducing who's who from Ravenshead Estate in this story

Henry Finchley (D 1917) -M- Martha Winstanley
     Offspring = Jane Finchley (B 1899)

Henry Finchley --- – /– Erin (O'Malley) Wilson (widow)
     Offspring = Darcy Wilson (B 1912) (illegitimate)

Jane Finchley (1899–1967) – M – George Creighton
     Offspring = Amelia (Amy) Creighton (B 1936)

Amelia (Amy) Creighton (1936–2024) –/– William Tingwell
     Offspring = Gabrielle (Gabby) Creighton (B 1961)

Chapter 1

"Sophie, would you have a few minutes to talk to me about something you will probably find a bit strange? I apologise if I am intruding. I can talk to you at some other time if you would prefer."

I looked up at a familiar face I hadn't seen in some time, standing beside my table in the coffee shop on the High Street.

"Gabby… This is a surprise, and yes, I definitely have time to talk to you. Besides, you made it sound so intriguing, I couldn't say no. Pull up a chair and sit down."

A few minutes later, armed with a fresh coffee, I slid back onto my chair across the small table from Gabrielle Creighton.

"Right, now I am all set, and I don't have anything booked for the rest of the day. God, I haven't seen you since your mother's funeral, and that was a few years ago now. Anyway, it's great to catch up with you again. Now, what brings you to my table today?"

"At the risk of sounding as though I've lost the plot, I've come to engage your services. I want you to investigate something for me."

"I am a freelance journalist… well, more of a correspondent really, so what could you possibly want me to investigate? Is it a crime of some sort? Has there been a crime? Do you want me to do some form of exposé?"

"No. It's a personal matter, not something that will generate column inches for you, but I was hoping you might apply your investigative skills to it for me."

"As you don't have a husband, unless you've acquired one since your mother died…." Gabby shook her head. "Okay, so it can't be a problem with a wandering spouse that's bothering you. So, what is it? Drink some coffee, relax, and tell me all about it." She took a couple of sips of her coffee before speaking.

"No cheating husband or bothersome lover to report. It's not as simple as that. I'm here because I think a crime has been committed. Well, I think a crime might have been committed, but it was a long time ago."

"Right, let's start with some basic facts and see where it goes from there. Who was the supposed victim of this crime? You said it was a personal matter, so was it you?"

"Me? God, no. If it had been me, I would have spoken to you long ago. No, it happened – *if* it happened – long before I was born and involved my grandmother, Jane. Well, I think a crime might have been committed, but it would have been decades ago."

"Decades? Perhaps I should hear the whole story before I comment further. I should warn you, though, that it is likely to be difficult, if not impossible, for you to take any action after so long."

"That's not an issue. I never thought to take any action over it. I just want to know if a crime was committed. I want to know if what I *think* happened *did* happen, or whether the notion is no more than a child's overactive mind's reaction to something heard and overheard."

"Perhaps I should hear the whole story before commenting. Right, let's start with basic facts and see where that takes us. All the usual details, please: who, what, where, and approximately when. So far, it appears our starting point is with your grandmother. Tell me about her, or as much as you know and remember."

"As I said, it involved my grandmother, Jane. Before you ask, she is long dead. It happened – if it happened – before I was born. I was only a child when she died, and I suppose it's true to say I barely knew her, but I do remember she had little time for me, and that, somehow, she terrified me from the moment I first met her. I know that's not helpful."

"It's a good start, but… what about the crime?"

"Ah, yes, the crime… Well, I believe some of Jane's books were stolen."

"Stolen books. Really? Is that what this is all about? What…? Were they rare and valuable first editions of something?"

"No, not exactly."

"Okay, Gabby. Please tell me about this mysterious crime that may or may not have occurred. Once I know more about it, I will be able to tell you whether I can do this or not.

"Well, we are talking about legends, not about hard evidence. It's about things I was told and things I overheard. Some of it goes back to when I was a child. That will give you an idea of how long ago it was. In fact, it goes back to when my grandmother, Jane Finchley, was a teenager.

"Why have you brought your suspicions to me? Surely, if you think a crime has been committed, there are others you should tell about it."

"Yeah, I suppose it does seem a bit odd, but I remember all the work you did and everything you found out about Aunt Lillian and her family. I know she wasn't your aunt, but you still managed to find out everything that had been covered up for so long. I hoped you might consider doing much the same for me, only this time it's my grandmother's and not Aunt Lillian's life you would be investigating."

"Am I to understand we are going to be talking about her various writings and not actual books that were stolen?" Gabby sighed and nodded. "Right, tell me how and what you came to know about all this." Gabby sighed again before continuing.

"When I came back to Ravenshead with my mother, I was about four years old. One day, I overheard Mum and Jane talking. The bit of their conversation I heard stuck with me until after Jane died. That's when I thought it safe to ask Mum about what I'd heard. Previously, I didn't want it to be known that I'd eavesdropped on a discussion about Jane's father, Henry Finchley. To my young ears, the discussion did not paint him in a favourable light.

That was the start of it, but the subject of Jane's writing was revisited often, and again on a couple of her more lucid days before she died."

"So, somewhere, there should be a monumental stack of stories in exercise books or whatever. Why do you think they've been stolen?"

"You would expect so, wouldn't you? I believe Jane was more organised than that. According to Mum, at some point, Jane employed a typist to turn her handwritten documents into more professional-looking copies. Later, Jane and Mum were at a fete held on the grounds of a nearby manor house. I don't know when it was, but I remember other stories I'd heard at different times, and I realised it was quite some time before Jane died. Anyway, at the fete, Jane was drawn to a bookstall and looked through its books with a view to purchasing some. Long story short… When she flicked through one of the books, she realised it was one of her stories. A search of a couple of the stacks of books on the stall identified at least another handful of her manuscripts."

"Ah hah, it sounds like the typist's employment was about to end, although finding the books was not proof that the typist was responsible."

"Well, Sophie, you are right about the immediate outcome. Miss Parker, the typist, was instantly dismissed without a reference."

"Does anyone have any idea how much of Jane's work was pirated? And I suppose the other big question is: how well did those pirated works sell? If they proved popular reads, there could be considerable money involved in the crime. Perhaps you had better tell me about Jane before we go any further. Who was she, apart from being your grandmother, I mean?"

"Right… Grandma Jane was the daughter and only child of the Finchley family of Ravenshead Estate."

Gabby stared off into the distance for a few moments. I allowed her to organise her thoughts before nudging her to continue.

"So, Granny Jane Finchley came from a monied background?"

"Yeah, that probably describes her situation. She was brought up to be a lady. Family legend has it that her father held the view that she would marry the only son of a neighbouring major landowner. He wasn't happy that Jane shunned her position in regional society, and showed no interest in taking over running Ravenshead Estate … or in the boy nextdoor."

"A bumpy time ahead for everyone involved, by the sound of that."

"It gets worse. After Jane outgrew her nanny, a governess, Miss (Dorothy) Glover, was employed to 'finish Jane off', so to speak. Her task was to ensure Jane was well-versed in appropriate behaviour for someone of her standing while advancing Jane's skills in music, painting, embroidery, and her fluency in French. During that time, Jane developed a love of books and reading, and it appears she also developed a love of writing."

"Sounds like a standard upbringing for girls in a similar position to Jane's. What else can you tell me about Jane's early life?"

"From what I've been told, I think Jane was pretty much ignored by her parents during her younger years. Perhaps it might have been different had she been a boy. Who knows? In Jane's case, she was left in the hands of a nanny for her basic upbringing and education before being handed over to Miss Glover, the governess.

Simply put, legend has it that Henry became annoyed that his only child, Jane, was spending so much time in her room when he expected her to be helping him in his office and learning how to run the place. On one particular day, he is supposed to have shouted, 'Does that damned girl ever come out of her room?'. His wife, Martha, tried interceding on Jane's behalf by suggesting that Miss Glover was keeping Jane hard at her studies every day.

That wasn't good enough for Henry. He bounded upstairs, burst into Jane's room without bothering to knock, and demanded to know exactly what she was doing. Miss Glover, unaware of Henry's views regarding Jane's spending so much time in her room, rushed to praise Jane's ability as a writer of both prose and exceptionally fine poetry. It resulted in Henry's announcement that, henceforth, Jane was forbidden from wasting time in such pursuits and that she should spend time every day assisting him in his office. Miss Glover departed Ravenshead a couple of days later, and Jane's education was deemed completed."

"It must have made life interesting for Jane. I don't imagine she had produced too much work before Henry put a stop to it. Do you have any idea how much work might have been involved?"

"Oh, that wasn't the end of her writing. She just had to be more covert about it for the next few years while Henry was still alive. After that, she was free to do as she pleased. She remained a prolific writer right up until shortly before her death – or so I'm told."

"Does anyone have any idea how much of Jane's work was pirated? And I suppose the other big question is: how well did those pirated works sell? If they proved popular reads, there could be considerable money involved in the crime."

"No. Even my mother had no idea how much work was involved, or if it was all of it, and we don't know how much of the pirated work ended up for sale on the open market. Come to think of it, Mum only had Jane's word that the books she saw on the stall were Jane's manuscripts."

Although I knew Gabby was waiting for me to say something more, my mind was far too occupied with trying to take in all I'd been told. I needed to process that before asking for more information. I heard Gabby fidget on her chair and then clear her throat to grab my attention again before she continued.

"Sophie, I know this is not the kind of investigative work you do, and I do appreciate how confusing this story must be for you, but I don't know who else to turn to. I really want…. No, I *need* to get to the bottom of this family legend before I drop off the twig. It has eaten at me since I was a child. Although I now know more than I did then, I still don't know how much of the stories of Jane's writing and pirated books is true, and how much of it is the product of overactive creative minds.

At the very least, please consider accepting this investigation. I promise to be a model client, and always pay well and on time. And, if your investigation uncovers anything interesting, you have a story to use if you wish."

"The fact that it is not my usual type of investigation doesn't bother me. What does bother me is the lack of evidence to work with. All I have so far is hearsay. Do you have any ideas about where we might start to look for evidence to confirm that Jane ever wrote anything?" Gabby shook her head and looked downcast. "Right, then, Gabby, perhaps we had better return to Jane's story and the rest of your family's history."

"Do you think we might have another coffee before I tell you more about it?"

"How about we have an early lunch instead? And, over lunch, you can finish your story and tell me why you have come to me now about all this."

Chapter 2

Gabby had seemed to be struggling with the Ravenshead story until lunch intervened. Whether the food revitalised her or it was the break that revitalised her thinking was unclear, but she was eager to continue her story. I eased her into it again while a good portion of lunch remained on our plates.

"Jane's father, Henry, died when she was about 18 years old, and she inherited Ravenshead Estate."

"She wasn't yet 21, so how did that work out? I mean, Jane was still a minor and had no legal authority, although she then owned the property."

"I'm not sure how that happened, but I think her mother, Martha, was bitter that the property wasn't left to her. Henry was still a young man when he died. I suppose he anticipated dying as an elderly man when leaving everything to his 'heir apparent' would have been the logical thing to do."

"It must have been a difficult time for both Jane and her mother. Do you know how life was after that or how Jane managed to keep the place running?"

"Not much... But it seems Jane wasn't about to follow anyone else's plan for her life. Despite her mother's best efforts, Jane refused to become a debutante and take her place in regional society. She didn't marry the boy nextdoor and remained single until about age 26 – and until not long after her mother had passed away.

When she inherited the property after her father's death, Jane employed a manager, George Creighton, to oversee the estate's management on her behalf. Soon after her mother's death, Jane married her estate manager, although he was a fair bit older than her."

"A feisty young woman by the sounds of it. Despite the age difference, I'd like to think they settled down to a happy life on Ravenshead Estate after that."

"Yes, it would be nice to think so, but I don't know. The couple continued to live in the big house on Ravenshead. Their only child, my mother, Amelia (Amy), wasn't born until Jane was about 28, and no others followed. Then, George Creighton died from a fall from his horse. His only child, my mother, Amy, inherited Ravenshead and everything else. His wife, Jane, spent the rest of her life as a widow at Ravenshead Estate. She was only 35 when George died."

"Amy was a young child when she lost her father, George. Like her mother before her, she wasn't legally able to run the property, but Jane had been much older when she inherited the place. How did they manage Amy's inheritance? As her mother, did Jane run the place on behalf of her daughter?"

"She tried to. George's solicitor was aware of what was happening and appointed a manager when Jane appeared determined to take over the place despite the terms of George's will. The solicitor, appointed by George as his executor, maintained oversight of the running of the property and, I think, he managed the finances until Amy turned 21."

"While Amy and my Aunt Lillian were good friends, and I met her on a number of occasions at Lillian's home, I never got to know anything of your mother's life. I hope the relationship between Amy and Jane turned out better in their later life than the relationship between Jane and her mother."

"I wouldn't go so far as to say that. It's more like an example of history repeating itself. Although you might not realise it from the person you knew as my mother, Amy was something of a rebel and more than a bit like her mother before her. Things were never sweet between Amy and her mother.

As happened in the previous generation, Jane expected to inherit Ravenshead Estate after her husband died. However, shortly after Jane and George married, the landholders next door experienced financial difficulties during lean years. Jane and

George pooled their resources to buy most of the neighbouring property. Somehow, as part of that process, the title deed for the amalgamated property was put in George's name – with no mention of Jane. As a result, on George's death, under the terms of his will, my mother, Amy, inherited the property. Jane was angry that it didn't revert to her, as it had been her property to begin with. She refused to leave Ravenshead and demanded to be kept in the manner to which she was accustomed – and would have continued to enjoy had she inherited."

"Oh dear, that must have made life difficult."

"Yeah. Jane went out of her way to make life difficult for Amy. To prevent Jane's interference, Amy waited until after she was 21 before leasing out all the Ravenshead lands, except for a small area around the big house, and then escaped Ravenshead to create a new life for herself elsewhere.

"So, you weren't born at Ravenshead?"

"No, in western Queensland. My parents were never married, and their relationship ended when I was about 12 months old. Subsequently, my father died of some sort of aggressive cancer when I was about four years old. That's when Mum and I came back to Ravenshead. Again, history repeated itself."

"If the property was leased out and Amy was receiving an income from it, I'm surprised she elected to return to Ravenshead."

"Although I didn't know much about it at the time, the doctor and family friends had been telling Mum that her mother, Jane, was not well and was nearing the point when she would need a carer. The lease over Ravenshead lands had only a couple of months remaining. We returned and set up home at Ravenshead so Mum could care for Jane."

"I notice you still have your mother's maiden name as your surname."

"Mum was just as much a rebel as her mother was. My mother, Amy, had a long-standing relationship with my father, William Tingwell, but they never married. I was born when Mum was about 34 years old. Tingwell was gone from our lives about a year later. She claimed never to have heard from him again. Obviously, I don't have any memory of him, and there are no photos or anything else to help me know anything about him.

Then, when I was about four and Mum received word that Jane's health was failing, she returned to look after her. My father was dead by then."

"I see what you mean about history repeating."

"It was an interesting time. We were not allowed to live in the main part of the big house. Instead, we were allocated a small suite of rooms to live in. It originally was part of the servants' quarters. Mum was upset but chose not to make a fuss because of Jane's deteriorating condition. However, she decided not to care for Jane herself and instead hired a full-time nurse. For a while, Jane had good days followed by periods of bad days."

"That was a bit rich… given your mother actually owned the property and the house. How did that arrangement work out in the end?"

"Mum talked to grandma for a few minutes every day, but apart from the first couple of days after we arrived, I was not allowed anywhere near her. Mum and the nurse seemed to confer constantly about Jane's condition, and about 12 months later, it was agreed Jane should go into care."

"Well, at least you would have the run of the full house once Jane went into care."

"No, it didn't happen like that. We continued to live in that small suite of rooms. Even after I was sent to boarding school and then went on to university, Mum continued to live in that small apartment."

"So when did you return to Ravenshead?"

"I was working overseas when I received word that Mum had dementia, and it was worsening. I came home and moved into that small apartment, where I cared for her until she went into a nursing facility. Then I leased an apartment in town so I could visit her easily.

Before you ask, yes, I have inherited Ravenshead Estate, but only now have I moved back to Ravenshead… where I plan to remain."

"Do you have any ideas about where we might start to look for evidence to confirm that Jane ever wrote anything? Are you living at Ravenshead now?"

"Yes, I moved back on the weekend, but still in that same small suite of rooms Mum had. I will probably continue to live there. I can't see any point in opening up the rest of the big house for just me."

"What about Jane's rooms, and her office in particular? Have you searched those areas?

"Argh, no, I haven't. I'm not sure what rooms she used, and I can't quite bring myself to go anywhere beyond my apartment. There's something about the place that terrifies me. Don't look at me like that. I know it sounds stupid coming from an adult, but it is the truth."

"Right… I'm not making any promises, but here's what we are going to do. Starting tomorrow, I will begin investigating Jane's stolen manuscripts.

Our first step in this case is to establish that Jane was, in fact, a writer. Once I have some evidence of that, I should be able to map out how to proceed with the investigation. So, first, I come to Ravenshead to begin searching any of the rooms Jane might have used – and any others that look interesting. Do you have any problems with any of that?" Gabby shook her head. "Okay then, do you confirm that you have engaged me to undertake this investigation on your behalf?"

"Of course, I do. That's what I've been trying all morning to get you to agree to do. Do I need to sign a contract, a release form, or something? Is there something you need me to do to help you get started?"

"Not yet. Let's see where the preliminary search takes us before we worry about signing anything or assigning tasks to you. Now, as it is way past lunchtime, we can continue to sit here and have the staff glare at us, or we can adjourn until tomorrow."

I spent the rest of the afternoon typing up my file notes from this morning and trying to get my head around the main characters mentioned. It didn't take me long to realise I needed a visual reference, a Ravenshead Estate family tree to refer to as I worked my way through the jumble of names I had already encountered and others that might pop up in the future.

I arrived home a little earlier than usual, but a late night followed after I decided to research online anything and everything I could find on Jane (Finchley) Creighton.

Having nothing definite scheduled for today, it made sense to work from my home office. My first task for the day was to review all the material gathered during last night's research. As I discovered then, most mentions of the Finchley and Creighton names were of the social variety. They offered no insights into Jane's literary endeavours or much else about the family's affairs, but there was one item of interest. It was the last thing I came across before quitting my search last night.

There was an inquest into George Creighton's death, at which Jane was called to give evidence. According to the newspaper report of the inquest's proceedings, Jane's evidence, not surprisingly, only provided timings for the various events that led to the discovery of her husband's body. It appeared George had come off his horse. When the horse arrived home minus its rider, a search was mounted for George. It was a couple of days after George left the house before his body was found. Although there appeared to have been some suspicions concerning his injuries, the inquest found that George died by accidental death.

"Okay, so it was an accident… Nothing helpful there," I murmured as I finished reading the newspaper report, "…Or was there?"

While the inquest, as it was reported, appeared quite straightforward and contained no surprises, there was something about it niggled me. I read it all again. That third reading produced no new clues and served only to strengthen the niggles it generated. I set it aside and tried to focus on the only other item of interest from my research.

Jane's mother was Martha Winstanley, the eldest child of the Winstanley family that almost passed as royalty in Victoria. So it appears that Henry Finchley scored himself a well-heeled catch. As Henry appears to have had a much lesser background, I felt it fair to assume that whatever Martha brought with her made a significant contribution to Henry's rise in standing in the community.

"Interesting but of no consequence to my case," I confirmed for my muse. "Come on. Where to from here? A wee bit of inspiration would be useful," I added as I went to make yet another coffee.

I had nothing else to work with, so my investigation had now stalled before it even began. The big house on Ravenshead Estate was where I needed to be. I had no doubts about that, but what would I do there? I needed a list of what to search for and where to search within the house. At least that way, I'd be a little more focused when I finally went to the house. That then brought the big question front and centre: When am I going to gain entry to the house? Gabby didn't rush to extend an invitation, and she seems reticent about venturing into the house beyond her small apartment. Maybe a more direct approach is required. I flicked through the contacts on my phone.

"Gabby, am I interrupting anything? … Good… I just wanted to ask when you might find it convenient for me to begin searching the house… Oh, I see. I didn't realise that was the case, and I was waiting for you to tell me when I could come. Well, if it's all right by you, I might make a start this afternoon… Okay, I'll see you then."

Having arranged to meet Gabby at one o'clock this afternoon at Ravenshead Estate, I needed to spend the rest of my morning planning what I would do there. That didn't take long. I knew nothing about the layout of the house, which rooms Jane used, or if any areas were sensitive for any particular reason. Given all that, it didn't take me long to realise the most I could do this morning was to set up files and go back over the transcript of yesterday's meeting with Gabby.

After a quick lunch, I packed everything I could need into my oversized tote bag, threw it into the car, and headed for Ravenshead Estate. Gabby came out to meet me as I pulled up, and after having ascertained that I'd already had lunch, she opened the front door of the big house and gestured for me to enter – while she remained outside on the doorstep.

"Aren't you going to come in and show me around?" I was surprised when she didn't come inside with me.

"No, I'd prefer not to. Besides, to begin with, I think it might be best if you take a look around on your own first. Then, come and join me for coffee at about three o'clock. That door over there opens into a short hallway that leads to my apartment. Does that suit you?"

Perhaps she had a point about my having a look around on my own being a good start. That way, when I join her for coffee, I'll be able to ask her any questions I developed in the course of my wander through the house. Obviously intent on not getting in my way and having delivered her invitation, Gabby promptly disappeared into her apartment. Stunned for a few moments, I stood there alone in the small entrance area and wondered what to do next. Finally, head and feet were in sync, and I set forth into the interior on my journey of discovery. At least, that's how it felt at the time. It felt nothing like searching a crime scene for clues.

For the best part of two hours, I wandered in and out of rooms, not really looking for anything in particular, just trying to get a feel for the layout of the place and the past function of various rooms. The whole house felt forlorn and abandoned in some way. It had nothing to do with dust and cobwebs. It was the vibes it gave off, and perhaps it provided an insight into how the house affected Gabby. By the time I started for Gabby's apartment, I still didn't know which rooms had been Jane's personal spaces.

Over coffee, I showed Gabby the rough sketch map I'd made of the rooms on the ground floor. There were a lot of them, and, to me, several of them seemed to have served much the same purpose. Gabby confirmed that, to the best of her knowledge, I had identified most of the rooms correctly.

"What about the upper floor?" she asked. "Have you been upstairs? Did you sketch that floor as well?"

"Yes, I had a quick look around up there, but it was obvious that, except for a couple of the rooms, all were bedrooms. Is there something in particular about up there I should have noted?"

"No. No, I just wondered whether they were still bedrooms or if they might have been utilised in other ways over the years."

We discussed my sketch of the ground floor for a few minutes before I became anxious to move on with what I had come to do. There was one last thing I wanted to check with Gabby before I went back to work.

"Gabby, can you indicate on my sketch which rooms Jane used? I'm not so interested in the earlier time of her life so much as the period after her husband died. My key interest is in which rooms she might have used as her office or writing spaces."

"I'm sorry, Sophie, but I really don't know. When Mum and I came back to care for Jane, she was using one of the small sitting rooms on the ground floor – that one, I think – as her bedroom."

After indicating the room on the sketch, Gabby seemed to study the sketch for a few moments. I was about to prompt her for more information when she continued.

"Yeah, I reckon it was that room. She had something like a daybed installed there and used it as her bedroom. A big cupboard was in that far corner of the room. I think she might have used it as her wardrobe. When we first moved back here, I visited Jane a couple of times in that room. Then, when Mum hired the full-time nurse, Jane was moved upstairs into one of the bedrooms up there. I don't know which one because after I saw her those couple of times, she didn't want to see me again. So, I never went to see her upstairs."

"What about her office or somewhere she did her writing? Was that down here somewhere?"

"Again, I don't know. By the time we arrived, she was no longer writing. Logic suggests that if she were essentially living downstairs, she would have used a room down here as her office. Another thing that supports that idea is her engagement of Miss Parker as a typist. Jane would not have her typist working out of one of the upstairs bedrooms. So, yes, I'm pretty sure Jane and Miss Parker would have worked out of rooms on the ground floor… but I haven't a clue which ones."

"Were you never tempted to explore the house after Jane died? I find it hard to believe you weren't tempted."

"You might find it strange, but apart from those couple of times I visited Jane soon after we arrived here, I have never ventured anywhere in this house other than this apartment. I've never been tempted."

"Why is that? You appear almost afraid to enter the main part of the house. Just standing in the entrance area talking to me earlier seemed to have you on edge. Did something happen in this house to frighten you? Maybe it was a long time ago rather than recently. Perhaps it was a story you heard as a child. Whatever it was, I would at least like to know about it before I spend too much more time wandering around in there."

"Please don't think I'm mad, Sophie, but I really don't know why I'm frightened to go into the house. I suspect your suggestion that something bad happened there might be right. Perhaps as a child, I did hear – or overhear – an incident being discussed. I just don't know, Sophie, but my feelings are real."

My questions had Gabby quite agitated. I felt concerned about how poorly I had handled the situation. After announcing that I needed to achieve a bit more before the end of the day, I stood up to leave. Gabby caught my arm and looked up at me.

"Sophie, I know it must appear that way, but I am not losing my faculties. Maybe having you wandering around in the house will give me the courage to explore the place myself."

"That would be good to see. I don't think you're losing your marbles, Gabby, but I hope that before I'm finished here, we get to the bottom of whatever prevents you from going in there."

Whatever had caused this situation for Gabby, I doubt it resulted from sitting around listening to ghost stories. To begin with, there were no other children around when she was a child.

Resuming my exploration of the house after coffee required a decision. Should I start a more thorough search of the downstairs rooms or take another look at the upstairs rooms first? Upstairs won. I didn't expect to find much of interest up there, so it made sense to tackle them first and tick them off the list.

It was all proving too easy. While none of the bedrooms appeared to have been in use recently, two of the rooms suggested that they had been used more recently than the others. After some consideration and a bit of to-ing and fro-ing between the two rooms, I finally assigned the smaller of the two to the live-in nurse and the other one to Jane.

"Well, that's progress. Little enough, I know, but still progress," I told the empty house as I scribbled the occupants' names on the relevant two rooms on my sketch.

Before heading downstairs again, I gave each of the remaining bedrooms another cursory inspection. That exercise produced nothing new, and neither of the bathrooms provided any clues as to which of them was used most recently – 'recently' being a relative description, I reminded myself. A dilemma prevented me from leaving the upper floor. Should I conduct a fingertip search of Jane's bedroom before going downstairs, or should I leave it and concentrate on finding where the writing took place? The latter won out.

Back in the entrance area again, I laid my sketch map out on a small hall table and studied it for a moment. Where to begin? The age-old answer came through loud and clear: Start at the beginning and work through until you reach the end. It made sense. I looked over at the first small room to my right. 'Yep, that's where I need to start,' I told myself, but my perverse 'other self' told me I had seen nothing exciting in that room before. My phone helped delay the inevitable. The call was not unexpected.

As seems to have become our regular practice, Detective Inspector Warren Tyson would be dining with me tonight. His call was to check whether he should pick up something for dinner on his way through town or if I was planning to cook tonight. Most of the time, we are both busy people. When I am not in the throes of some investigative journalism exercise, I do love to cook. Tonight, there will be no home cooking, but there will be plenty of discussion of Jane (Finchley) Creighton.

Nevertheless, if I didn't head home now, Warren and our dinner would be there before I was.

Chapter 3

Tonight's fare consisted of a couple of pasta dishes and garlic bread that Warren had picked up on his way through town. A few minutes after I arrived home, he marched in, carrying the pasta, a tub of gelato, and one of fruit salad. My contribution to tonight's dinner was the wine, coffee and after-dinner port. As is often the case, having come straight from work, we required a few minutes to relax and unwind before conversation began to flow. Tonight was no different. We took our glasses of wine out onto my back deck and settled down in silence for a minute or so. Warren roused himself first.

"Were you working today? I thought you didn't have any projects on the go at the moment and were relishing a few days of reading books and hanging out in coffee shops."

"That was the case until my new investigation. I'm not even sure whether I should call it an investigation or a case, but I suppose it is just an investigation."

"Sounds intriguing. A case, eh? Tell me more … and whether I might be involved with this one."

Warren's eagerness for details was evident in his voice, and his body language confirmed it as he slid forward onto the front edge of his chair. I considered his request for a few moments before replying. My problem was that I wasn't sure how to describe what I had agreed to do.

Once a copper, always a copper… That's what they say, and in Warren's case, it seems about right. I first encountered Detective Inspector Warren Tyson a few years ago, following the death of Lillian Cavendish. Although I had only ever known her as Aunt Lillian, I was never able to prove whose aunt she really was, but I proved beyond doubt that she really wasn't mine. A lot of mysterious information and events followed her death, and my investigation into her background. Suffice to say, DI Tyson led a police investigation when events turned from mysterious to criminal. The friendship developed at that time has continued and, at times, threatens to become something more than just friendship. So far, neither of us has felt brave enough to venture down that track.

He brought me back to the here and now by reminding me he was waiting for information.

"How can you not be sure whether it is a case or not?" he demanded. "You either have a crime to investigate or not. What's so different about this investigation? ... Or is it the client that's a problem?" He added after a moment's pause.

"Argh, you're reading too much into what I said. My client is someone I've been acquainted with for most of my life. Our mothers were friends, and that's how my client and I know each other. We were not close friends, just two people who happened to encounter one another occasionally over the years."

"So what's the case about?"

"As I said before, I'm not sure it is a case, and I won't know until I've completed my investigation. I'll give you the story so far. Gabby, my client, has returned to the area after being away from here for quite some time. She came back when her mother became ill, but after her mother's funeral, Gabby returned to her job overseas. On her mother's death, Gabby inherited Ravenshead Estate and has now returned to live there."

Warren let out a low whistle. "That is one well-heeled client you've added to your list. You're not going to tell me the case is about problems with the inheritance, are you?"

"No, there's no problem with that. This will sound weird, but my case appears to be about manuscripts that possibly were pirated decades ago."

"Possibly...? Surely, they were either stolen, or they weren't. So why the apparent confusion?"

"It's a long and convoluted story involving family history, and it's one I'm not sure I've got my head around yet. The crime, if there is one, was committed against my client's grandmother at some unknown date in the past. So, I have embarked on an investigation without too much in the way of hard facts and absolutely no evidence."

"You said you've known Gabby for some time. How would you rate her? More importantly, should you be wasting your time on something so imprecise?"

"That's an interesting question, and it's one I'm not sure I can answer honestly. Gabby is an extremely intelligent woman and quite lucid in every way, but there is something not quite right there."

I explained how, when Gabby was growing up, she and her mother had lived in a small apartment attached to the big house on Ravenshead Estate rather than in the house itself. Gabby, having recently returned here, has moved back into that apartment.

"Why is she living in the apartment? If she inherited the estate, she owns the big house and is free to live in it. Is she planning on having renovations or something done before she moves in?"

"Not that I'm aware of. What do you make of an elderly, intelligent woman who claims not to be afraid of ghosts but can't bring herself to enter that house?"

Not unexpectedly perhaps, Warren cocked his head to one side and studied me before responding to my question.

"Are there ghosts associated with the house – psychological ghosts, I mean? There must be a deep-seated reason why she refuses to enter the house. Maybe something unpleasant happened to her there, or she witnessed something that happened there that has traumatised her."

"She says not, but admits she doesn't know why it happens or what it's all about. I know it's real because I witnessed it this afternoon. She let me into the house and followed me a little way into the entrance area, where she spoke to me for about a minute before retreating to her apartment. Over that brief period, I watched her become increasingly agitated before she fled to her haven. It was the first time she'd actually set foot in the house since she was about five years old."

"So, whatever the problem, its origin lies way back in her childhood. If she can't identify what happened back then, I don't like your chances of helping her sort herself out. But what about this supposed crime? Do I want to know about that, or more precisely, do I need to know about it?"

"Who knows? I've already pointed out to her that if a crime were committed back then, there would be little chance of taking action against it now. Apparently, she's not interested in compensation or anything else. She simply wants to confirm whether her grandmother's manuscripts were stolen or not. Watch this space… This exercise could drag on for a long time – or it could be all over in a couple of days. So far, my thinking leans towards the latter." I reminded him that our pasta dishes, kept warm in the oven, would be quite dry if we didn't eat soon.

It wasn't late when Warren left. I wasn't disappointed. After so much discussion about my new case, I was eager to act on a couple of ideas that had come to me during the evening. The big issue, of course, was the need for an inquest into George Creighton's death. Although I had no idea how useful it might be, I also considered researching the Finchley family history.

George's inquest details would involve trawling through the State Archives' online index to files. I gave it priority on the basis that it was more likely to provide useful information than the family's history. After a short spell and with minimal bad language, I located what I thought was the appropriate file. I ordered a copy after checking the number of pages and performing a quick calculation of the cost. I knew it would take a few days for my copy of the file to arrive, so I turned my attention to the Finchley family history. It felt like repeating history. My work surrounding Aunt Lillian's estate had given me a crash course in family history research.

My research into the Finchley family history didn't provide much information other than the fact that Henry Finchley snagged himself a valuable, well-heeled asset when he married

Martha. A thorough search of birth indexes for most states produced only one recorded live birth for the couple: Jane. It wasn't a complete waste of time, I told myself. At least I had confirmed the true nature of the Finchley family at that time.

By then, it was almost midnight. My eyes were telling me they had endured enough staring at screens for one night, so I went to bed and lay awake for what felt like hours, trying to think of where else to search for clues.

With no new ideas to pursue, there was no alternative except to return to Ravenshead today to conduct a detailed search of the house. I thought my chances of finding anything helpful were slim, given the lack of evidence my preliminary search uncovered. I had seen no evidence of writing and not even a reasonable amount of writing paraphernalia to support the notion that any serious writing had occurred there.

After letting myself into the house, I took a deep breath and made my first serious decision of the day: where to start my search. The layout of the ground floor was interesting and obviously designed to create the impression of affluent living. An impressive front door opened into a small entrance foyer, which, in turn, opened into a large entrance space dominated by a grand staircase, situated centrally about halfway along the room's length. The staircase swept majestically up to a first floor balcony that fronted the bedroom area of the house. On the ground floor, rooms lined both sides of the grand entrance space and continued beneath the upper floor. Each room was the mirror image of its twin on the other side of the entrance space.

My memory of yesterday's search results suggested the first small rooms on either side of that entrance area were not a high priority. Nevertheless, in the interests of thoroughness, I did quick circuits of the interiors of both of them without discovering anything new. After making appropriate notations on each of the rooms on my sketch, I moved on in the hope the next couple of rooms might prove more interesting.

Those next rooms, situated on either side of the grand entrance area, were larger than the first two and contained more furniture. I felt my spirits lift a little as I entered the room on the right-hand side of the space. Built-in bookshelves complete with a travelling library ladder lined one end wall. The other dominant piece of furniture was a mahogany desk. Huge and impressive-looking, it seemed to shout 'male' to me. I paused for a moment to consider why I thought it was a man's desk. Of course, it could have been a woman's desk, but its size and general appearance suggested it was more to a man's taste.

Various other items scattered around the room, including the pipes rack and ashtrays, also contributed to the sense of male ownership of the space. A couple of small cabinets, a number of mismatched chairs and various side tables were scattered around the room. It all suggested this had been a man's study, his private den, but I had scant evidence to support such an assumption. Still, I knew instinctively I would be spending more time later exploring this room.

I started across towards the mirror image room on the left-hand side of the entrance space, but only made it as far as the foot of the grand staircase. It seemed to beckon me to come up, so I did. After all, I have to inspect the upper floor as well at some point, so it might as well be now. No surprises awaited me upstairs. There was evidence of only two of the bedrooms having been in use most recently. On closer inspection today, I found nothing of any consequence to my case. After scribbling a couple of notes on my sketch of the upper floor, I returned to the ground floor and turned my attention to the room I was about to search before the staircase lured me upstairs.

Although the furniture that remained looked dated and tired, it was obvious it had been the main dining room. After searching the few places where manuscripts might be lurking, I stepped outside the room and ran my eyes along the wall towards the next room on this side. It appeared the dining room didn't quite mirror its counterpart on the other side of the entrance space. The dining room was longer, and I could see that the next room along from it was smaller than expected. That was the room I searched next.

In another time, it had been a sitting room, probably the sitting room the ladies retired to after dinner while the men went elsewhere to drink and smoke. No more than hints of its former glory remained. A couple of faded and worn overstuffed chairs and a few side tables remained, but little else worthy of mention remained in the room.

Rather than crossing to the other side, I chose to stay on the left-hand side and proceeded to the next room. It was another sitting room, but this one had a distinctly different feel. By the time I had finished searching it, I had decided it probably had been the private sitting room of the lady of the house. If the thought ever crossed my mind that this might have been where Jane did her writing, I found nothing to confirm it.

It was lunchtime. My stomach rumbled to remind me, but I still had a couple of rooms on the right-hand side of the entrance space to search. I was unlikely to succumb to starvation if I searched those rooms before doing anything about lunch. In the end, I found both rooms were so empty, it looked as though all the furniture had been removed from them some years before. I was finishing my search of the last room when I heard my name being called. Surprised, I rushed out into the entrance area.

Gabby was standing on the doorstep outside the open front door. She waved at me to catch my attention, but I was already on my way to meet her.

"Have you done anything about lunch today?" she asked in a concerned voice. I shook my head in reply, and she continued. "I intended to talk to you earlier, but time ran away from me this morning. Anyway, I haven't had lunch yet either, so will you join me now?"

"Thanks, but you're not expected to feed me while I'm working on your investigation."

"No, I know, but I would appreciate the company, and I do want to talk to you. It will only be sandwiches if you are okay with nothing more exciting."

"Sandwiches will be fine. In fact, they will be wonderful as an alternative to hunger. You said you wanted to talk to me. Does it have something to do with my investigation?"

"Yes, but let's eat first and then talk," she said as she sliced through the last of the sandwiches we had made.

The sandwiches were much better than anything else I might have found for myself, and they were washed down with long glasses of iced tea as my curiosity about the 'talk' Gabby wanted skyrocketed. After a couple of minutes, I couldn't restrain myself any longer.

"You said you had something you wanted to talk to me about," I said in the hope of progressing the matter.

"Eh? Oh, yes. I wanted to let you know that I'll be away for a few days. I'll be on the other side of the country, but please feel free to call me if you need to discuss anything. Something has arisen regarding the last major project I managed. It's not a problem for me, but I do need to be there to help sort things out. So, I will go into the city this afternoon and overnight there before catching the early morning flight. As I said, I'll be gone for a few days… Well, probably for at least a week. You have your own key, and you should continue to come and go as you please. Come into my apartment to make coffee and lunch, or whatever, while I'm away. Please feel free to make yourself at home whenever you are here. Before I go, is there anything I need to do, or anything you want to talk to me about?"

After thanking her and assuring her there was nothing I needed to discuss with her, I went back into the house and left Gabby to her packing or whatever she had to do before she left. A little while later, I heard Gabby drive away. I perched my backside on the edge of the nearest sturdy-looking table and took a few moments to consider 'what's next'. It was already three o'clock. I decided that giving myself an early mark might be the best next move, so I locked up and went home, but I knew my working day was far from over.

The quote for the inquest file had come through, so I ordered it before turning my attention to what to have for dinner tonight. About half an hour later, a casserole went into the oven, and I sent Warren a message that dinner was sorted for tonight. Then it was time to return to Jane Creighton's manuscripts and devote some serious planning to how to progress over the next couple of days.

Warren arrived just before six o'clock and, although the casserole was ready, we indulged in our customary pre-dinner drink on my deck before eating. I had no doubts about what my preferred topic of conversation would be this evening, and I waited only until after a couple of sips before launching into it.

"Warren, please put your copper's hat on for a moment and tell me what factors might trigger a coroner's inquest into a death."

"Depends on the death, I suppose. I mean, if there were anything out of the ordinary or even vaguely suspicious about the cause of death, an inquest would probably be held. Does this have something to do with the current story you are working on?"

"It's an investigation at best, but not a story. And, yes, there was an inquest into a death that seemed fairly straightforward to me. I wondered whether the need for inquests might have changed over time."

"Well, I suppose, like most things in life, changes do occur in legal procedures. How long ago are we talking about?"

"Oh, about the mid-1930s.

"Come on, give me the details. I need more information if you want a reasonably accurate answer. Tell me about the death."

"A bloke came off his horse…."

"…Allegedly came off his horse. Sorry, do go on."

"I'm not sure 'allegedly' is the right word either. Maybe 'supposedly' might be more accurate. Anyway, the bloke in question rode out to where the fencing gang was camped and didn't come home."

"Okay… was he expected home that same evening?"

"No, I don't think so. While I don't know all the details, I gained the impression George wasn't expected home that night. The expectation was that he would return when he had finished whatever he had to do out there. Hence, no one was concerned about George until two days later when his horse returned home without him."

"So, no one witnessed the accident or came across him soon after it happened. That might have been enough to consider it a suspicious death and for it to trigger an inquest. Were there any arguments about his will, either before or after the inquest?"

"Dunno, but not as far as I know so far. I think the terms of his will were quite clear. His daughter, Amelia (Amy), inherited the whole of his estate, and that amounted to all of the Ravenshead Estate and its operations."

"Hmm… It appears the inquest might have been nothing more than routine. As no one witnessed the accident, the inquest might have been a way to gather all the information and have it officially recorded. How significant is the inquest to your investigation?"

"While it could be a significant part of the family history story, it's not important to my investigation as far as I know. However, my gut keeps suggesting otherwise."

"Right. Well, we must await the arrival of the inquest file. When is that likely to be, by the way?"

"That depends on whether the file has already been digitised or not. Anyway, instead of wasting more time discussing inquest files, perhaps we should rescue my casserole before it's too late."

After Warren left and I cleaned up the kitchen, it was still early. I decided to allow myself about half an hour in my office before calling it a night. So far, my plan for progressing my investigation amounted to about three words on an otherwise blank sheet of paper. When getting started seems almost impossible, you resort to a safe activity: checking your email inbox.

Tonight, it proved not to be a waste of time. The George Creighton inquest file had arrived from the archives. As its cost had indicated, it was huge. All thoughts of planning my investigation went out the window as my printer spat out page after page. Once the pages were sorted and safely secured in a binder, I started reading. When my eyes refused to focus properly after only a few pages, I realised midnight had come and gone. Within minutes, I was in bed and willing my mind to slow down so sleep might catch up with me.

Chapter 4

Last night, it was a foregone conclusion that this morning would be spent on George's inquest file. Copious notes were added to a pad as I worked my way through the pile of pages. Not much before 1.00PM, I turned the last page and abandoned my office in search of lunch. After finishing my sandwich, I took a coffee out onto my back deck and sipped it as I considered the information contained in the inquest file. By the time my mug was empty, I was convinced that the accidental death verdict arrived at by the coroner was not correct. But was that important?

That was the question niggling me as I rinsed my mug, and it then accompanied me on my drive to Ravenshead Estate. For some reason, my gut kept insisting it was important. Try as I might, it wouldn't go away, but kept churning away in the back of my mind as I strode into Ravenshead's grand entrance hall and laid out on a small table my sketch of the ground floor. It was almost no contest. The most interesting thing I had discovered so far was the room with the bookshelf-lined wall. The room that I had decided was the master's den.

If I were searching for a woman's manuscripts, why search a man's study? While it was a reasonable question, that room was the only one so far to make my antennas twitch. I began my fingertip search of the room with its huge desk. With so many drawers to search, there had to be something interesting in at least one of them. Disappointment is a terrible emotion.

The only real assumption made after searching all the desk drawers was that the last person to work at the desk probably was right-handed. All the drawers were empty except for the top right-hand one that contained some (dated) writing paraphernalia. The only surprising things amongst it were two expensive-looking fountain pens –no ink for them. I had held such high hopes of finding something – anything – interesting in those drawers, and I voiced my disappointment as I considered where to search next. The bookshelf-lined wall was the obvious place.

Climbing the ladder allowed me to peruse the sparse volumes on the highest couple of the seven shelves. It didn't take long to establish that everything on those upper shelves was likely to be more to a man's taste than a woman's. Nothing stood out to me as being exceptional or special in any way, but I don't pretend to be an expert in any of the topics covered. After descending the ladder, I stood back and surveyed the lower five shelves.

These were more tightly packed than the higher ones, except for the bottom and fifth shelves. Those two shelves, probably being less easily accessed, still held many books, but they were less tightly packed than the intervening shelves. A glance along the spines on a couple of the shelves confirmed they were probably a woman's books and not subjects I would associate with a man. In particular, some classic tomes and books of poetry caught my eye. I told myself that a man might read such works, but in this case, they were so far removed from the focus of the books on the top two shelves that it was unlikely they belonged to the same man.

I perched on the corner of the desk and took a moment to consider what my survey of the bookshelves had revealed. It almost seemed a no-brainer. The room, once a man's domain, appeared to have been taken over by a woman at some point.

"Now, how does that fit with my investigation?" I asked the empty office. "Very nicely, I should think," I assured myself.

This room might well have been George Creighton's private study, and possibly Henry Finchley's before that. Then, in more recent times, following George's death, the room was taken over by a woman … presumably Jane. Many of the volumes on the lower bookshelves are in keeping with what little I know of Jane (Finchley) Creighton's interests in literature. Did she claim this space and turn it into her office? Is this where she did her writing? That grand-looking mahogany desk would certainly be enough to tempt anyone to sit and work at it.

While my assumptions seemed solid, there was one major flaw in my thinking. If this was Jane's office and where she did her writing, why is there no evidence of such activity to be found anywhere in the room? That sent me back to the bookshelves. Had some of Jane's writing been bound and now resided on one of the shelves? Another question slammed in on the heels of its predecessor. Having discovered some of her work published in book form, did she, by whatever means, acquire those publications? Perhaps she might have bought a copy of each of the works that were published without her consent or acknowledgement.

My slow and careful inspection of all the books on the lower five shelves failed to produce anything that could be attributed to Jane. I took a deep breath and thought about having found nothing useful. That's when it occurred to me how pointless my search had been. I had searched the shelves for anything that appeared to have Jane as the author, but that was probably a waste of time.

If Jane's manuscripts had been pirated and published illegally, would the culprits attribute the works to Jane? It seemed highly unlikely. I thought it was most likely that an author's pseudonym would have been employed. After giving the matter a few minutes thought, I decided that, if a pseudonym had been used, it was likely that, along with all the other work on the shelves, there would be a number of books bearing the same author's name. My search had not discovered a frequently appearing author's name.

In the end, I accepted that none of the volumes was Jane's work. Regardless of how they came to be published, would an author not acquire a copy of her own work if an opportunity arose? None of the writers that I knew would pass up such an opportunity, even if the reason for acquiring the copies was to use them as evidence in legal proceedings. So, why didn't Jane? Legend has it that, when she discovered what had happened, she was incensed enough to sack her typist. Despite what little I knew of Jane, I hardly think sacking her typist would have been her only reaction to the situation. So, where are Jane's manuscripts, pirated or otherwise?

With no inspiration forthcoming from my muse, I took myself off to Gabby's apartment to make myself a coffee and ponder the situation. I took it back to the study and flopped down onto one of the remaining chairs in the room. A cloud of dust and who knows what else erupted to engulf me. I barely managed to get my mug down on a side table before succumbing to a coughing fit. Then I resumed studying the bookshelves from a distance. After a couple of minutes of sipping coffee and staring at the bookshelves, a thought from somewhere deep in the back of my mind managed to struggle through to the forefront.

There was something wrong with those shelves. I shook my head to clear my mind before studying the shelving more intently. There was definitely something wrong with those shelves, but it wasn't until about five minutes later that I had any level of enlightenment. I sprang out of the chair, creating another cloud of dust as I did so. I could die of some nasty lung disease if I keep disturbing the furniture this way, I told myself as I marched towards the shelves. Then, with my back pressed hard up against the shelving, I shuffled along in front of them until I reached a point that offered an unobstructed path through the room to the opposite wall.

I paced out the distance to that opposite wall, and then, to make sure I hadn't miscounted, I repeated the process from the wall back to the shelves.

"Right, now let's see what the story is outside the room," I suggested to the universe.

While standing in the entrance space, I ran my eyes along the length of the wall that separated all the rooms along the right-hand side of the space. It was relatively easy to identify the locations of the walls separating each room. I paced the distance between to two end walls of the study… and then repeated the exercise twice more. There was no denying it. A major discrepancy existed between the internal and external lengths of the room. Some quick mental arithmetic told me the discrepancy was a little more than a metre. I needed to accurately measure the internal length of the room. That required a long tape measure. With any luck, a suitable one might still be in the box of tools I carry about in my car.

Long ago, while still employed as a journalist, I often found myself needing to establish certain measurements or to confirm information provided by other sources. I had put together a few useful tools that had proved handy when reporting on location. I dashed out to my car.

"Eureka!" I yelped as I dragged a builder's 30-metre tape measure out of my box of tools. "Definitely long enough for what I need…," I assured the universe, as I had a quick look around to check if anyone was around and heard me.

Armed with the tape measure, it took no time to confirm that the distance between the wall supporting the bookshelves and the opposite wall was 150 centimetres shorter than the distance between the room's exterior dividing walls.

"So, a hidden space, eh? Now, why would that be necessary? What was it for, and when might it have been created?"

No answers were forthcoming from the empty room, but it didn't matter. A frisson of excitement was coursing up and down my spine. Could this be the Aladdin's cave I searched for? A quick inspection of the shelving's length provided no immediate new information, but if there were a hidden space behind it, there had to be an entrance to it. A more thorough inspection produced the same result as the previous one. I realised the shelving was fabricated from continuous long planks… except for the last metre or so at the external wall end of the installation. No surprises in that. It was amazing that such long, straight lengths of beautiful timber were available, but not long enough to traverse to entire width of the room. Hence, that last section had been an added small separate set of shelves.

Having noted and marked it appropriately on my sketch map, I was about to resume my search of the shelving when inspiration slammed in. What if there was something more significant about that short set of shelving? What if it had resulted from something other than the length of planks available? That focused my attention back on the small set of shelves.

Nothing about them excited me. Fabricated from the same timber as the rest of the shelving, it was obvious they were intended to appear as a continuation of the rest of it and a necessary extension to traverse the length of the wall. No amount of pushing and prodding produced any exciting effect. Noting moved. Nothing sprang open or sprang out at me. Disappointment is a terrible emotion, and for a few moments, I knew it well. After some serious internal dialogue, I accepted that it had always been a long shot that this might be the entrance to a mysterious hidden space.

Fresh out of ideas, I perched on the edge of the desk and took some time to consider what else I could do. There had to be a way into that hidden space. My gut had kept suggesting that the small set of shelves was somehow the entrance to it. As I sat there thinking dark and disappointed thoughts, I ran my eyes slowly over every inch of that small set of shelves.

"Well, in the absence of any better ideas, maybe removing all the books from that section might reveal something," I shared with the empty office.

I eased myself off the desk. As I stood up, my eyes dropped to the floor in front of the small set of shelves. I caught my breath.

"What's that?" I hissed as I bounded across to the shelves. "I'm sure it's a scrape mark."

Down on my hands and knees, I studied the faint mark on the floor. "Could be a scrape mark," I told the universe as I explored the mark with my fingertips. "Yes, it feels as though the surface is abraded. Now, how might that have happened?"

An unnecessary question. To my mind, there was only one way it might have happened. Something scraping across the floor multiple times at that one point had left scratches in the surface of the polished timber floor. The only thing that could have caused it was something opening and closing at that same spot. Something like a set of shelves swinging open and closed across the floor.

My excitement revitalised and disappointment swept aside, I began hauling books off that set of shelves. Nothing obvious resulted. Then, with the shelves empty apart from dust, and my excitement wavering, I was down on my knees again. Running along the full length of the shelving and set back about one and a half centimetres from the front edge of the lowest shelf was a low kickboard. I ran my hand along the length of the kickboard below the small set of shelves and found nothing. I started to scramble up off my knees, but was halted by a thought slamming in from left field that forced me to drop back down. The kickboard had produced nothing, but what about under the leading edge of the bottom shelf?

"Bingo…!" I yelped as my fingers found something unexpected. It felt as though a small circular piece of wood had been inserted into the bottom of the shelf. With my face pressed hard on the floor, I tried to see what I had discovered. "Okay, if I can't see it, I'll have to explore it by feel," I counselled myself. "A button of some sort?" I suggested.

How ridiculous am I? There's no one within miles of this place, and I'm having a conversation with an empty house. Perhaps it is as well there is no one around. If this thing I've found is a button that operates some form of release mechanism, logically, I need to either press it in or slide it sideways. Not convinced about the sideways idea, I tried that first, and nothing happened. What I had found felt like a round button set in a round hole. Of course, it wasn't going to slide anywhere. Right, I'll press it in to see if that moves anything. Nothing happened.

Despite several attempts, still no result. 'Give it one last try,' I told myself before summoning all the strength I could muster.

"Alleluia! This time, the jackpot – I think."

I heard a loud clang. The left hand edge of the small bookshelf sprang out about three centimetres. Running my hand up the edge of the frame, I located a notch that felt like it should be a hand grip of some sort. For a moment, I hesitated. What if I had it wrong, and that notch wasn't intended as a 'handle' to pull the shelves away from the wall? I had no idea what might happen if I tried pulling on that notch. Perhaps the shelves might swing wide open, revealing an entrance to the secret space. A less appealing prospect was that the shelves might fall over on top of me. Just in case the latter would occur, I shuffled along the floor so that my body was no longer in front of the small set of shelves.

Although at a somewhat awkward angle, I took a firm hold via the notch and gave it a tentative tug. Nothing happened. I tried again, this time giving it an almighty yank. It was clear no one was meant to easily enter this secret space. The mechanism release button was a challenge for my hand and would have been almost impossible for arthritic fingers. Then, with the set of shelves slightly ajar, it took considerable strength to open the gap wide enough for a person to enter. Despite the hard work involved, I had revealed what I hoped was the entrance to that mysterious space.

Another trip to my car was necessary to fetch a headlamp before proceeding further. Once I had the shelves swung open from the wall behind them, I could make out the lines of the door set in the wall. It was too dark to see much else without some form of artificial light. The batteries in the headlamp in my toolbox in the car were a bit suspect and hadn't been changed in quite a while. Nevertheless, I figured they would at least give me enough light to examine that door I had discovered.

I tightened the strap around my head and switched on the torch. A dull glow lit up the door. A negative thought rushed in. What are the odds that a key is required to open that door? Although I hadn't carried out a detailed inspection so far, my search hadn't revealed a key of any sort anywhere.

"No point creating problems before you know they actually exist," I told myself and anyone else in the universe that was listening. I eased in behind the shelving and stood in front of the door. "Moment of truth…." A keyhole was obvious immediately below the doorknob, but I reached out and grabbed the doorknob. A deep breath, and I tried turning the knob. There was no resistance. The door wasn't locked.

The doorknob turned sluggishly, and after so long without use, the latch seemed reluctant to withdraw. Not about to be defeated after reaching this point in the exercise, I employed the age-old tactic of wriggling and jiggling, and applying a bit of solid persuasion to the recalcitrant locking mechanism. Finally, the latch released with a solid clunk. It took a moment for the reality of the situation to sink in. I had opened the door, albeit by no more than a couple of centimetres so far.

"Stop messing about and get in there," I chided myself. "You are unlikely to encounter savage beasts, and there are no such things as ghosts." I swung the door wide open, stirring up an almighty cloud of dust that forced me to step away from the door for a few moments until it was safe to breathe again.

As tentatively as a kitten, I snuck my head around the door and slowly swung it around to allow the torch to reassure me that nothing resided in the secret space to attack me. What that first tentative look around did show me was a cord hanging down from the ceiling. It reminded me of those old-fashioned cords used to turn lights on and off. I reached up, grabbed the cord, and pulled gently. Pale yellow light from a low-wattage bulb in a 'lady's skirt' type light fitting affixed to the ceiling dimly lit up the space.

The wall in front of me was lined with shelves from ceiling to floor. It was obvious from first glance that those shelves were tightly packed with whatever secrets were stored in there. From where I stood just inside the doorway, a narrow space about ninety centimetres wide ran from the shelves at my far left to those at my far right, effectively creating a narrow walkway bounded by shelving on three sides. I turned my attention to the shelves on the end wall to my left. Somehow, the material on those shelves appeared different from that stored on the long shelves in front of me. Regardless, at first glance, all shelves appeared almost packed to capacity.

Of course, the temptation was too much. I had to see what treasures lay stacked on those shelves. The first thing worth noting was that the shelving in this hidden space was of significantly lower quality than the bookshelves outside. Those not meant to be seen by anyone were made from rougher, less expensive timber and featured no fancy joinery during their fabrication or installation. The weak lighting installed also suggested that no work or research was meant to be carried out in the space. It was just for storage. But, now the burning question was what had someone gone to so much trouble to store away from everyone's eyes?

Without any thought to a systematic approach, I walked forward a couple of paces from my position just inside the entrance to the space, and reached for the folder immediately in front of me. Millions of disturbed dust mites swirled around in the airless space. I stood still and held the folder away from me at arm's length until the swirling cloud settled a little and I felt it was now safe to breathe normally again. Then, careful not to release a further dust storm, I brought the folder closer and studied its cover.

Covered in a good layer of dust and grime, no lettering was immediately apparent on the cover or its spine. Bugger ... If I want to know more, I'll have to look inside ... And of course, I wanted to know more. So, I gingerly lifted the cover until it was about half open, and I was able to read some of the first page of its contents.

I caught my breath. Abandoning all safely considerations and due care, I flung the cover fully open. There it was. The proof I needed to give credence to the legend that Jane (Finchley) Creighton was a writer. Crikey, was all of this material her manuscripts? As I stood there, stunned and holding the open folder out in front of me as though it might explode at any moment, I ran my eyes over the horde of material on the shelves.

Such weak lighting made reading the old documents difficult. After a few moments, common sense kicked in. The next step was not something to take without first being prepared. I needed a plan – and I needed better lighting. Better lighting as would be provided by the set of site work lights I have at home. A glance at my watch told me that outside this hidden space, it was fast approaching six o'clock, and the time when I should be focused on dinner and a pre-dinner drink.

After turning off the light and closing the door, I stepped out through the gap in the bookshelves. For a moment, I stood there considering whether to push the small bookshelves back into place or to leave them ajar. Although it was unlikely anyone would enter the house before I returned tomorrow, it seemed foolhardy to leave the shelves open. I leaned heavily on the small bookshelves and pushed against them. My efforts were rewarded with the resound clunk of the locking mechanism thumping back into place.

Now I knew how to enter the hidden space, tomorrow, it would be easy. The hard part was waiting until then to access that material.

Chapter 5

All the way home, I was cursing myself for not having checked what was on the two end sets of shelving. That material looked different from the rest of the stuff, but was it? Perhaps it was just more of Jane's writing, but instead of being written on loose pages, it had been scribbled in hardcovered journals and exercise books.

Warren sent a text to tell me he wouldn't arrive until at least seven o'clock for dinner. That suited me fine. It allowed me a quiet time alone to ponder today's discoveries and think about how I might conduct a thorough investigation of the material hidden in that secret space. The construction of the bookshelves and creation of the hidden space must have been Jane's doing. Surely, if someone else had created it at an earlier time, there would be some of someone else's treasures. Of course, a thorough search might uncover stuff belonging to others.

The moment Warren arrived, he realised my excitement level was off the chart, and was foolhardy enough to query it. That opened the floodgate for an account of my day to gush forward. While I recounted finding the hidden space and its contents, the roast dinners Warren had brought for our evening meal were keeping warm in the oven. It was about 45 minutes later when Warren suggested we might eat now and resume our discussions after dinner. Although difficult for me, that is what we did. Then, as soon as we had eaten, we took our coffees through to the lounge room and discussing my day at Ravenshead house resumed. My story continued at a pace until Warren threw in an unexpected question.

"What's your gut telling you about the material you've discovered?"

His question confused me. I shook my head to indicate I didn't understand.

"Do you think there is a chance some of it might have major implications for people associated with Ravenshead today? Or, perhaps, might it have consequences for people previously associated with the place? I suppose the real question I'm asking is whether you have had any thoughts about the material stored in that space being anything except Jane Creighton's manuscripts."

"No, none at all. What else might she consider so sensitive that she felt compelled to hide it there?"

"I don't know, and there probably is nothing apart from those manuscripts, but it is possible there could be other material of a totally different nature amongst it. I'm not talking about State secrets or the security of the realm; nothing quite so significant or of interest outside this immediate area."

"Again, all I can say is that, no, I haven't entertained any such thoughts. For a start, I'm fairly sure Jane is responsible for the creation of that space. As I haven't heard anything to suggest she was involved in anything other than her writing, I'm sceptical about such a possibility. Granted, according to family stories, Jane was miffed when she discovered she didn't inherit everything upon George's death, but I don't think there was anything she could do about it. Her daughter, Amy, inherited and retained ownership until her death, when it passed on to my client, Gabby. All fairly straightforward, I would have thought. Do you know something different?"

"Well, of course, I don't know anything. I was simply suggesting that creating that hidden space was a lot of effort and expense just to hide a few odd bits of writing. There had to be a more substantial reason for it."

"God, you coppers spend your whole lives looking for criminal intent in everything. If I come across any dead bodies or gold bullion secreted away in there, I'll let you know."

Fortunately, a phone call soon after that exchange of ideas had Warren on his way to a crime scene somewhere. I wasn't looking for an early night, but I did want time to plan tomorrow's assault on that hidden space.

The first thing I'll need beforehand is a detailed layout sketch of the interior of that hideaway. On a blank A3 sheet of copy paper, I drew the interior of the space roughly to scale and ruled across it the appropriate number of lines to represent the shelves. After marking the position of the entrance door, I sat back to admire my handiwork. One question bothered me: should I also mark and detail information relating to that one manuscript I briefly looked at today? A few moments later, I had convinced myself it would be better to systematically record the contents as I examined them, so my drawing was complete for now.

"Where to start on the contents?" I asked my empty office. "Should I start at one end of the top shelf on one of the end walls and work my way along the top shelf on all three sides before moving down to the next shelf to repeat the process?"

That seemed an untidy approach, but a better solution came to me as I sat sipping a nightcap. With a plan of attack now clear in my mind and my layout drawing ready, all that remained for me to do tonight was to load a couple of bits of equipment into my car, ready for an early start tomorrow.

While I hoped my preparations for tomorrow would help ensure a sound night's sleep, I knew that was wishful thinking as I climbed into bed a turned off the bedside light. Sleep was a long time coming and brought with it a load of ugly dreams, thanks largely to Warren's suggestion of something bad possibly lurking in that secret space.

Entering the space was a lot easier this morning. Armed with my battery-powered vacuum cleaner and wearing an appropriate mask, I removed as much visible dust as possible from the floor, shelves, and material on the shelves, where it was safe to do so. Then, after running a long lead from a power outlet in the study, I set up my work lights just inside the entrance to the hidden space. Their bright, white light was almost blinding after the dull glow of the low-wattage overhead light.

"Right, time to find out exactly what's in here," I murmured as I pulled out my layout drawing from last night and a lined pad.

My intention was to inventory as much of the material on the shelves as possible, starting with the two end sets of shelving first, before moving on to the enormous amount of material on the main set. Last night, when I had thought through my plan of attack for today, I hadn't quite decided which end would be my starting point. As I stood in the doorway into the space, the shelves along the internal wall were to my left, while the shelves mounted on the external wall were to my right. With no real logic driving the decision, I decided to start on the shelves to my right.

Moments later, I discovered that the material there consisted of various financial records. A quick riffle through the material revealed a number of ledgers, journals, and folders containing what I assume were bank statements. This was not what I was supposed to be doing. Today, I was supposed to conduct an inventory, and that involved listing every item on every shelf. It did not allow time for rummaging through the various pieces of material to satisfy my idle curiosity. With the small ladder I had brought positioned in front of the set of shelves, I climbed up to start work on the top shelf.

When I stopped for mid-morning coffee, I had completed listing about three-quarters of the contents on that set, and only had the lowest two shelves to complete. For a moment, I considered completing the last two shelves before I stopped for coffee, but my caffeine level urgently needed topping up. I headed for Gabby's apartment and hesitated at her door. I was filthy. Although I removed as much dust as possible before starting work, the residue of ages remained and transferred itself to almost every part of my clothing. My need for a caffeine fix outweighed everything else. So, after making coffee, I drank it in the study to avoid messing up Gabby's kitchen.

Listing the contents on the shelves was taking much longer than anticipated. I expected to have both end sets completed by lunchtime and possibly start on the other big set of shelves. Reality set in as I sat sipping my coffee. The financial records on the shelves I was dealing with at the moment were not so tightly packed. A glance at the opposite end wall suggested that the material on those shelves was crammed in on every available inch of shelving. I realised I'd be lucky to complete both sets of end shelving by the end of today. It made me question why I was in such a hurry. What did it matter how long it took, as long as I did a reasonable job? Revitalised by that thought, I set to work on the remaining two shelves.

I had barely started on the left-hand end wall when my stomach grumbled. It was one o'clock, and I had just started listing material on the second highest shelf. I was in need of water. I decided it was lunchtime and retrieved my lunch and a bottle of water from my esky. Rather than make more mess in Gabby's kitchen, I opted to have lunch in the study. A lunch break gave me time to ponder the material I was uncovering on the second set of shelves. Although I hadn't progressed far, much of the material appeared to be Jane's diaries, dating back to when she was barely a teenager. They were not traditional style diaries. All of these were large, hard-covered books with lined pages on which Jane recorded her daily thoughts and activities as she felt inclined.

Often, there would be a string of entries on consecutive days, followed by a gap of one to two days or, sometimes, several days with nothing recorded. Scattered amongst the diaries were a few thin files containing various documents. It appears a locked filing cabinet never appealed to Jane. I couldn't help but wonder why, when there were so many rooms in the house begging for use, Jane felt compelled to create this hidden space. Any doubts I held previously about when and who created it were gone. So far, nothing encountered on those shelves belonged to anyone other than Jane.

At some point, had she become paranoid about privacy and security, or was there a deeper, perhaps darker, motivation behind the hidden space? …Or were Warren's suspicions well-founded after all? Was there something in Jane's life that she needed to keep hidden? While finding some of her manuscripts had been pirated would be upsetting, once the guilty party, the typist, was dealt with, would such a major secure construction be necessary? Perhaps the beginnings of dementia had set in and prevented her from implementing the final act in her strategy. If she had remained of sound mind, although seriously ill, until the end, would she have revealed all this to Amy? Somehow, I didn't think that was ever part of her plan.

Within a few days, I would have to face a significant question. How to explain all of this to Gabby? So far, everything I'd uncovered only amounted to a strange situation, but what if I uncover something more, something unsavoury? I haven't been able to form a clear opinion of how Gabby regards Jane. She has indicated that Jane didn't care for her, but Jane was Gabby's grandmother. Did Gabby hold a sentimental attachment to Jane, or were they completely estranged?

Enough time wasted on lunch and speculative scenarios, it was time to go back to the dust and the grime. A shower and a change of clothes held greater appeal, but I was soon lost in Jane's world as it existed in the confines of the hidden space. There was so much to catalogue. The more I did, the more overwhelming the magnitude of the task became. Despite such growing feelings, I forced myself to maintain a steady pace until I finished all the items on the second set of end shelving. It was just after four o'clock when I stood up and stretched my back… and became aware of how weary I felt.

"Time to go home," I announced to the empty space, and promptly set about preparing to leave.

I left the set of work lights, the ladder, and the vacuum cleaner in the space overnight. A fleeting temptation to leave the space open overnight was soon replaced by more cautious thinking. It was my responsibility to keep everything safe, so

I closed the door and pushed the bookshelves back into place before grabbing my bag and heading home. It was some time later that evening when I found myself questioning my one last act before closing the door on that repository.

Put it down to a rush of blood to the head or some other equally implausible reason, but as I started to close the door, something made me dash to the shelves on the right-hand end of the space. I grabbed a random item from eye level on the shelf and stuffed it in my bag. I was alone this evening. Now that I was clean, had eaten, and was relaxing with a glass of wine, that 'borrowed' material stirred my interest. 'I'll just have a quick look at what I grabbed,' I told myself as I untied the tape and gently eased back the package's brown paper wrapping.

Its contents were a mix of financial transaction records and a slim, soft-covered ledger-type book. I managed to convince myself that the material probably would prove interesting if I found the energy to read it.

"First things first," I reminded myself aloud. "Check the dates on all of this stuff to see if any of it aligns with known significant events in Jane's life."

After a long day of cataloguing similar items and other material, I was brain-dead. It took a while for the dates of the material in the package to capture my attention. All the items appeared to date from the same month of 1934. That year, 1934, rang a distant bell somewhere in the back of my mind. To avoid wasting time and energy trying to remember why, I reached for the rough timeline I had created from the information Gabby had given me at our first meeting.

There it was! George's death occurred in 1934. That revelation caused a flurry of research as I tried to tie information in the financial documents with the likely events associated with George's death. At first, nothing unusual jumped out at me. Various bills relating to his funeral were paid, including ones from the undertaker and a local minister. That caused pause for thought. Where was George buried? Did he end up in the local cemetery, or was he buried somewhere on Ravenshead? I made a note to ask Gabby about it, but my gut was telling me he was not buried on the property. If Jane were so incensed at not inheriting, I suspect she would not allow him to be buried there. God, I'm developing a distinct dislike of Jane. I was making judgments supported by almost no evidence about her.

Having established what I thought to be all the expenses associated with George's death, I began a more detailed inspection of the documents. What Jane had been paying for at the time might help me understand what was going on in her life and what life was like generally at Ravenshead in the mid-1930s. While I had to make educated guesses about a few payments, most of the expenses appeared fairly straightforward for the day-to-day running of the property. However, one large payment made shortly before George's death baffled me.

Try as I might, I could not think what the payment might have been for. The payee's name didn't provide any clues. Another trawl through all the documents confirmed that there had been only one large payment to that particular creditor. Although I was reasonably versed in our local history, the name did not ring any bells and wasn't associated with any of the businesses that I knew operated in the town at that time. I sat back and thought on it for a few minutes before deciding it would remain a mystery for now, and I might as well wrap it up again and go to bed.

As I carefully restacked all the documents, I was shocked to discover something I hadn't noticed before. I had incorrectly assumed all the payments were from what appeared to be the property's operating account. Only the single, large, mysterious payment was from a separate account: Jane Creighton's personal account. Now, why would that be? What significant purchase would she have made so soon before becoming widowed?

Of course, she could spend her money on whatever she liked, but it was a substantial amount, even by today's standards. The question such thinking generated was whether other payments to the same payee were amongst other financial documents Jane had seen fit to hide. I had not intended to conduct a detailed inspection of each of the financial document packages. Perhaps that might now prove necessary if Gabby were to truly understand her grandmother's life.

As I climbed into bed, another thought slammed in from left field. Did Gabby want to know about Jane's life? We had spoken only about the mysterious legend of the pirated manuscripts. After thinking about it for a while, I accepted that my brief from Gabby had only mentioned the manuscripts. I realised I didn't know if Gabby was interested in anything else that might have been a part of Jane's life. How much longer was Gabby going to be away? How was I going to contain my curiosity until she returned? That question succeeded in making me wait a long time for sleep to arrive.

This morning's challenge was to stick to my original plan and start cataloguing all of the material on the long shelves running the width of the space. Nevertheless, I struggled to resist the temptation to abandon cataloguing in favour of searching through more of the financial records. The question that lingered in the back of my mind was whether that large mysterious payment from Jane's personal account was the only one to that payee or whether it might have been one of some periodic payment arrangement.

While cataloguing the material on the top shelf, my mind was elsewhere. If nothing else came out of my research last night, I was now aware of how little I knew about life in the 1930s, and in particular, that of the landed gentry of that era. My mind roamed over various questions about such lifestyles before focusing on one particular aspect: What was Jane (Finchley) Creighton's married life like before her husband's death? I was astonished to discover that I had been considering Jane's existence through the lens of my knowledge about the lives of today's average married woman. Did Jane have the same degree of independence and freedom as today's wives, or did she experience a more rigid and controlled life? If 'controlled' was the standard for that era, would Jane's wealth and position in society have afforded her more freedom?

All good questions, but irrelevant, I told myself. In reality, it all came down to George, the sort of man he was and what he expected of his wife. And there was only one child, Amelia (Amy). Does that reveal something about their marriage and relationship? This line of thinking and the questions it generated were far outside the work I had agreed with Gabby. Nevertheless, while I knew I must and would concentrate on Jane's manuscripts, those other thoughts and the questions they raised were not going to go away.

A full day's work ended with slightly less than half the material on the long shelves catalogued. As I was dining alone again tonight, I worked through until six o'clock before calling it a day. Totally unplanned and almost an involuntary act, as I was about to close up, I grabbed another brown paper-wrapped parcel from the financial materials on the end shelves. I was driving away from the homestead before the realisation of what I had done hit me.

Why was I taking home another bundle of financial records? At some point during the day, I had convinced myself not to do further snooping until I had spoken with Gabby and at least had an idea of whether she was interested in any of this or not. But I had brought the material home, and I was alone this evening....

Well, it wouldn't hurt to take a quick look through this bundle of documents, or so I told myself… and another late night ensued. By the time I climbed into bed, I had only deepened the mystery and increased my curiosity about a certain payee who had again received payment from Jane's personal account. The three payments were comparatively small, made at irregular intervals, and occurred during the year following George's death. All that aside, I also noticed other unusual transactions. Small amounts of money were being paid into Jane's account, but not by the previously identified mysterious payee.

This morning, while I dealt with breakfast, I sent thought messages on a continuous loop to Gabby: Please come home today. Obviously, reception was poor at either my end or hers. By lunchtime, there was still no sign of Gabby, but I was hopeful of completing the cataloguing by the end of the day.

I didn't finish the cataloguing. Gabby arrived home when I still had about half a shelf left to catalogue. I was too excited to care about the cataloguing. We had coffee together as soon as she arrived and arranged to meet first thing the next morning. It was obvious Gabby was tired, so neither of us initiated any discussion of my work, but I did ask her if, before I went home, she might like to see what I had discovered. She said it sounded as though I was excited by whatever it was, but she would rather find out about it tomorrow, when she would be able to appreciate its significance.

As soon as we finished our coffees, I left her to unpack and relax while I closed up and left. Somehow, I managed to slip another of those financial bundles into my oversized tote bag before I locked up.

Chapter 6

This morning, I had to force myself to dawdle over breakfast to prevent me from arriving at Ravenshead before Gabby was out of bed. Excitement and anticipation had built up all night, despite my knowing that today could be a disappointment. It was possible that Gabby would show no interest in anything I shared with her at our meeting. Somehow, but I don't know how, I need Gabby to see the hidden space I have discovered. I know persuading her to enter the main part of the house will not be easy – if at all possible – but she needed to see it to fully understand its discovery.

The moment I pulled up out front of the Ravenshead house, Gabby called out to me.

"Good morning, Sophie. I know you've probably just had breakfast, but could you manage another coffee with me?"

Of course, I could handle another coffee. I tend to be caffeine-powered, so a coffee at any time is fine. This morning, I hoped coffee would be accompanied by a long discussion of my work so far – and my slight deviation from the original brief. As soon as we sat down with our coffee, I sensed Gabby wanted a progress report, and she confirmed it a few moments later.

"Can you spare me some time now to tell me what's been happening in my absence, or should we schedule it for later today?"

"Now would be fine, thanks. I hope you have some time available. There is a bit to share with you."

She nodded and gestured to indicate I had the floor. I launched into my report, starting with the discovery of the hidden space, and enhanced it with the various images I had taken on my phone. My heart sank. Gabby didn't display a flicker of interest, let alone excitement, in the news of my discovery. I pushed on.

Perhaps the material I found would ignite her interest. Although she appeared to listen attentively, I didn't detect even a spark of excitement. As I concluded my findings report, I decided it was time she became involved in what had been a one-way conversation to that point. The best way I knew to make that happen was to ask questions, and if needs be, demand answers. So I did.

"Right, I have part of the last shelf to finish cataloguing, but then I will need further direction from you. Now you know what has been achieved so far, how do you want me to proceed?"

"What do you mean? I don't understand what you are asking me to do."

"As I understood it, my brief was to prove or disprove the family legend of Jane's manuscripts having been pirated.

"Yes, and that's still what I want you to do. Don't worry about the time it might take or the cost. Money is not a problem. Just keep track of everything and bill me for it as you would with any other client."

"That's not the problem, Gabby. Think about all I've told you I've found so far. There are shelves full of manuscripts in that hidden space. How am I supposed to work out which ones are missing, or if any of them are missing? Amongst all those on the shelves, how will I identify the ones that were pirated? And before you suggest it, none of them has any such indication scrawled across the front of it. I would appreciate your thoughts on the subject."

"Well, no, I don't have any ideas at all about how to proceed."

"Okay, let's talk about that legend. As I recall from our conversation, Jane went to a fete or fair in the grounds of some big house, and discovered on a stall a number of her manuscripts published as books without her permission. When was this? I know you can't be sure exactly, but roughly at what point in Jane's life did this occur?"

"Uhmm, as you say, I can't be sure, but I think it was late in her life. I don't remember any major uproar occurring after we returned to Ravenshead, and at that time, she was too sick to attend a fete or anything else."

"Gabby, try to think back on when you heard that legend to see if you can find any clues that might indicate when it happened."

"Sophie, over the years, I've replayed that story in my mind so many times, but it provides no clues to help you. All I have is a feeling I gained when I first heard it. The feeling was that it hadn't been so many years ago when it happened and, therefore, it was late in her life. I will consider it, though, to see if I can link it to something else that might establish a timeframe for it. This is going to sound like a really stupid question, but is when it happened really so critical?"

"As I pointed out earlier, one of the bookshelves on the end walls holds Jane's journals from when she was barely a teenager to almost the end of her life. If we had a rough idea of when the pirated manuscripts were discovered, we could check her diary entries from around then that might shed light on the matter. If we are working with nothing more than 'towards the end of her life' as a timeframe, there are a hell of a lot of journals to peruse."

"I see … And you don't know of any other way we might be able to do it?" I shook my head emphatically. "Right, then I will try to think back on whenever I've heard that legend repeated."

While our conversation yielded nothing to work with, I had other questions to ask. Questions that may not be directly related to the brief I was given, but whose answers could help inform some aspects of it.

"Who was Darcy Wilson?"

"Darcy Wilson? I've no idea. I don't recall ever hearing the name before. Is he important?"

"Dunno. He could be, and I was hoping you knew the name from somewhere in your family's stories. Perhaps he was an old faithful retainer from your grandmother's days, maybe a gardener or such like."

"He could have been, I suppose, but I don't recall ever having heard mention of him – or any others of the household staff, for that matter. I think there might have been staff back then, but I don't know who or how many, and I certainly never heard any names mentioned. You have me intrigued, though. Why's that Darcy bloke important?"

"Wish I knew...."

As I wasn't about to learn anything about Darcy Wilson, I decided to finish my cataloguing. Then, as I went to stand up, another line of questioning demanded my attention. I indulged it.

"On another matter, Gabby, please indulge me for a few moments as I believe it is important." She nodded. I took a deep breath and dived in. "What happened to make you now so reluctant to enter the main part of the house? I realise it must have been when you were just a child, but can you tell me about it... And, before you ask, yes, it is important to the work I'm trying to do for you."

"It's going to sound ridiculous, but I honestly don't know. You are right, though. Whatever it was goes back to my childhood."

"You had never been to Ravenshead until you returned here when you were about four or five. Is that correct?"

"Yes, Mum brought us back here when Jane had reached the stage that she needed care. That was the first time I had set foot on the place."

"If I remember correctly, you said you had visited Jane a couple of times in the house before she was taken into care."

"That's right. Mum took me to see Jane three times, or maybe four, before Jane demanded I shouldn't visit her again – and I didn't. I haven't been into the main part of the house since then."

"Why...?"

"Eh? What do you mean by 'why'?"

"Why haven't you been into the house since then? Jane was taken away, so she was going to kick up a fuss if you went into the house. Surely, your mother would have gone into the house to tidy up and deal with things after Jane died. You could have gone in with her. Did you, or were you not allowed to accompany her?"

"A strange question, and one I'm not sure how to answer. Yes, I have a vague recollection of Mum's having gone into the house at least a couple of times… to clean up, I suppose. However, I don't recollect being told I couldn't go with her. If anything, my memory is of not being interested in entering the house. So, if I weren't looking to go with her, she wouldn't have told me I couldn't.

Sophie, is any of this really important at this time? I mean, does it matter if I choose not to enter the main part of the house ever again?"

"Perhaps…. What do you plan to do with the Ravenshead Estate now it's yours? Do you intend to keep it and continue to live here, or are you thinking of selling it, or perhaps leasing it out?"

"I won't be selling it, and in due course, it will pass to my daughter, who has never even laid eyes on the place and who is currently too busy with her career overseas to even visit me here. Is that a problem?"

"No, it's not a problem for me. But, if the house remains unoccupied, it could become a problem for both you and your daughter. By the way, your comments about your daughter sound like something your mother probably moaned about in the past."

"Quite possibly…."

"Please try to think back to anything that might have triggered this fear about the house. I believe it is important not only to the work I'm doing, but in other ways as well. Anyway, I have cataloguing to finish, so I'll leave you to your day."

"Okay, but have another coffee before you go, and then I will see you again at lunchtime."

After yet another (quick) coffee, I was back in the hidden space and striving to complete the cataloguing, but my mind was elsewhere. I really needed Gabby to become interested in everything related to this hidden space because I believe that the information stored in here might put a few of those ghosts that haunt her to rest. There was so much going on in my mind that I hadn't noticed the time slipping by until a voice brought me back to reality.

"It's lunchtime. Are you coming?" Gabby shouted at me from the front doorstep.

"Give me ten minutes. I'm almost done here," I yelled back.

I strode into the kitchen after a quick wash to remove the grime, and was stunned to see the table set for lunch.

"You're not expected to feed me, Gabby. I've brought my own lunch."

"Stick it in the fridge. Take it home and have it for dinner tonight, or leave it in the fridge for lunch tomorrow. I've made a salad for lunch. Now, tell me, did you finish that cataloguing that you seemed hellbent to do?"

"Yeah, I've just finished it. Now, everything in that hidden space has been catalogued, and the list goes on for pages. There is so much about your family's history contained in those records, more than you could imagine, and certainly more than I expected. Still, it's up to you how much you want to know, or not know. The one thing you need to be aware of is that nothing I've done so far will answer your questions about the possible pirating of Jane's manuscripts. I have no doubt that the information you require is held in that space, but winkling it out from all the other information is the real issue. It will not be easy, and it will not be achieved without a great deal of reading.

Now, at the risk of ruining our lunch, I do need to know how you want me to progress from this point, and how much more you want me to attempt to do for you."

"Is time critical to you? I mean, do you have other work demanding your attention that limits how much more time you might devote to Ravenshead?"

"No-o, I don't have anything demanding immediate attention, so at the moment, I am free for at least the next week, but things might change after that."

"So, you will be all right to keep working here at Ravenshead for a bit longer?"

"In theory, that's possible. However, the situation is not quite so straightforward. Unless you engage with the material stored in that hidden space, it's unlikely to yield a satisfactory outcome for either of us, regardless of how long I work for you. Yes, I understand you're having trouble entering the main part of the house. I accept the problem exists. I also know that, unless you come and look at the material, nothing will be achieved. The only information guiding this project at the moment is your recollection of a distant, spurious conversation. The problem is, whether we like to accept it or not, with the passage of time, your recall of that story might have changed."

"I remember the story about the manuscripts. I heard it several times over the years."

"Right, and I'm not suggesting you imagined it. What I am suggesting is that it would have been better if you had remembered a bit more detail. Any additional information may help us discover the truth. The way things stand at the moment, I have no belief that will be the case."

"Sophie, I hear what you're saying, and I am beginning to appreciate how difficult this is for you, and how little help I'm giving you. Is it really so critical for me to enter the house and look at that hidden space?"

"More than you can understand at the moment. You don't know what you don't know, and therefore you can't understand why this is important. All I can say is that, without your involvement in some of the material stored in that space, we are both wasting our time pursuing this further. Even the work I've done so far will ultimately be nothing more than a waste of time.

Argh, I'm at the point where, Gabby, if you cannot become involved as I've indicated, there is little for me to do here. I'll type up the inventory of all the material I've catalogued and give it to you, but then, disappointing as it will be, I think my work here will be done."

"Allow me a little more time… Please. Take a few days to process the inventory, and then get back to me. Please, Sophie, let's talk again in a couple of days. I need to do this."

What else could I do but agree? She sounded so desperate, although I didn't know why she should be. Not confirming the story of the pirated manuscripts is hardly life-threatening. After not knowing whether the story is true or not for so long, not confirming it one way or the other hardly seemed cause for concern. Yet, I wasn't mistaken. There was clear desperation in Gabby's pleading for me to continue with the project. Well, I agreed to produce an inventory document of all the materials in the hidden space, so I needed to get started.

It was two days later when I received a phone call from Gabby. When the caller ID indicated it was Gabby, I was convinced the call was to end the project. I was a roiling mass of mixed emotions when I answered it.

"I hope I'm not interrupting anything, Sophie, but I do need to speak with you. You don't need to come all the way out to Ravenshead. If you can spare me some time, we could meet in town somewhere, even over lunch, if that would suit you better. Please say you have some time to talk with me."

"Of course, I have time. Has something happened that I should know about? You sound a little anxious about something."

"Anxious? No. Well, perhaps a little, but nothing has happened… Other than I devoted some time to thinking things over, and particularly the things you said."

"How do you feel about making lunch?" She indicated it wasn't a problem. "Good, make us lunch, and I'll be out there to have it with you in about an hour. Does that suit you?"

She agreed, and I stuffed a few things into my tote bag before having a quick shower and heading for Ravenshead. On the drive out to the property, I kept warning myself not to get excited. If there had been a change, it might not be in the direction I wanted. My attempt at keeping calm was an abject failure. It was all I could do to restrain myself from dashing straight into the apartment as soon as I pulled up but, somehow, I managed to saunter to the door and wait for Gabby to usher me in. She took me straight to the table where lunch was already waiting for us. As I was still settling myself on my chair, Gabby started the conversation she was obviously keen to have.

"At the risk of giving us both indigestion, would you mind if I dive straight into the conversation I want to have with you. I've been practising what I wanted to say all morning, and now my mind is a woolly mass of nothing intelligent.

Sophie, the most important point I want to make is that I want you to continue to work on the material you found in the hidden space. No, don't interrupt or I'll never manage to say what I want to say."

"Okay, but everything I said previously still holds true today. So, how do we work around those problems as I see them?"

"I'm not sure, but I've done a lot of thinking over the last couple of days and, maybe, I've dredged up something worthwhile. It probably will sound ridiculous, but might we sit more comfortably in the lounge while I try to explain what I think might be the cause?"

We moved to the lounge room and did the usual faffing about until we both were settled comfortably. I suspected Gabby was about to employ delaying tactics instead of jumping straight into her story. It wasn't surprising, I suppose, if she found it difficult or embarrassing in some way to discuss, so I encouraged her.

"Right, Gabby, remember that no one in this room is here to judge or criticise. Take your time to tell me in the way you feel most comfortable about whatever it is you think you have remembered." I watched her take a deep breath and swallow hard a couple of times before the words started to flow.

"Although I can't remember exactly how old I was at the time, I know I was only a child. As I think I told you, Jane was quite ill and became a virtual invalid towards the end of her life. She also lost her mind. Oh, I don't mean that she forgot everything and everyone. It was as if she had lost touch with reality. She would ramble on about past events, becoming upset and hostile when Mum couldn't recall them. I questioned Mum about it. She said that often the things or events Jane talked about happened before Mum was born. Sometimes they happened when Jane was only a young girl.

There was something else about Jane's state of mind at that time. I suppose, to put it politely, she had lost her social compass and tended to say things she shouldn't. Just before Jane went into care, I heard Mum and the live-in nurse discussing something Jane had said that seemed to have upset the nurse. A couple of days later, Jane left Ravenshead."

"Did your mother give you all the details of the incident?"

"God, no, and I couldn't ask her about it either. It was supposed to be a private conversation between Mum and the nurse. I would have been in all sorts of trouble if Mum found out I had been eavesdropping on the conversation."

"When did Jane actually upset the nurse? I mean, was there some sort of upsetting conversation between the nurse and Jane that sent the nurse running to your mother?"

"Oh, I haven't explained things well. No. The conversation I eavesdropped on was sometime after Jane's death. Mum and the nurse had become friends. They kept in touch and occasionally caught up for coffee. I think on the occasion in question, the nurse had come to Ravenshead to collect a reference or something from Mum. Anyway, back to the story, and please note that I did not hear the entire conversation.

It appears Jane had told the nurse some aspects of her marriage that she would never have mentioned if she were of sound mind. The key detail was that George, Jane's husband, was playing away with a young widow in a cottage not far from the Ravenshead boundary. Jane claimed that George thought he was being cautious and that Jane didn't know about it, so he was safe. Jane had other ideas. It's obvious there wasn't much love between the couple. According to the nurse, Jane claimed she arranged for George to be killed. Jane believed Ravenshead was hers, and George was trying to cheat her out of it. After all, he was only there because he had wormed his way into her bed. Now she wasn't about to suffer being embarrassed by his womanising."

"Jesus… It could be nothing more than the raving of a demented mind, I suppose, but there had to be something that made her think she had arranged his death. Maybe she just wished she could do that, and then Fate stepped in and delivered for her. Was there more to the conversation?"

"I don't know. I remember Mum became really upset. She began shouting and swearing – I think it was swearing – and the nurse was trying to quieten her down. The nurse kept apologising for having told Mum the story. I don't know what happened after that. What I had heard, coupled with Mum's behaviour, frightened me. I ran to my room and hid until Mum dragged me out for dinner. The nurse stayed for quite a while after I scarpered, but I have no idea what was said then."

"Yeah, I can understand how that whole episode would have been upsetting to a child, but I don't see what it has to do with the house or why all this frightens you about entering the main part of the house."

"Well, this is the *really* strange part of the story. According to what the nurse told Mum, Jane claimed George's ghost still roamed the house with murderous intent to avenge his death. I know … I know… If you asked me if I believed in ghosts, my answer would be 'of course not', but for some reason, in this particular case, that response doesn't apply, and never has since I heard the story."

"Right… It seems we both agree there are no such things as ghosts. That's the first step. Now, let's apply that – and some common sense – to your particular situation. Perhaps Jane's 'ghost' that roamed the house looking for revenge was no more than a guilty conscience that had bothered her since George's death. Whether she had any involvement in his death is another matter, and one we might explore. I suspect maybe a number of other issues stem from it.

Now, shall we go into the house so I can show you the hidden space? I'll even hold your hand, if it helps."

Chapter 7

Having it out in the open and discussed, I hoped Gabby would be at least a little enthusiastic about exploring the treasure trove of material I had discovered. That's not exactly how it happened. Things went well enough until she actually had to step into the main entrance foyer. She balked, and I feared she would turn and run.

"Come on, Gabby. We can do this together. Just take your time and come with me to the study."

"No. No, I can't do it."

"Yes, you can. Gabby, there are no ghosts here; nobody looking for revenge. George didn't die here in this house, so why would his ghost be here? …And there are no such things as ghosts, remember." Then, to have her focus on something else, I asked, "You told me that when you and your mother returned to Ravenshead, Jane was using one of the rooms down here as her bedroom. Which room was that? Do you remember?"

"Uhm, yes. It was that little room over there. It's only a small room, so with a bed, a wardrobe and a big old padded chair in there, it was pretty crowded."

Gabby had indicated the small sitting room beyond the dining room on the opposite side of the house from the study. I sensed she relaxed a little as she explained about Jane's bedroom, so I encouraged her to talk more by asking more questions. The ploy worked well, and we found ourselves standing outside the study.

"I don't need to ask you about this room. I know it was the study and probably belonged to the man of the house in the past."

"Oh, yes. They used to have their own den, where women had to be invited to enter, didn't they?. How can you be so sure that's what the room was used for?"

After a brief explanation of the remnants of a man's world found in the room, I explained my assumption about its more recent use.

"That's how I believe it was originally. In more recent times, I think that was swept aside and it became Jane's domain."

She looked sceptical, so I explained the changes, including the bookshelves and how the books had been shelved, with all the men's books on the upper shelves out of easy reach. To illustrate my point, I led her over to the bookshelves and indicated the positioning of various titles that tended to confirm my assumption. Then, although I still held some reservations, I decided it was time to introduce her to the hidden space. I started by pointing out how the long shelves didn't quite reach the far end wall and how a small extra set of shelves was used to fill the gap.

"Nothing is surprising about that. It's amazing that they found straight timber long enough for those shelves, and it would have looked strange if they hadn't filled along that wall with more shelving." As Gabby spoke, I positioned myself in readiness for the big reveal.

While she continued to run her eyes over the books on the shelves, I reached under and pressed the button. The clunk as the mechanism unlocked and the grind as the end of the small set of shelves slid out of alignment startled Gabby. She looked ready to bolt.

"It's okay, Gabby. Come and take a look. All I've done is opened the entrance to the hidden space. Come on, have a look."

Hesitantly, she did as I asked, and I witnessed her face light up.

"That is sneaky. What a brilliant piece of engineering. When do you think that was installed? Was the shelving there to begin with, and it was later altered to create this?"

"No, I don't think so. My feeling is that the whole installation is a relatively recent addition to this room. Look in here. See, there is the door that opens into the hidden space," I said as I hauled the small bookshelf wide open.

"What does 'relatively recent' mean? Who built this? Was it in George's time? If it was, I'll bet it got up Jane's nose and wouldn't have improved relations between them."

"True, Jane probably wouldn't have been happy if George had been responsible – but he wasn't. I believe Jane commissioned this work."

"Jane…? Why would she want to install something like this? Was this some strange form of *up-yours* to George?"

"Again, it's only speculation, but I think this dates to after George's death. Perhaps once you've seen what is stored in there, you will understand why I think that to be the case. Come on. Allow me to take you in and show you around."

I heard her gasp as she followed me in. I spun around to check that she was okay. I was prepared for her to be surprised, but I hoped for no worse reaction than that. She stood behind me, sweeping her head from side to side as she tried to take in the magnitude of the contents of the space.

"Don't try to take it all in immediately, but I will give you a quick tour of what all this is. In front of us, those long shelves across the width of the room hold Jane's writings. The shelves on the end wall to your left contain Jane's diaries from when she was barely a teenager. The shelves to your right contain financial documents, contracts and other legal documents. That material, too, all relates to Jane."

"Sophie, I'm speechless. I don't know what to say. You are right, I can't take it all in – yet. Do you think we might retreat to my apartment for sustenance while I recover, at least a little, from the shock of all this?"

"What a good idea … But only if you promise to return here with me later."

'Sustenance' proved to be a slice of a Victoria sponge to accompany our coffee. Although she was initially subdued, I was relieved when the questions started flowing.

"There is so much stuff in that room. It must just about cover Jane's life story. I can understand that it took a while to catalogue everything. What stands out amongst it?"

"Because I know your interest is in the manuscripts, that had to be my focus, but just about everything else in there is more exciting for me… And I think you are going to have to become interested in some of that other stuff. While there is a massive amount of Jane's writing stored there, we have no way of knowing if any of it is missing, or which, if any, was illegally published. Our only hope of finding out, as far as I can see, is to find clues in other material, like her diaries."

"Oh, I've been meaning to ask you about that name and keep forgetting. Now that I've remembered it again, why did you ask about Darcy Wilson? Who is he, and what was his association with Ravenshead?"

"Odd though it might sound, I don't know that he was associated with Ravenshead in any way. His only known connection, so far, was through Jane. She paid Darcy Wilson a significant sum of money from her personal account not long before George's death. Before you ask, no, I don't know of any connection between the two events. All I know is that Jane paid some bills from the business account, and at the same time, she made a payment to Darcy Wilson. Her diary for that time might tell us more."

"Well, we need to have a look at that," she said emphatically. I felt a hint of accusation in it, and I suspect my face let it be known. "No. No, I wasn't having a go at you about not having read the diary to find out more. All I was admitting was that WE have some work to do … And WE should get on with it instead of sitting here eating cake. I don't know how to do this stuff. So, how do we begin?"

"Well, I think our first move is to look at the catalogue to establish which diaries we need to read."

That's what we did, but having aroused Gabby's interest, time was spent poring over other entries in the catalogue besides those for the diaries. After some time, and once attention refocused on the diaries, it was discovered that the period of time that included George's death was split between two journals. The last few entries in the earlier of the two books covered the time of the payment to Darcy Wilson, while comments on events surrounding George's death probably appeared in the latter.

"If it's all right with you, I'll take the earlier journal home for a bit of light reading tonight," I suggested, hoping she wouldn't mind if I took the other one. Darcy Wilson had me intrigued.

"Yeah, that's fine. I'll take the other one to see what I can find in it."

So far , so good, I told myself as I retrieved the two journals from the shelf and handed one to Gabby. Now, if only I can keep her interest alive, who knows what exciting things we might find hidden in all this stuff.

Long shadows heralded the evening when we again emerged from the house. Gabby walked me to my car, and I told her I planned to start work early tomorrow, hopefully to progress whatever I uncovered tonight. As I drove home, I realised I hadn't heard from Warren today, although he should have returned from his conference by now. Was it too much to hope that I might have another evening alone, I wondered, and caused myself a moment of guilt.

Luck was on my side. With not a murmur from Warren, after a quick shower and some leftovers reheated in the microwave, I put my feet up in the lounge room and settled down to read Jane's journal. The problem with the fairly random process I applied was that many other journal entries were encountered before the required date was found. While not of any immediate relevance, I had become lost in Jane's scribblings and it took me ages to find the approximate date for the entry I wanted.

At last, there it was. Darcy Wilson's name caught my eye from amongst the words of a long diary entry. After locating the start of the important entry, I carefully read through it. Jane's handwriting was quite tidy, if a little fancy at times. It seemed to me that Jane might have been distressed or upset as she recorded that day's thoughts and activities. Frequently throughout the long entry, Jane's handwriting degenerated into an almost unintelligible scribble. Each occurrence required time, patience, and repeated attempts to decipher it before it was understood. Yes, this was the critical entry.

Once I was sure I had accurately deciphered the entire entry, with the book held out in front of me like some unexploded munition, I rushed to my office. Grabbing my digital recorder, I took a deep breath to steady my nerves before slowly and clearly reading the entire entry into the recorder. Then, as my computer transcribed the recording, I slumped back on my chair and considered the magnitude of my discovery.

How the hell was I going to tell Gabby about this? Perhaps I should simply hand her the journal and direct her to the relevant entry, so she can read it for herself. No, not only was that cowardly, but Gabby's recently developed acceptance of the house and things about Jane would be knocked for six. Ghosts would again inhabit the house. Gabby might never be persuaded to enter it again. No, better I wait for some appropriate time, and then share the truth with her – gently, if that's at all possible. In the meantime, I had to find a way to digest the information myself, and that's when I realised how cryptic the entry was.

My hope was that earlier in her writings, Jane would have noted other details of the events leading up to the main event and the payout of so much money. I located the start of entries for 1934 and began skimming every entry, stopping only to carefully read those that appeared to have some relevance. I hadn't gone more than a couple of pages when Darcy Wilson's name caught my eye. I read the brief mention of the man, and then reread it. Shaking my head, I sat back to consider what it told me, and the question it raised: *Why did Jane pay the grocery delivery boy such a huge sum of money?*

I searched for other mentions of Darcy Wilson to gain a better understanding of him and of Jane's relationship with him. It didn't take me long to find that Wilson visited Ravenshead every fortnight. It appeared his arrival always coincided with morning tea time, and he would always have a cup of tea with Jane in her private sitting room. It posed more questions than it answered.

It didn't take me long to find the subsequent entries that dealt with Wilson's visits and his morning tea interludes with Jane. Surely Jane was not so lonely and deprived of other company that she had resorted to entertaining the delivery boy. Long before I reached the entry regarding the 'main event', I realised Darcy Wilson was not so much a lad as a young man, who had worked at the local general store in town for a number of years, since he was a lad, in fact. Somewhere during that time, he was promoted to delivery driver and then spent some time every week delivering orders to the various properties in the area. His run alternated between the different sides of the district, meaning that he visited each property on a fortnightly basis ... And always took tea with Jane when he called at Ravenshead.

A quick review of a few entries from the previous year showed the practice was in place then as well. It raised the question of how long the arrangement had been in place, but I reminded myself that it was not my mission at this time. Nevertheless, it did have me wondering about life after George's death. While I hadn't developed any suspicion that Jane had acquired a toyboy, I couldn't help but wonder how her relationship with Mr Wilson survived after Jane became widowed.

There weren't too many more entries after the one relating to George's death before I reached the last page of the journal I had selected. Any further mentions of Darcy Wilson would be in the journal Gabby intended to read tonight. How frustrating. There was nothing more I could do to satisfy my curiosity. After sulking about it over a glass of wine, I turned to the start of Jane's journal and began skimming its entries. Some entries recorded the minutiae of daily life. While others hinted at more significant events, but did not provide sufficient detail for the reader to understand the full story of what was happening. And, yes, Mr Wilson's visits were recorded, and some of those entries included reference to a particular item of local news he brought.

All of the entries were interesting. Frustrating, yes, but interesting nevertheless, as they provided a glimpse into Jane's life. If only they had included more detailed information....

Reading such sketchy entries was like glimpsing life through a dirty window. Things were happening out there, but you couldn't see exactly what was going on.

When I sat back to ponder all I had discovered, I realised it was gone midnight. I had planned to be at Ravenshead early tomorrow, and I needed to be at my best if I was to share with Gabby the unpleasant details I had discovered. It wasn't much later when I fell into bed, but sleep was a long time arriving. My mind kept working at breakneck speed as I wrestled with the dilemma of how to tell Gabby about her grandmother – and confirm for her at least one part of a family legend.

My plans for an early start at Ravenshead this morning were the stuff of good intentions and went the way of so many other good intentions. Out of bed later than usual, I struggled to find traction. Breakfast seemed to take an inordinately long time, and packing my tote bag for the day at Ravenshead seemed almost beyond my capabilities. Then, to top it off, as I reversed out of the garage, I realised I had left Jane's journal on my desk. More time was lost retrieving the book before finally setting off. A bleary-eyed Gabby was waiting for me when I arrived.

"I don't care whether you've had breakfast or not. I need another coffee. Please come and have one with me before we do anything else."

"While I don't mean to be rude, Gabby, you look about as bad as I feel this morning. What have you been up to?"

"It's amazing how easily this research lark can run away with you. I had some work stuff to attend to after dinner last night. After that, I sat down to read Jane's diary. In my wisdom, I didn't start at page one. I picked it up, let it flip open, and began from the page that it opened to. While I admit it took me a while to get the hang of her writing and language, I soon was lost in the book. It was well after midnight before I realised how late it was. Anyway, I only had a few pages left to read by then, so I kept going until I finished the book."

"Funny how that happens. I had a similar experience last night – until early this morning. You mentioned having something to do for work. I thought you had retired when you came back here."

"Yeah, I thought so, too, but they keep asking me to do bits and pieces for them. I'm not complaining. It gives me something to do, something to keep the grey cells working."

"Right… Well, what about the diary? Did you find Jane had written anything interesting, particularly about any major events that might have occurred at Ravenshead?"

"Not really. There were occasional mentions of Darcy Wilson, more frequent earlier in the part I read, but they tapered off to occasional mentions as time went by. At one stage, I wondered if he might have been more than just an acquaintance, but if he was, it seems the flame went out. I didn't come across any comments to explain why he barely rated a mention in the later part of the diary, but it seemed as though something had changed between the pair of them."

"Did you note when or how long after George's death you noticed a change in their relationship?" Gabby shook her head and looked upset.

"Sorry, Sophie. I didn't think to make a note of it. Argh, I'm afraid I don't know how to do this. Anyone else would have picked it up as an important development, but I was more intent on just galloping along through the story. Do I have to go back to read it again? I will if that's what you need me to do, but I was looking forward to moving on to the next diary."

"No, that's not a problem. Just grab the next diary and get stuck into it whenever you have the time to do some reading. I'll return these two to the shelves. Should I fetch the next diary for you while I'm about it?"

Gabby indicated she would come with me, but Fate intervened. Gabby's phone played its tune. After checking the caller ID, she indicated that she would join me in the hidden space after attending to the call. That made things simple. I didn't intend to return the diary Gabby had read to the shelves. I wanted to read it, particularly the first part that Gabby hadn't read, but I didn't want her to see me put it in my bag. While I didn't want her to feel that she hadn't done a good enough job, I did want to check for myself any mentions of Darcy Wilson. I hurried across and let myself into the hidden space.

While dealing with the diaries, a thought slammed in from nowhere. Perhaps I should take the file containing the financial transactions for the period covered by the diary Gabby had read. That way, I would be able to check on any mentions Jane made about Wilson and whether any further cash went his way around the same time. I slipped the relevant bundle of financial documents into my tote bag alongside the diary. As I heard Gabby enter the study, I picked up ê Gabby's next diary from the shelf.

"Here is the next diary you wanted to read. Is there anything else in particular you would like to look at while we are here?" I realised I sounded like I was taking charge, but I didn't know what else to do.

"What else can we look at? I know there is plenty in here, but without a goal in mind, we could spend a lot of time looking at things for no reason. I suppose, as our original goal was to prove or disprove the story of the pirated manuscripts, that's probably what we should aim to do."

"You're right. That's what we should be trying to do, but do you have any ideas about how we should do that? I believe that, until we find some mention in her diaries of that fete Jane attended, we really don't have a sound starting point."

"Well, Sophie, you're the expert, and I will be guided by your advice, but the only way I can see to establish a reliable date for that fete is to keep reading Jane's diaries until we find something."

"See, you do know how to do this. Stop putting yourself down, take that diary, and start reading. That's all we can do. The only thing to remember is that you don't actually have to read every word if it doesn't have any relevance. Just skim, and only read those entries that grab your attention. Otherwise, you'll be reading diaries for years to come."

Armed with our next lot of reading material, we returned to Gabby's apartment for lunch, before I went home to read in the peace of my office.

Chapter 8

It didn't take me long to realise that by not reading Jane's diary from the first page, Gabby had missed what appeared to be some important information. How important wouldn't be determined until I checked Jane's financial records, but in the meantime, my excitement level was running high.

While not exactly cryptic, Jane's diary entries dealing with Darcy Wilson suggested she was applying a modicum of caution to what she wrote. Because I was on the lookout for further cash payments to Mr Wilson, her carefully worded entries still caught my eye. The question was how to proceed without wasting too much time.

I decided the most efficient and effective approach was to continue with the diary, noting the date of each reference to Wilson. Once I reached where Gabby had started reading this diary, I could set it aside while I searched for corresponding entries in Jane's financial records. While references to Wilson weren't many, they were more frequent than I expected. It didn't take me long to detect a pattern in the payments to him, and the financial records provided an intriguing detail.

Some of the payments were from the Ravenshead account, while others were from Jane's personal account. None was a large amount, and the amount of each payment varied. Then, suddenly, payments to Darcy Wilson from any account appeared to come to an abrupt end.

"Why?" I demanded of the universe. "What changed, and why so suddenly?" With no enlightening response forthcoming, I pondered the situation over another coffee.

About half an hour later, and still no wiser, I flicked through the rest of the diary, the part Gabby already had perused. Gabby had confirmed mentions of Wilson in the latter part of the diary.

Maybe the earlier mentions of him had stopped because he had gone away on holidays – or been in goal – and mention of him only resumed after his return. When there was a significant gap before Darcy Wilson again appeared in any entries, I felt my suspicions regarding his absence confirmed. It posed questions about such an absence. Why was he absent? Where did he go? What brought him back to town? All good questions, I decided, but none with an immediate answer.

No later mentions of Wilson contained any comment, veiled or otherwise, regarding money. Was money still changing hands, but Jane had refrained from documenting it? Eager now to search the financial records for the period, I rushed through to the end of the diary, simply noting the date of any mention of Darcy Wilson. Then, armed with a long list of dates to check, I pushed the diary aside and opened the folder containing the financial documents.

Perhaps the results were not as surprising as they might have been. As I suspected, prior to Wilson's absence from the diary, Jane continued to pay him small, variable sums of money. Then, after his return, no further payments occurred, at least not during the period under review. As I idly flicked through the ledger relating to Jane's personal account, something caught my attention. Initially, it was unsuccessful because my focus was on the apparent cessation of payment. Some part of my mind nudged me to look more closely at the ledger, to look not just for payments to Wilson, but for anything else unusual that might have been happening at the time.

"What the…?" I yelped. "How did this come about, and why now?" I demanded of the universe, as I sat up straight and pulled the ledger closer.

A feverish scan began of those pages of the ledger that aligned with the diary. Nothing unusual occurred until Wilson reappeared in the diary after a period of absence. My feverish scan became a careful search of every subsequent ledger entry. There they were: small, fairly regular payments into Jane's personal account. It wasn't difficult to identify larger, regular payments from the Ravenshead account to Jane's account. I assumed they were some form of allowance that was paid to her, although I couldn't understand why anyone would have felt such an arrangement necessary. Those small payments that had caught my attention were for something else… but what?

No bright ideas about the origin or the nature of the payments came to me. It was late. I hadn't stopped for dinner. Food might help fire up my grey cells, but I didn't want to waste much time preparing it. Cold chicken and salad doesn't take long, and I was soon sitting at my breakfast bar with my dinner. It probably was a tasty meal, but I didn't notice. My mind was preoccupied with those odd payments. As I added my dishes to the dishwasher, something I had overlooked sprang to my attention.

Darcy Wilson was no longer visiting Ravenshead on a fortnightly basis. When did that change occur? Was it before his lengthy absence from the diary, or after his return? Telling myself there was only one way to find out sent me hurrying back to my office. With both Jane's diary and her ledger open in front of me, I started checking every mention of Mr Wilson against entries in the ledger. That confirmed something I hadn't realised earlier.

Jane's brief mentions of Darcy before his long absence indicated she did not have regular fortnightly contact with him. Her encounters with Wilson appeared to have been erratic rather than aligned with any regular fixed interval. There was no consistency in timing or payment amounts. That's when it occurred to me that I should have paid more attention to the period of his supposed absence. I abandoned the diary for a while and focused on the ledger. Moments later, I was chiding myself for sloppy work.

Payments, small and almost to the point of being insignificant, were made into Jane's personal account. Those payments were not accompanied by any mention of Wilson in Jane's diary. It was not until after Wilson's supposed return that the payments increased slightly, although they remained quite small. After spending another hour cross-checking the diary and ledger entries, without generating any inspiration, I closed both books and set them aside. There was no point spending more time on them tonight.

Moments after I crawled into bed, an idea occurred to me. Flinging off the bedclothes, I rushed to my office and dragged in front of me the bundle of financial records that accompanied the ledger. Now, to try to answer the question that occurred to me moments after I switched off my bedside light. *Who was making those payments into Jane's personal account?* Because they coincided with entries in Jane's diary, I assumed Darcy Wilson made the payments. Again, I suffered a flood of dark thoughts about my sloppy workmanship.

The other documents bound up in the same parcel as the ledger related to the various transactions in the ledger, and included bank statements. I felt my pulse quicken as I rifled through the documents and realised what they were. In my haste, I seemed to fumble through the pile without seeing anything useful. After a couple of deep breaths, I checked every document as I worked my way through the pile. I found the information I needed. All those small payments into Jane's account were from the same payee.

"Ri-ight, that is useful," I told my empty office, "but who that is, and why, would be even more useful. Who or what was Kennedy's Store… And for what was the store paying Jane?"

I sat back to ponder my latest discovery. Back in the 1930s, what would a store pay one of its customers for? That only gave rise to two more questions: What type of store was Kennedy's, and what could it possibly be buying from Jane? The country had suffered a terrible depression in the 1930s. Were the payments, small though they were, Jane's attempt at making ends meet? Probably not, I decided. After all, she was paid an allowance on a regular basis, and according to Gabby, Jane's continued rent-free existence at Ravenshead came with free food and domestic staff.

Perhaps Kennedy's was one of those 'general' stores that sold everything from mousetraps to fresh fruit and vegetables.

Did Jane have a garden and sold her excess vegetables to the store? Maybe she had chickens and sold the eggs. Was it due to the late hour or a long day that my mind seemed barely able to function? While it took me a while to work it out, I eventually realised I couldn't progress further until I knew more about Kennedy's Store. It's as well Google doesn't mind late hours.

Not exactly at my brightest at that hour of the night, it took me a while to find what I wanted. It wasn't until I finally remembered the National Library's Trove archive that I made any progress. Once I logged into Trove and typed the name of Kennedy's Store in the search bar, I was off and running. Nevertheless, the search produced only a few hits. I read them in chronological order, starting with the earliest reference to the store. The first couple of hits I looked at, while useful, were not particularly exciting.

Both were copies of an advertisement that the store ran in the local newspaper. In reality, they told me what I had wanted to know. Yes, as I suspected, Kennedy's Store was one of those 'general' type of stores that flourished in the more rural areas of the State. A place to buy anything from bootlaces to bales of hay and everything in between. The advertisement also advised readers that the store delivered to outlying properties.

"Ah hah," I chirped. "So, our Darcy Wilson was a delivery driver for Kennedy's Store. That fits with what we know."

After a couple of moments of feeling smug about my earlier suspicions being right, I crashed back to earth. That bit of information didn't explain why he stopped being a regular visitor to Ravenshead, or why he appeared to have no contact with Jane for an extended period in the middle of 1935. I pressed on with the other Kennedy's Store hits Trove had found for me… And struck gold.

The next hit was an item from the Social Notes column. It reported that following the death of his only son about a year previously, Mr Kennedy, the owner of Kennedy's Store, was considering disposing of his business. With both his wife and their only child gone, Mr Kennedy was looking to take steps to organise the remainder of his life, and that could well include selling the store.

If Kennedy did find a buyer for the store, Wilson's employment might have been threatened, and it could explain the dramatic change in contact between Jane and Wilson, as well as his long absence in 1935. Now, well and truly hooked by the ongoing saga of Kennedy's Store, I had to read the remaining two hits Trove had found. The next one came as something of a surprise.

I expected it would follow the previous comments and include references to the sale of the store and its new owner. I was wrong on all accounts. The hit again came from the Social Notes column, but it was from more than two years after the previous mention of the store, and ran under the headline *Store Sold.*

"Hmm, looks like it took old Kennedy a while to find a buyer. Having gone so far, I suppose I should find out what happened to the store," I told my empty office as I started reading the article. "Oh my God… I did not see that coming!" It took me a while to take it all in.

According to the article, Kennedy's Store had a new owner *after the remaining half of the business was sold.* It went on to explain that a partnership formed a couple of years earlier had resulted in a buyer purchasing 50 percent of the business. That same buyer had now purchased the remaining half, to become the sole owner. It stated the name of the store would remain unchanged.

Nothing exciting in all that, perhaps, except that the buyer referred to was named as Mr Darcy Wilson. The article went on to report Mr Kennedy's comments on the sale. He claimed that due to his advancing years and continuing ill health, Mr Wilson had been running the store since he bought into the business. Kennedy claimed he felt it was time to tidy up the arrangement and offered to sell his interest in the store to Mr Wilson, who accepted the offer.

The final article I had to read again came from the local newspaper's Social Notes column and was a report of an interview with Mr Darcy Wilson, the owner of Kennedy's Store. The reporter prefaced the article with an indication that it was a problem-child-made-good type of story.

"Damn! Just when I thought I had all the answers I needed, that just adds to the intrigue and poses more questions."

I told myself it didn't matter. I had the information I needed to press on with the investigation into the supposed pirating of Jane's manuscripts, but I wasn't successful. I knew there was more to the Darcy Wilson story, and it was important to uncovering Jane's story. I also knew that not much of the remaining night would be wasted on sleep.

The morning got off to a late start. I felt as though I hadn't closed my eyes for more than a few moments before the sun shining through my bedroom window woke me. Finding top gear felt like a challenge too great as I eased myself out of bed and stumbled to the bathroom. Zombies were real, I discovered when one draped itself over the breakfast bar as it waited for the kettle to boil. Everything happened in slow motion. It was almost two hours later before I felt sufficiently awake to drive out to Ravenshead.

Gabby wandered out to meet me when I arrived. Not her usual enthusiastic welcome, I thought, before I noted her looks mirrored the way I felt.

"Coffee, black and strong, would be great," I told her as I scrambled out of my car. "And what have you been up to all night, or should I not ask?"

"Whether you wanted it or not, coffee will happen before anything else today. Come in. I'm ready for it. And, in response to your question, it's your fault I'm this way this morning. If you hadn't got me hooked on reading those diaries, I would have had a good night's sleep last night," she growled at me.

"You're a big girl now. Take responsibility for your own bad habits," I chided her as I followed her into her apartment and slumped on a stool at the kitchen bench.

No further conversation occurred until we were sitting, sipping our coffees in her lounge room. I had lowered the level in my mug to about halfway before I felt up to further conversation.

"So, did you learn anything new last night? Find anything interesting in that diary?" I asked and watched her cock her head to one side as she considered her answer.

"It's so fascinating to read about Jane's everyday life, but that's all it is, everyday stuff. I can't say I came across anything of import, or even particularly exciting. Anyway, you're on your own this morning. I have an online meeting. It's to do with the work from which I thought I had retired."

"Okay, I want to work in the study and the hidden space today, so no problems if you are tied up with other things."

We agreed I would return to the apartment for lunch. I intended to swap last night's diary and financial records for the next instalment in Jane's life. As I dumped my bag on the big desk in the study, something occurred to me. I still hadn't established why Jane was receiving small, semi-regular payments from Kennedy's Store. Perhaps, before I move on, I should check that I haven't missed something important in the material I examined last night. I opened the diary and the ledger and spread them out on the desk before searching for a suitable chair to use at the desk. A few minutes later, I returned and spent a little more time walloping the chair to remove as much dust as possible before using it.

My gut kept suggesting I had missed something in the material Trove found regarding Kennedy's Store. I returned to the most recent article and read it (carefully) a couple of times, but still nothing jumped out at me. My gut kept insisting that what I needed to know was in that article, so I pushed my chair back from the desk and stared off into the distance as I pondered what it had to say. In summary, all it told me was that Darcy Wilson purchased the remaining half of Kennedy's Store after having been a half-owner of the business for the previous two years.

The previous two years…? Hang on a minute. When did he first buy into the business? A quick check on the article's date revealed that two years prior, any mention of Darcy would have been recorded in the diary I examined last night. After setting the financial material aside, I placed the diary squarely in front of me, flipped through to the approximate relevant date, and began reading. A few moments later, I reached for the bundle of financial material and pulled out the ledger. I read the diary entry again before turning my attention to the ledger.

There was nothing specific about the diary entry, but something kept bringing me back to it. In fact, the entry said nothing. Initially, I had wondered why Jane had written it. Perhaps she had meant to say more, but was distracted, and ended up leaving out the 'punch line'. Somehow, that didn't fit with my picture of Jane. There had to be more to that entry than the words in the diary.

"Let's see what the ledger has to say," I said hopefully as I flicked through to a corresponding page in the ledger and began examining every entry in minute detail. The shock came three entries later.

"How did I miss that?" I yelped. "How the hell could I have missed that payment last night?"

Now that I had found the payment, the words of the diary entry started to take on some meaning, but not enough to solve the mystery. I pushed the ledger aside and dragged over the other material in the financial bundle. A quick rifle through the slips produced gold.

"Gottcha…," I whispered. "How could I have missed that?" Again, I asked the question, but the answer was becoming clearer by now.

No mention of Darcy Wilson's name appeared in any diary entry at the time that suggested Jane had paid him money. Yet, there it was in the bundle of slips recording transactions relating to Jane's personal account. She had paid Darcy Wilson the sum of £2,000. Although not of the same magnitude as the earthshattering amount she had paid Wilson previously, it was a significant sum back then. Now the question was why? Why had she paid him that money?

A little more sleuthing provided a possible answer. The timing of the payment was significant. It appeared to coincide with the first contact with Wilson after a long period of no mention of him. It also appeared that the payment occurred shortly before Jane started receiving small payments from Kennedy's Store. More significant, perhaps, was the timing of all this. It all appeared to happen at about the time the article from Trove's archives suggested Wilson had bought a half share in Kennedy's Store.

I sat back for a few moments to savour the glow of satisfaction, but it was a short-lived interlude. It took me no time to realise that, in this case, 2 + 2 didn't quite add up to 4, not yet anyway. Payments to Jane from Kennedy's Store would suggest she had become a shareholder in the business, but she hadn't bought into the business. She had paid money to Wilson, who had then bought into the Store. Even if Wilson was paying back the money Jane paid him, the subsequent payments to Jane's personal account should have been from Wilson, and not Kennedy's Store. Did I have it wrong? If so, at what part of my assumption had I gone off on the wrong tangent?

Gabby's appearance in the study prevented further deliberation of the matter. "I thought you were coming to have lunch with me," she reminded me. I agreed. "Then, come on. It's almost past a civilised time for lunch."

Somewhere between the study and Gabby's apartment, a plan of action for the afternoon formed, but was forced to the back of my mind by a decision I knew I had to make: When to tell Gabby what I had learned of her family history so far, especially the bit about George's death? After tossing the problem around in my head all through lunch, I finally decided that, as I suspected there was so much more to discover about Jane's story, it might be best to wait until I knew the whole story, or at least a good deal more of it. One of us turning ourselves inside out while trying to work out what was going on back then was enough. There was no point in telling Gabby half the story, only to have her struggle with the same questions that were tormenting me.

Our lunch break proved fruitful for me for another reason as well. Not only had I decided about sharing Jane's story, but I also now knew exactly where to look for the next instalment in the enthralling story of Jane (Finchley) Creighton's life. In the near future, I suspected I would look back on that decision and remember the slight churning in my gut it had caused at the time.

Chapter 9

Gabby had to go into town this afternoon and said she would select something to read tonight after she returned. That really didn't suit me. I had hoped to take at least one diary and its matching financial records home with me to work on them in the quiet and comfort of my own office. That meant Gabby needed to learn how to access the hidden space. While it is a straightforward procedure, it does require reasonably strong fingers to depress the button. It took her several attempts before achieving success.

Then, confident Gabby would be okay to manage on her own, a few minutes after she left for town, I fetched the material I wanted from the hidden space and headed home. As I drove into my garage, Warren called to say he would be coming tonight and would bring something for dinner. I tried to sound pleased while I groaned internally. It was a few days since I last saw Warren. While it would be good to hear what he had been up to, I was anxious to work on Jane's stuff I brought home.

Well, don't mess about, I told myself. Grab a coffee and get straight down to work to make the most of the time you have before Warren arrives.… So I did, and it was slow going. Not wanting a repeat of my previous performance when important clues were missed, I read every word and considered every entry before moving on.

My list of mentions of Darcy Wilson grew steadily. Every mention of his name, its date, and an outline of each entry was meticulously recorded and ready for cross-referencing with the financial records. I had reached what appeared to be a period of interesting activity when Warren arrived.

Having to abandon my office just when things looked like becoming interesting made it difficult to be enthusiastic about

Warren's arrival. I'm not a good actor, and he soon sensed that something was off about me. After I claimed late-night research had left me tired, Warren made comforting noises and left almost as soon as we had eaten dinner. Yes, I did experience a moment of guilt, but it was fleeting. By the time he reached the end of my driveway, I was back at my desk with Jane's diary open in front of me.

Full marks to Jane for what I came to appreciate as her cautious wording in her diary entries. I might flatter myself, but I quickly became quite adept at deciphering the hidden meanings in her words. After all, I suppose that's not surprising, as she was supposedly a writer. Any entries on my list that I assessed as containing more information than was initially obvious were highlighted in fluorescent pink marker. They were the entries that I thought might have corresponding financial information. By the end of the night, more pink appeared on my list than I expected.

The night had slipped by unnoticed, and it wasn't until my eyes struggled to stay open that I realised how late it was. I still had a long way to go with cross-checking my highlighted diary entries, but the excitement running up and down my spine told me I was about to uncover something important – *really* important. It called for drastic measures. A cold shower and another coffee helped keep my eyes open for a bit longer.

Early in my reading of the diary, I had started a second list of noteworthy entries. With only one or two exceptions, they referred to her employment of a typist to produce typewritten copies of Jane's handwritten manuscripts. The earliest of such entries suggested Jane found the typist quite competent, and Jane was happy with the quality of the woman's work and her efficiency. I managed to glean from Jane's comments that the typist was not accommodated at Ravenshead, but continued to live somewhere off the property. The woman must've either been from a wealthy family or had done well from her work as a typist, as she appeared to own her own vehicle and preferred to drive to and from work at Ravenshead.

As usual, after crawling into bed, my mind continued to analyse all I had learned over the preceding few hours, and that included the fact that Miss Parker, Jane's typist, was sufficiently affluent to own a motor vehicle and could afford to drive it to work every day. Surely that was unusual, given that the 1930s were renowned for their depressed state of the economy. So, what was Miss Parker's story? If she were from a wealthy background, I doubt she would have trained as a typist or be earning her living in that capacity. Would there have been much work around for a privately employed typist at that time? The more I thought about Miss Parker, the more my antennae twitched. While she must've been a competent typist, or Jane would never have retained her as an employee, there was much more to be discovered about Miss Parker.

Slumped over at the breakfast bar, I lowered the level in my second mug of coffee this morning as I reminded myself of what Gabby had employed me to do. While Miss Parker is relevant to my brief, it is only her involvement in the reputedly pirated manuscripts that is of any consequence. Her family history and the source of her apparently plentiful cash are not. That didn't work. I was intrigued by Miss Parker and wouldn't be able to restrict my interest to just the relevant issues.

While there remained plenty of work to do on the diary and financial records I brought home yesterday, I called Gabby this morning to tell her I would be working from home for at least part of the day. She mumbled something I couldn't understand, but I eventually discovered she was thanking me for waking her up. She also had a late night and now faced the real prospect of being late for an appointment in town this morning. Needless to say, my call was short, and as soon as my brain was capable of clear thought, I was back at my desk with the diary and financial material spread out before me.

Curbing my inclination to rush through the remaining pages in the diary was not easy. There were few pages left to read. I had yet to find any comments related to Jane's pirated manuscripts, Miss Parker's termination, or Darcy Wilson's purchase of the remaining interest in Kennedy's Store. Dates, as mentioned in the social columns, tend to be somewhat flexible. However, I may have misjudged the timeline, and the material I brought home might be too early for the events I'm researching.

Somehow, I curbed my impatience and worked methodically through to the last entry in the diary… and was pleased I did. Some cryptic entries, almost at the end of the diary, reignited my excitement. Knowing I needed to be sharp and focused to decipher what was written 'between the lines', I took myself outside to jog around my yard a couple of times. Then, only after splashing cold water on my face, did I feel up to the job ahead.

Rather than carry on from where I left off, I flipped back a few pages in the diary and began rereading the entries. During my laps around the yard, I had realised my focus had changed as I neared the end of the diary. Instead of carefully reading every entry, I scanned and only read those that mentioned Mr Wilson or Miss Parker. "Not good enough," I reprimanded myself. "Go back and do it properly." Sure enough, I had missed important information.

"Ah hah… Here, we have Jane attending a garden party. What is a garden party? Is it the same as a fete?" I asked the universe before telling myself to keep reading. A few moments later, I let out a yelp.

"Yes!... Here it is. This is what I was looking for." In the family legend, Jane's 'garden party' has translated into a 'fete'. It doesn't matter. I think this is the event that triggered everything that followed. Having told the universe of my success, I settled down to read – carefully – the next few entries.

The first entry I found told me that Jane had accepted an invitation to a garden party at the manor house. I found it interesting that the biggest house in the district was referred to in the very aristocratic English way as a manor house. I couldn't help but wonder whether it had been built along English lines or if it was an Australian version of such dominant structures. I reprimanded myself. Did it matter what the house looked like? I didn't need to know about the house.

Jane's next entry told me she had bought a new hat for the occasion, a new hat that proved to be of no practical use whatsoever, as it protected her from no sun at all. I also learned that she had regretted her moment of weakness in accepting the invitation. It seemed that garden parties, fetes, or whatever, were not something Jane enjoyed or bothered with, but for some unknown reason and in a weak moment, she had accepted this invitation.

She lamented the usual horde of stalls peddling often substandard domestically produced wares. Two stalls received particular mention for standing out from the crowd. One was selling quality handmade leather handbags, while the other was a book stall.

"Oh, we have mention of a book stall…," I murmured as I turned the page to see what else she had to say about it…. And there it all was. Jane's interest in books lured her to the stall, and the rest of the diary entry is the stuff of the family legend.

It appears she didn't recognise the titles of some of the books. Nor was she familiar with the authors' names, but that didn't deter her from examining some of the volumes. There followed a sentence or two detailing how she scrabbled through the books on sale, checking random pages here and there in each volume in search of passages she recognised. The lengthy entry concluded with the information that Jane had bought five books from the stall and managed to haggle the price down for the bulk purchase.

While the diary entry in question said enough to confirm that the books Jane bought were pirated copies of her own manuscripts, the tone of the entry clearly suggests she was angry. To me, it didn't portray the level of anger and the state of mind that must've prevailed at that time. I was disappointed when the next entry was from some days later and offered nothing more about the garden party or the books.

The next entry, however, did mention Darcy Wilson. While the entry was short and cryptic, it contained sufficient detail for me to glean that Jane had made a special trip into town to meet with Mr Wilson at his lodgings (not at Kennedy's Store) to discuss some urgent business matters. She did not expand on the nature of those business matters either in that particular diary entry or in subsequent entries, but Miss Parker, the typist, did warrant further mention a few days later.

"Well, well…" I whispered. "So, there it is. Confirmation of the family legend of the pirated manuscripts." As an afterthought, I added, "Hmm, perhaps not, but it does hint at it. It's a clue that might lead to the confirmation we seek."

Jane was kind enough to record that she had dismissed the typist on the grounds of unacceptable professional behaviour and the theft of Jane's personal property. No further mention of Miss Parker or the event appeared in subsequent entries up to the end of the journal. Had I missed something else? Something about those entries niggled me. I sat back to consider this latest information.

Perhaps a timeline of events that reflected the diary entries might prove helpful in future, as well as put to rest whatever wasn't sitting well with me. A couple of minutes later, a major 'lightbulb moment' sent me scurrying to Google for more information. I typed in the date Jane had used in reference to the garden party, and asked Google what day that was. Google's reply was swift. The garden party was held on a Saturday. Okay, no surprises. Even today, such an event is most likely to be held on a Saturday – or possibly a Sunday. With that, it was easy to work out the days on which other subsequent diary entries occurred.

Of particular interest was that Jane's visit to Darcy Wilson occurred on Sunday, the day following the garden party. It explains why Jane met him at his lodging and not at the Store. Being a Sunday, the Store would have been closed. It also raised several questions about why Jane would rush into town on a Sunday, when, apart from visiting Wilson at his lodgings, there would have been little else she could do there. I returned to the timeline I had created.

The next diary entry was dated the following Wednesday. It noted that Miss Parker had been ill and had not reported for work on Monday and Tuesday, and had arrived late on Wednesday morning. According to the diary entry, sometime during that morning, a heated discussion had taken place between Jane and her typist. It resulted in the typist being given her marching orders and leaving Ravenshead around lunchtime.

On Thursday of that week, according to her note in the margin, the postman, on his weekly delivery to outlying properties, delivered only two items of mail to Ravenshead, both addressed to Jane. I mentally thanked Jane for her foresight. Her custom was to record in the margin of her diary's pages the items in each mail delivery, and that Thursday, she recorded that one of the items was from Miss Parker.

Jane's diary entry for the same day recorded that Miss Parker's letter threatened Jane with legal action for wrongful dismissal unless Jane paid her a significant sum of money. Jane did not indicate how much money. Jane had underlined 'significant', but made no further comment. That gave me pause for thought. It was completely contrary to how I had expected Jane to react, given the picture I had developed of the woman. Granted, my assessment of the woman was based solely on her writings, but the demand for money suggested that I should examine the financial records from around that time.

I flipped through Jane's personal ledger for any payments to Miss Parker. There were two. One appeared to be a routine monthly payment for services rendered. The second one, made on the day Jane sacked Miss Parker, appeared to be payment for Parker's services for about a week's work after the previous monthly payment.

"So, no severance pay…," I murmured as I finished reading the final payment details. "Parker was game threatening Jane, given the reasons for her dismissal."

A check on subsequent payments recorded in the ledger showed none to Parker or to any associate of Parker. Well, it suggests that Jane was not only cranky about her manuscripts but that she might have been inclined to tightfistedness as well. However, scrolling through the entries in the ledger did reveal one other significant payment from Jane's personal account. Darcy Wilson was once again the recipient of a large sum of money from Jane. Now, what might that be for? Maybe a more careful search of the diary might tell me.

Again, I had missed the entry earlier when I read through the diary, and I could see why. A diary entry from the Monday of that tempestuous week provided me with enough information for a fairly sound assumption. After visiting Wilson on Sunday, Jane paid him a substantial sum of money on the following Monday. That was the day after visiting Wilson in town, and two days before she terminated Parker's employment as her typist. It might have been dismissed as a simple business transaction had it not been for one telling comment in Jane's diary entry: *To be for the same service, and under the same terms and conditions as previously.*

While the comment was innocuous in itself, I knew exactly what it meant. Previously, Jane had only ever made one similar payment to Darcy Wilson. From my research over the last few days, I guessed what he was paid to do. I couldn't believe what my mind was telling me. Surely, she wasn't paying Wilson to have Parker terminated (as in 'permanently eliminated') just because some of her manuscripts had been pirated. But I couldn't think what else it might be for?

"Aw, hell. This really complicates things." I was struggling to work out how I was going to tell Gabby about George Creighton's death and the role Jane – and Darcy Wilson – played in it. Now, it looks as though I'm also going to have to tell her how Jane had her typist murdered. Could I be wrong, and in this case, that's not what the payment to Wilson was for? Was I wrong on both counts, and that's not what Wilson was paid to do? The little voice in my head was having none of that.

No. Cryptic though they were, Jane's diary entries at the time surrounding George's death said it all, and the coroner wasn't convinced George fell off his horse either, or there wouldn't have been an inquest. In the 1930s, did women go around paying people to bump off other people whom they were unhappy with? That seems more like the criminal underbelly of today's world. Despite my efforts, I couldn't persuade myself there was any other explanation for the payments other than my initial assumption.

A little more cross-checking of the diary and financial records showed that almost immediately after that second substantial payment, Wilson purchased the remaining share of Kennedy's Store. It was all there, and the timing was right. Even the approximate date of Wilson's buy-out of old man Kennedy's share of the Store fitted with the rest of the evidence. Christ, how will Gabby cope when I give her this information about her grandmother … And how am I ever going to tell her? For a few moments, I even considered not telling her and claiming I hadn't found anything, but that wouldn't work. Now I had her hooked on reading Jane's diaries, Gabby would work it out for herself, and that would result in my being asked a lot of difficult questions.

Although my initial plan this morning was to drive out to Ravenshead as soon as I finished with the material I had brought home, now, I couldn't bring myself to do so. I couldn't face Gabby, not yet anyway. My phone interrupted my rapid slide into a blue funk. The caller was Gabby, and I hesitated. Somehow, I didn't feel up to talking to her. I avoided the situation. She ended the call. Moments later, I heard a message arrive. I had no doubt it was from Gabby. It was, and it was brief. She had been delayed and would now overnight in town and come home sometime tomorrow.

"Wonderful…," the coward in me crowed, "now I can put it off at least until tomorrow."

My problem was what to do next. Should I go to Ravenshead and do more work out there, or should I fetch another set of records to work on at home? Suddenly, I realised there was something more immediate demanding attention. I was hungry, and it was way past lunchtime. I made a quick sandwich and ate it on the back deck. It was a balmy afternoon with a light breeze. I soon felt a wave of drowsiness sweep over me. Jumping up off my chair, I reprimanded myself.

"No… This is not a time for snoozing. You have work to do. Make a coffee and then sit and think about all you've discovered so far." It made sense, so I did.

What had I discovered? In my mind, what stood out was that Jane (Finchley) Creighton was not a nice person, and one you wouldn't want to cross. What about what I was supposed to be working on? The manuscripts were supposed to be my focus. So far, I had established only the apparent date when Jane discovered some of her manuscripts had been pirated and illegally published. In effect, that confirmed the family legend, but didn't provide sufficient detail. Right then, more research required on that matter.

What else do I need to work on? Maybe the question should be: Is there anything else I need to investigate? Was there? Yeah, there was, but I doubt it had anything to do with the Creighton family legends. Darcy Wilson… What's his story? One of those articles from Trove suggested his was a 'bad boy made good' story. The 'made good' bit probably reflects his becoming the sole owner of Kennedy's Store… Even if how it was achieved stayed hidden.

The first we learn of Darcy Wilson from Jane's diaries is that he was a delivery driver for Kennedy's Store, who used to take tea with Jane whenever he visited Ravenshead. While it seems a strange relationship, there was nothing obviously illicit about it, and it had been in place for a while before George's death. At first glance, investigating Darcy Wilson's background might not appear part of my brief, but I felt it might provide important underpinning information. So, the first question might be *what became of Darcy Wilson?* I knew I'd be disappointed if I found he died a natural death in his old age and was buried in the local cemetery.

Thoughts about death and cemeteries brought something to the fore. What about the typist, Lois Parker? If Darcy Wilson 'dealt' with her in the same way as he did George Creighton, what happened to her, and where is she now? Without knowing more about Miss Parker's outcome, everything I thought I knew about her was mere speculation … And that put the veracity of a whole lot of other stuff in doubt.

It appears I have a couple of lives to investigate, and I also need to know more about those supposedly pirated manuscripts. The first question about the manuscripts is whether copies of them still existed in Jane's secret archives. Finding the answer was a realistic and legitimate direction for my research.

Chapter 10

About seven o'clock, Warren arrived with a collection of takeaway dishes from our favourite Chinese restaurant. After spending the last of the afternoon combing through births, deaths, and marriages indexes, and the local historical society's burials index, I wasn't much company. It took a couple of glasses of wine before the fog in my head cleared and I became capable of intelligent conversation.

I told Warren of my frustrating search for anything on the lives of Darcy Wilson and Miss Lois Parker, hinting at what I thought might have happened to Parker. Of course, Detective Inspector Tyson wanted to know more. Who were these people? Why was I interested in them? What did I think, or know, that made them so interesting? All reasonable questions, but not ones I could answer easily or honestly – yet. After some internal debate, I decided it was safe to discuss Wilson, but only insofar as he was a significant contributor to the town's development. Given his prominence in local history, I was surprised to find no information about what happened to him.

After retrieving his laptop from his car, Warren interrogated various police files for me. His results didn't differ from mine. I was disappointed, but Warren was more positive and told me that not finding any mention of Wilson was a good thing.

"No mention of him in any of our police files indicates he did not fall foul of the law, or end up in court for any reason, even as a witness. Perhaps, after some years of running the Store, he sold up and moved away from here, interstate maybe."

"Yeah, I thought of all that, but selling the Store to new owners would have been a big thing in the town, and would have merited at least a mention in the local newspaper's social column."

"As for Miss Parker, Sophie, you have to remember women are difficult to track through history. They get married, change their name, move around the country, and even go to live overseas."

My hackles were rising, and I felt the red mist gathering. Who did Warren think he was trying to teach how to conduct such research? I am a journalist. This type of research is what I do on a daily basis when I am working. I did not want tonight to end on a sour note. So I forced myself to smile politely and agree with his comments. I also yawned to hint that perhaps it was time he went home. He took the bait and departed about 20 minutes later. As I tidied the kitchen, a new thought slammed in from left field.

All afternoon, I had concentrated on researching Wilson's and Parker's names. That approach had yielded nothing. What if I tried researching Kennedy's Store? Maybe that might provide at least an insight into what was going on in town at the time. It looked like I would be disturbing Google again tonight, along with the National Library's Trove newspaper archive.

Trove took a while to produce a surprisingly short list of hits in response to my request for information on Kennedy's Store. Then I realised I had made an error when I typed in the date range to search. Date range amended, I sent Trove off to search again. This time, it brought back a long list of hits. I groaned. That list meant I would spend all night checking the various hits. I made a less than enthusiastic start on the list.

Early hits on the list were repeats of those I had downloaded previously. Then came a long run of advertisements that appeared in the local newspaper on a regular basis. They told me nothing and simply informed the reader about the products stocked by the store. The list of hits also included the social jottings article about Darcy Wilson purchasing the last of Mr Kennedy's share of the Store. With heavy eyelids, I continued checking to the end of the list. The last few hits were advertisements, including a couple announcing huge sale price reductions on certain goods. It appeared that, once Wilson had his foot in the door, an entrepreneurial approach was introduced. Then, the advertisements ceased. The list of hits ended abruptly, and for no apparent reason.

As I climbed into bed, the abrupt end of that list crawled in with me and kept me awake for some time. It was as I was finally drifting off to sleep that a lightbulb moment occurred and had me out of bed in a flash. Something I had glanced at while I was checking the list of hits had come back to haunt me. It had nothing to do with Kennedy's Store as such. An article in the next column of the newspaper had caught my eye. I skimmed it. Finding no mention of Kennedy's Store, I moved on to the next hit on my list. I needed to find that article again, and I have no idea where to start. After a moment's thought, I decided it was towards the end of the items I had checked. So, I began rechecking the hit list in the reverse order, working backwards from the most recent hit.

About half an hour later, I found the required article. This time I read it carefully. No, there was no mention of either Kennedy's Store or Darcy Wilson, but it did paint a realistic picture of the state of the town at that time. While the town had survived the depression of the 1930s reasonably well, in the latter 1940s, it was struggling to survive. The article squarely places the blame for the parlous state of the district on the rapid development of the nearby town and its surrounding area.

Many farmers in the adjacent district found themselves in financial straits after the depression, and only too happy to sell their properties to a developer when it came knocking. First, a manufacturing industry was developed on some of the former farmland. A short time later, a processing plant was established to turn milk from the local dairies into butter, cheeses, and yoghurt. While employing locals where possible, the new industries created an influx of new residents and the need for more houses.

As the town grew, other facilities followed. That included supermarket chains, major stock and station agencies, and machinery supply firms. So, as the neighbouring township grew and developed some 14 kilometres away, things stagnated here. With a motor vehicle commonplace in many households by then, a shopping trip to the supermarket in the neighbouring town became easy and increasingly popular. I sat back to ponder the article's content.

While the neighbouring town remains the larger of the two, it seems our town somehow managed to claw its way back from the brink. Although without any evidence to support my thinking, I suspected that, as available land in the neighbouring district was taken up by developers and became scarce, latecomers looked to our district. By the late 1940s, it was possible that some of our rural landowners didn't require much persuading to sell. Quite a few of those landowners had lost their only sons (and male heirs) in the recent war. For the parents, now in the twilight of their lives, and with no one to hand the farm on to, the opportunity to sell up – at the right price – and move into retirement would have been hard to resist.

Was Kennedy's Store a casualty of such progress? Access to the major retailers and their ability to offer 'the right price' to attract customers probably sounded the death knell for the likes of Kennedy's Store and other small, independently-owned retailers in our town. That scenario fitted with the several sales of various stock advertised by Kennedy's Store in the days before it was no longer mentioned in the local newspaper. It appears Kennedy's Store went out of business around that time.

"Okay, so what became of Darcy Wilson?" I demanded of the universe. After a moment's thought, I added, "Does it matter what became of him?"

The short answer was no. It was of no relevance or importance to the work for which Gabby engaged me. At least, at the time, I didn't think it was important. As I delve further into Jane's life and what was happening at Ravenshead, I may need to review that assessment. So, with Darcy Wilson and Kennedy's Store parked on the sidelines for the moment, what about Miss Lois Parker?

"Do I need to know about her after she left Ravenshead?" It was a silly question, when both my gut and I knew my suspicions about it probably had a lot to do with Jane.

It was about three o'clock when I climbed back into bed. In about an hour, the sun would start lighting up the sky as it prepared to creep up over the horizon. "My day will have a late start," I murmured as I succumbed to Morpheus.

I was right in predicting a late start today. It was gone eight o'clock before I opened my eyes. After that, everything seemed to happen in slow motion, and it was a little after ten o'clock before I climbed into my car and headed for Ravenshead. Gabby rushed out to meet me when I arrived.

"Are you all right? I was worried about you. I thought I might have upset you when I wasn't here to help with the research," she babbled by way of a greeting.

"Whoa, slow down. Take a breath and calm down before you implode or something… And… yes, thanks, I will have a coffee before I start work on Jane's archives this morning."

A few minutes later, as we both sat nursing our mugs of coffee, I asked, "What's this nonsense about me expecting you to help with the research? You didn't engage me, so you could do the work yourself. Mind you, if you wish to continue exploring the contents of Jane's archives, please feel free to do so. Just remember to show me anything interesting or exciting you happen to come across."

"Well, I hate to disappoint you, but I haven't found anything like that. The fact that I haven't done anything over the last couple of days might have something to do with it."

A lengthy explanation followed of how, having supposedly resigned and retired before returning to Ravenshead, her former employers continued to call on her services. Despite her protests, it was obvious that she wasn't ready to retire. Occasional calls back to work would probably be beneficial for her. However, having already wasted a large slab of the day, I grabbed the first opportunity to escape to the hidden space.

Although I had no clear work plan when I left Gabby's apartment, by the time I entered the hidden space, I had identified a couple of things I was going to look into over the next couple of days. The first of those was Jane's involvement with Kennedy's Store. Two questions demanded my attention. Did Jane continue to receive small, reasonably regular payments from the Store? The other question was whether Jane's diaries from the late 1940s provided any insight into what happened to Kennedy's Store and its proprietor, Darcy Wilson. Unfortunately, I began with the mistaken belief that finding answers to those two questions would be a mere formality once I got started.

My first problem was deciding which question to tackle first. It should take only a few moments to check Jane's financial records for the period immediately following Wilson's purchase of the remaining part of Kennedy's Store. I selected the financial records bundle for the relevant dates and opened it on the big desk in the study. Although unsure what to expect, my findings didn't immediately answer many of my questions.

It took me only a few minutes to confirm that the payments to Jane had continued after Wilson became the sole owner of the Store. What was intriguing, however, was that the payments had become smaller and more sporadic. Although the payments had never been regular, they then seemed to occur at quite random intervals. Did it signify that the Store was already struggling to survive? I convinced myself that the period in question was too early for the change to be due to the development occurring in the region.

As I bundled the records up again, I thought to check if the payments continued through to the end of the period covered by the records in that bundle. They did, and they appeared to remain unchanged, still small and sporadic. So, the question became whether to continue following the 'money trail' period by period to see if it changed or when it ended, or if I should jump ahead to the records covering the period when I suspect the Store closed down. Gabby's arrival delayed a decision.

For the next half hour or so, silence filled the study, broken only occasionally by the scrape of a chair being adjusted, or a murmured exclamation, the latter by Gabby. I made a mental note to ask her later what she had found so fascinating in the diary she read today. I hoped there might have been something, but Gabby hadn't recognised it as being relevant. As for me, I had found what appeared to be Jane's final payment from Kennedy's Store.

Although no further payments were received in the subsequent couple of months, something about that last payment didn't feel 'final' somehow. If that payment had marked the closure of the Store, I would have expected at least a brief note to that effect scribbled across the payment slip. Back to the diaries, I told myself as I wrapped the bundle of financial records I had been working on.

Several minutes later, any hopes I had that the diary would provide information about the Store or Darcy Wilson were dashed. As previously discovered, Jane obviously thought the Store's small payments unworthy of mention in her diary. This one was no different from that last payment I found, and the diary had no comment about it. I clasped my hands behind my head and stretched back in my chair to ponder my next move. No progress had been achieved before Gabby announced that it was gone one o'clock and we hadn't stopped for lunch. Maybe if I took on more fuel, my thinking would become clearer. I leapt off my chair and followed her to her apartment.

Maybe it was activity, not food, I needed to clear my head. By the time we sat down to lunch, I knew exactly what I would look at on returning to the study. As soon as we had eaten, I rushed back to the study… and encountered a hurdle. I wanted Jane's diary for the time when Kennedy's Store was last mentioned in the local newspaper. I already knew that date, but was it when the Store actually closed? I needed to read diary entries from a reasonable time before then until a while after that last advertisement. The question was how long to allow on either side of the known date. In the end, I discovered I had to peruse the latter part of one diary and the early part of the next one.

Gabby was a while returning to the study, but when she resumed reading her chosen diary, she mumbled and murmured as she read. It wasn't loud, but it was distracting. I kept losing my train of thought, unable to concentrate on the page in front of me. After suffering it for the best part of an hour, I announced I was taking the two diaries home to work on them tonight. Gabby's stunned look turned to hurt. I felt compelled to make some excuse for suddenly dashing home.

"I'm half expecting a phone call late this afternoon or this evening, and I might need to refer to my files during it. I'll take these diaries with me now, and I'll see you again in the morning."

I felt confident my excuse had worked when I saw her face brighten. Rather than waste time, I grabbed my bag and the diaries and headed home. After arriving home, I checked the fridge. Yes, I had a couple of nice-looking steaks that we could barbecue to have with a salad and jacket baked potatoes for dinner. With dinner sorted, I escaped to my office to work until Warren arrived. I found myself sitting in semi-darkness, experiencing eyestrain, when my phone disturbed me at six o'clock. Warren would not be joining me for dinner tonight. He likely would be dealing with a crime scene until the wee hours of tomorrow morning.

"Good… No need to bother with steaks. A tuna sandwich will do just fine," I told my empty house as I switched on the kitchen lights.

Time slipped away unnoticed before I realised I had become engrossed in reading Jane's entries, instead of looking for the information I wanted. I reached the last page of the first of the diaries I brought home before anything caught my attention. Although they didn't mention Kennedy's Store or Darcy Wilson, something made me pause and reread the two entries carefully. I still had no idea what they were about. While Jane's entries were generally cryptic, I hadn't found it too difficult to read between the lines to discern what she was writing about in the past. These two entries had me stumped.

After reading them again and considering them for a while without gaining even a clue what she was talking about, I decided the best thing was to push on. Perhaps, if I started reading the second diary, some of the early entries in that journal would help interpret the earlier ones. Even if they didn't, they might at least shed some light on what the issues of the day were.

As I reached the bottom of the first page of the second diary, I groaned. Was this the start of Jane's dementia? The entries on that page made no more sense than the previous ones that had me stumped. None of them made any sense. I couldn't even figure out what she was talking about, but one thing came through loud and clear. Jane was angry when she wrote those entries. Now, if I can work out what might have caused her anger, maybe I'll be able to decipher what she had to say about it.

For the third time, I reread the first page of that diary, carefully considering each sentence and the choice of words used. A breakthrough of sorts occurred as I re-read the last entry on the first page. I realised that it felt as though the entry had been left unfinished, as though there should have been more to follow. Responding to that thought, I flipped over the page. There it was, the last few lines of the entry started at the bottom of the previous page. After berating myself for having behaved worse than a novice, I took a couple of deep breaths to clear the red mist that had descended, and read the entire entry again.

Nothing came easily. I read and reread the entry multiple times. The only inspiration I gained from it was that this entry, and probably all those on the first page of this journal, were about the same topic as those on the last page of the previous diary. If I were honest, I'd admit that was nothing more than a gut feeling. Now, if I could just determine what the topic of all that rhetoric was, I should be able to work out why it had upset Jane so badly.

"Well, at least I've almost convinced myself the entries weren't born of dementia," I admitted to the universe as my mind wrestled with the entries, while I sipped a glass of wine.

Perhaps the wine was a magic elixir. It seemed to help clear some of my fog. My glass was empty, and I was rinsing it when the lightbulb moment occurred.

"Why the hell would she be writing about that? What possible interest would she have in it?" I demanded of the universe, but it was either deaf or had gone out for the night, as no response was forthcoming.

Chapter 11

After moments of elation at having deciphered Jane's several cryptic entries, reality slammed in, bringing me down to earth again. All I had managed to do was to work out that the entries related to abandoned shafts, a legacy of an earlier gold rush that had gripped so much of the country. The question I took to bed with me was why Jane would suddenly develop an interest in them.

While I might have been ready for sleep, my mind was still on duty and working at breakneck speed to dredge up more questions to confound me. I suppose the underlying question was whether Ravenshead lands had been involved in the gold rush. I knew there had been mining at different places in the district, but I didn't know where exactly. From the little I knew of the topography of Ravenshead lands, only one small area looked suitable to have seen some mining activity in the past. I don't recall hearing of anyone striking it rich in this area, so Jane's interest in such mining activity was intriguing.

As I dawdled over breakfast, some of my thoughts from last night began to coalesce with my other memories from other earlier research. Decades ago, there was considerable concern about abandoned mineshafts being left in unsafe condition wherever there had been goldfields. I recalled from earlier research that there were two types of mine shafts involved: those that ran off into a hill, and those that were basically a hole in the ground that dropped down into a deep shaft.

Landowners were concerned that stock would fall down shafts or wander into those running into the hills, and if a cave-in occurred, they would be trapped in there. Where the hills on some properties were pockmarked with shafts, the landowners were resorting to explosives to create rockfalls that would fill the shafts. There had also been concern during the Depression that some of those who found themselves down on their luck and took to the roads were using the shafts as makeshift shelters. Then, during and after World War II, the abandoned mineshafts were suspected of being home to all sorts of nefarious activities that were carried on out of the prying eyes of the law.

By the time I had driven out to Ravenshead, my morning's mental activities had boiled down into two questions. Were there abandoned mineshafts on Ravenshead property? What had triggered Jane's cryptic references to it in her writings? One other thing had become clear by the time I was having coffee with Gabby. None of the research I had done was in any way relevant to Jane's pirated manuscripts and, therefore, not what I was engaged to do. The latter wasn't an issue. It simply meant I wouldn't charge Gabby for the hours I spent researching personal interests yesterday.

"Well, thanks for the coffee, Gabby, but it is time to get to work. While I have a whole raft of questions about what was happening at Ravenshead over a lengthy period, I suspect they don't have anything to do with the manuscripts. So, I intend to leave the diaries alone for now while I concentrate on the manuscripts in Jane's archives."

"Okay, but what does that mean exactly? How will you determine if any were stolen? And, do you need my help with it?" I shook my head. "Good… If you don't need my help, I can continue reading the diaries."

"Good idea, but don't forget to make a note of anything exciting – or even just out of the ordinary. You never know. We might want to come back to it later, or it might be that it holds the key to some aspect of the story about the manuscripts."

Leaving Gabby to clear away after our coffee, I strode off to Jane's hidden space alone and grateful for the time, however brief, to work in splendid solitude at that big desk. The solitude ended as I entered the hidden space. Gabby, having thrown our coffee mugs into the dishwasher, followed me into the hidden space.

"Sophie, I know this is going to sound ridiculous, but how are you going to know if something is not there? I mean, if a manuscript is missing, how will you know? There could be dozens missing from all those on the shelves, but no one will have inserted a marker to indicate that one is missing from there. Oh, God, Jane wasn't considerate enough to have placed markers where something was missing, was she?"

"If only…. No, I doubt I'll find any markers, but I do have a couple of clues that might help."

Gabby eventually selected her next diary to read and left the space. I fiddled with the manuscripts on the shelves until she was seated back at her little table, then pulled out the list from my pocket to work from. I had copied Jane's diary entry relating to her attendance at the 'garden party' and what she found on the book stall. In it, she had listed the copies of the books she bought and the names of her corresponding manuscripts. By the time I found that information, I had already catalogued all the manuscripts on the shelves. Regarding the works Jane claimed to be her own, I noted the changed names under which the books had been published.

Back at my desk, I placed the three manuscript parcels I had selected along the front edge of the desk. I intended to bring out all of the suspect manuscripts, but common sense prevailed. There wasn't enough room to work safely on them all, even on such a huge desk.

"Anything you need a hand with?" Gabby called out as I started unwrapping the first of the bundles.

"No, thanks. I'll call you if I find anything interesting." I would have preferred to study the manuscripts alone, and I certainly didn't want someone yapping in my ear as I did so.

In the first bundle I unwrapped, the manuscript was secured in a soft cardboard folder. The surprise came when I discovered the folder contained not only Jane's handwritten manuscript, but also a typed copy of it.

"Now that is interesting," I murmured, and quickly glanced up at Gabby, and heaved a sigh of relief. She either hadn't heard or chose to ignore me. What was particularly interesting was a small smudge on the back of the first typed page: a smudge of colour from carbon paper. Why use carbon paper unless you harboured an illegal plan for the second typed copy it produced?

Change of plan. Instead of studying the contents of each bundle separately, I now wanted to check the contents of the other two bundles on my desk. A couple of minutes later, I stood back to consider what I had discovered. The contents of each of the three bundles were the same. Each contained a cardboard folder that held both the handwritten and the typed versions of Jane's manuscript.

The question now begging for an answer was how many of the manuscripts had been typed before Miss Parker was sacked. The three bundles I had selected were neither the earliest nor the last on the shelves. Was it safe to assume Miss Parker had started from the earliest manuscript on the shelves and then systematically worked through them? An alternate scenario might be that Jane selected her favoured manuscripts to be typed first. 'Stop dithering,' I told myself. 'Concentrate on the bundles on the desk, and worry about the others later.' It was sound advice, so I did.

So engrossed in studying the contents of my first folder, I didn't know Gabby was standing beside me until she spoke.

"Is that one of Jane's manuscripts? I mean, one of her manuscripts that had already been typed?"

"Yeah. Both the handwritten and the typed versions are bound in this one folder. Apart from that, I haven't discovered anything else yet."

"Should I unwrap these other two bundles for you?"

"Thanks, Gabby, but no, please don't do that. I don't want cross-contamination between the bundles. Only one unwrapped at a time is the safest way to proceed."

"Okay, but I really came to see if you were ready to take a break for lunch. I was planning on making tuna salad. So, if you're ready for lunch, I'll go and rustle it up for us." Reminding her that she wasn't expected to feed me was pointless, so I admitted I was starving and would join her in her apartment in a couple of minutes.

Lunch proved a trying interlude for me… and probably an exasperating one for Gabby. I wanted to sit in silence to consider what I had discovered about the first manuscript, little enough though that was. On the other hand, Gabby wanted to speculate about what we might discover and kept coming up with wild speculative scenarios.

My first task on returning to the study was to unwrap the other two manuscript bundles I had selected from the shelves this morning. They told much the same story as the first bundle. I spent the rest of the afternoon studying the manuscripts. I wasn't looking for anything in particular, just hoping for something useful to leap out at me. It didn't. The only thing noticeable about the three manuscripts on the desk was that they shared similar storylines, albeit not identical, and all fell within the same genre.

Having found nothing exciting or interesting so far, I sat back to consider what I had learned. There had to be something that singled them out from the dozens on the shelves. Was that particular genre popular at the time? Were the books Jane bought from the stall the only manuscripts that had been pirated, or were there others that I didn't know about yet? While I was tempted to fetch the other manuscript bundles that corresponded to the rest of the books Jane bought, Gabby's announcement that coffee was ready put that idea on hold.

Although I wasn't aware of it, over our coffee break, my mind applied itself to the matter of the manuscripts, in particular, what to do next. Once coffee was over and I escaped to the study, I knew exactly what my next move would be. How accurate were Miss Parker's transcriptions of the handwritten documents? It would be a daunting task, but my gut kept telling me it was important. When Gabby returned to the study, she was in a yappy mood, and foremost on her mind was what I had found out about the manuscripts. When I told her 'nothing', she turned to speculating about why those particular manuscripts were chosen. Fair enough, I suppose, but I was getting nothing done.

"I'm expecting someone for dinner this evening. I might leave a little early today so I can put a roast in the oven." How easily the lie rolled off my tongue, but it might not be entirely false. Warren might be coming for dinner tonight. "Gabby, I'll take one of these manuscripts home to study the writing and its storyline while the roast is cooking," I added.

With no fictitious roast to bother about, I was able to start work on the manuscript as soon as I dropped my bag in my home office. First, I pulled the folder apart to facilitate my comparison of the two documents. Then, with the two stacks of pages lying side by side on my desk, I began what would be a long, tough job. It was clear that a simple yet effective process was needed, so I established one. I would skim a handwritten page of Jane's manuscript, and then skim Miss Parker's corresponding typed version of that page. When Warren arrived at about seven o'clock, I was only about a quarter of the way through the manuscript.

"Apologies for not checking what you would like for dinner beforehand, but I took a punt on your being happy with roast dinners. On my way over, I picked up a couple with all the trimmings from that new takeaway place."

"A roast dinner sounds wonderful, and if they are as good as they smell, let's not waste time getting stuck into them." The aroma of the dinners Warren brought had my stomach growling.

Warren didn't stay late. The locals had kept the detectives busy over the last few days, and he was looking forward to his first early night this week. I had no objections to his departure soon after eight o'clock. It wasn't that I was finding Jane's story enthralling. It was a case of wanting to have the job over and done with – and I wanted to see how the story ended.

When I next checked the time, it was almost midnight. My eyelids were becoming heavy, but there wasn't too much of the manuscript left to peruse. I splashed cold water over my face to wake up, and continued to the end before crawling into bed at almost 2.00AM. As I turned off the light, I groaned at the thought of another day of the same ahead of me.

"So, how did it go?" Gabby asked almost as soon as I set foot in her apartment this morning.

"How did what go? You will have to be patient with me today. I'm not sure all of me is functioning yet."

"The manuscript! How did it go? Did you find anything interesting? What about the story? I'm dying to read her work to see what sort of writer she was. She must have been all right, though, or no one would have bothered stealing her work."

That's when I realised how ridiculous it would sound if I confessed I hadn't actually read the manuscript and didn't know what the story was about. But that was the reality of the situation. All I did was compare each page of both manuscripts for variations. There had been some. What remained unclear was whether the changes were Miss Parker's initiatives or were made in consultation with Jane. The changes mostly tidied up phraseology to correct the tense of a sentence.

As I suspected, Gabby wasn't impressed that I hadn't 'read' the story and, therefore, didn't know what it was about or if it was any good. With an edge to her voice, she announced she would read the damned thing to find out for herself. I offered her the bundle containing the manuscript, told her to proceed, and insisted she provide a review afterwards.

"No, not right now. I'm only a little way into the next diary, and I want to finish that first. Anyway, you have other manuscripts to work on in the meantime. Maybe one of them will hold greater appeal for you."

I tried to explain the situation and why the next manuscript was unlikely to be any different. I knew I was wasting my breath, but the conversation had sparked an idea, and I was now eager to be alone to let it develop fully. I didn't want to appear rude and upset Gabby further, but struggled to think of an acceptable way to escape.

My admiration of Gabby's phone increased further. It seems able to accurately sense when I need it to distract Gabby by demanding her attention. Right on cue, it played its tune. As she rushed to take the call, I bolted for the study and its hidden space. It wasn't a long journey, but it was long enough to allow sufficient time for that germ of an idea to develop. After opening the manuscript folder to the first page of Jane's handwritten work, I scanned the bookshelves for what Jane believed was the corresponding published version of her writing. Those books Jane had bought at the 'garden party' were grouped together at eye level.

"Okay… Now let's see how the two of you compare," I murmured as I positioned the novel next to Jane's manuscript on the desk and opened it.

It was slow going. The pagination of the two works no longer aligned. Page 5 of Jane's manuscript was on page 3 of the novel, with the last couple of lines continuing onto page 4, and so it continued from there. Although I didn't read either of the works, I did manage to gain a rudimentary understanding of what the story was about. When Gabby finally appeared in the study, I still hadn't made much progress, and I was instantly aware progress would become stymied thanks to her arrival.

She marked her arrival with a string of questions about what I was doing, why I was doing it, and what doing it again, when I had already done it once, might achieve. After a couple of deep breaths, I explained the reasoning behind what she obviously considered a waste of time. She was quiet and stunned-looking after my explanation, but soon found her voice again.

"Well, it will be quicker and better if we work on it together. Which do you want, the handwritten version or the novel?"

Uncertain about what she was planning, I said I was happy to work from the handwritten version, but I needed to know what to do.

"There's nothing earth-shatteringly complicated about how we are going to do this. One of us will read from one version, while the other checks it against the same passage in the other version. Now, do you want to read, or will I?"

"As I have the handwritten version, and I am now familiar with Jane's handwriting, I will read – if that's okay with you."

"Right... You read, and I'll follow along in the novel. I'll stop you, make notes, and tell you about any variations I encounter."

Her approach seemed logical and would save time, so I agreed and we began what I knew would be akin to an endurance test. Apart from anything else, I probably would have a raw throat long before the day was over. We crawled along for about an hour before Gabby announced it was lunchtime and she needed to fix something for us to eat. I dragged over to me the pad on which she had been noting any variations we encountered. There had been some, but I didn't realise how many we had found. That provided food for thought.

If enough variations were made (whatever number that might be), would it avoid intellectual property and copyright infringement? An interesting question to which I didn't have an answer, and I doubted Gabby would know either. Nevertheless, by the time I joined her for lunch, I knew I would be exploring the question with her.

"I've had a little to do with copyright law, but more to do with issues of intellectual property. I'll think about it for a while, but my initial thinking is that there would need to be considerable substantial changes to avoid copyright infringement."

"Oh, I see. I didn't realise you would have dealt with such matters. How did that come about?"

"Sophie, I'm a lawyer, a corporate lawyer. Granted, most of my work has dealt with contracts of various sorts, but depending on the work I was doing, there were occasions when I needed to be up to speed on copyright and such matters."

"What about the volume of variations we've discovered so far? Would that be close to avoiding an infringement?"

"No, not by a long way, I don't think. As I said earlier, I would need to review it again to be sure. And, yes, I know laws change over time, but copyright law has remained fairly consistent in this country. Now, if you have finished your lunch, I'm keen to return to Gabby's manuscript."

She was right. If we were to finish that manuscript and have a better understanding of what had happened, we needed to get back to work. I groaned internally at the thought of more reading aloud. Despite constant sips of water, my throat already threatened rebellion. Long before I go home today, I will be hoarse, and we won't have finished the book yet. And tomorrow will require a repeat of today. That's when it occurred to me that it could take days to read the whole of the manuscript… and it was just the first one we needed to check.

Coffee was a welcome excuse for a break. While the coffee machine was doing its thing, Gabby rummaged in a cupboard in the bathroom and returned with a bottle of something she insisted I gargle with. I succumbed to her insistence, but not until after I had finished my coffee. It was as foul-tasting as it looked, but I managed a little gargling in between gagging. Although I wasn't about to admit it, I did feel some minor relief within a few minutes. By the time I returned home, I was hoping Warren wasn't coming for dinner. I did not want to have to speak another word today.

As I dumped my bag in my home office, I realised I didn't have to entertain Warren tonight. I had the means to ensure a peaceful, nonverbal evening. So, I sent him a text explaining that it wasn't convenient for him to come tonight. It was something of a white lie, but I felt it necessary and acceptable under the circumstances.

Chapter 12

It was a relief this morning when Gabby suggested we swap roles. Today, she would read Jane's manuscript while I compared it to the book, noting variations as they occurred. With my throat still raw from yesterday's ordeal, I was dreading having to read aloud again. Another positive aspect of this morning was that Gabby was ready to start work as soon as I arrived. For a moment, I even allowed myself to wonder if we might finish the first book today.

Gabby took a while to warm to her job. It was slow going until she became comfortable reading aloud, but once she settled into it, we made good progress. By the time we stopped for morning coffee, I was again toying with the possibility of finishing the book today. Then, when we stopped for lunch, Gabby was barely able to croak and begged off having to do any more reading aloud today. I knew how she felt, but the end of the book was in sight. I reluctantly suggested we swap roles again. With no argument from Gabby, after a short lunch break, I returned to reading the book aloud.

By taking only a brief afternoon coffee break and then pushing on until a bit after five o'clock, we finished the book. Neither of us was capable of conversation by then, and my departure for home followed no more than a brief 'see you tomorrow'. After advising Warren I wasn't available again tonight, a shower, a glass of wine and the solitude of my back deck were all I needed. Despite my best efforts, my mind was not about to stop working on the book. I took the rest of my wine with me to my office.

With the book, Jane's handwritten manuscript, and our longish list of variations lined up across the desk in front of me, I encouraged the vague thought wafting around in the back of my mind to come forward. It took a while to happen. When it did, I wished it hadn't. The prospect it presented was not one I wanted to contemplate tonight, but it had brought forward a valid point: When did the variations occur?

The question was whether Miss Parker had altered the wording from the original manuscript or if it had been altered at a later date, probably by the publisher. All I could envisage was that we should have conducted a three-way comparison instead of comparing just two versions as we had done … And having to carry out another comparison was not something I wanted to do, if it could be avoided. I sat back to consider the matter, but the only thing that came to me was the fact that I was hungry.

"Right… I'll ponder the situation while I make and eat dinner," I promised the universe as I marched out into the kitchen.

Something not particularly exciting on toast does not take long to prepare and eat, but it took long enough for my grey cells to come up with a possible solution. I hurried back to my office and cleared a space on the desk in front of me. The aim of the exercise was to check the typed version of the manuscript against either the book or Jane's version. I turned to the list of variations we recorded from the reading of the published book. It might require careful application, but I was almost convinced that the listed variations shouldn't be too difficult to check in the typed manuscript. That made me think about the nature of the variations.

Did they have any significant impact on the storyline? Did they alter the plot in any way? I sat and stared off into the distance for a minute or so as I considered the nature of those variations I could remember with any clarity. They didn't actually change anything about the story.

My memory suggested that, in most cases, the variations did nothing more than tidy the language used in Jane's manuscript. Sometimes, pedantic, verbose passages were condensed into more readable forms. There were also instances where Jane's language seemed antiquated. The variation 'modernised' the words without altering the meaning or the intent, although by today's standards, some of the upgraded passages still felt dated or 'old-fashioned'. I hadn't found anything too disastrous about the variations, so all that lay ahead was to check the list of variations against Miss Parker's version.

Although the process wasn't arduous, it was fiddly in some instances. Long before I had worked my way to the end of the list of variations, it was obvious there was no one consistent outcome. Sometimes, Miss Parker appears to have been responsible for improving the wording of various passages. In other cases, the changes appeared to have occurred subsequent to Miss Parker's typed versions, suggesting they were the publisher's initiative. I couldn't help but wonder whether Jane ever conducted a similar exercise and identified the variations between her manuscript and the published novel.

A new question arrived to occupy my mind as I prepared for bed. Was it necessary to repeat this comparison exercise for all the other books Jane bought from that stall? Although, in the interests of thoroughness, all the books should be subject to the same scrutiny, I was inclined to believe the evidence we had collected might apply in a similar fashion to the other books as well. Having accepted that, by the time I crawled into bed, I was feeling confident of a sound night's sleep.

That assumption was wrong. A new question snuck in as I snuggled down amongst the bedclothes. Were the books Jane purchased from the stall the only ones of her manuscripts that had been pirated, or had others been acquired as well? Perhaps the books Jane bought were the only ones on the stall she recognised as hers. What if there had been others? Maybe others had been published but were not on the stall, either because they had already been sold or were not yet available for sale.

Like all the other questions those manuscripts have generated, finding answers to them won't be easy. The only confirmation we have that any of her manuscripts were pirated is thanks to Jane's entry in her diary about them. If Miss Parker were facilitating the theft of Jane's work, it's not unreasonable to expect that other manuscripts were involved as well. Why would the theft involve only so few from the vast collection of Jane's writing?

My eyelids were heavy, and my mind too fogbound for further thought, and I drifted off to sleep. Strange dreams resulted in a restless night that promised a thick head in the morning.

For the entire drive to Ravenshead this morning, I was seriously distracted by a question for which I needed an answer before I arrived at the property: What to tackle this morning? By the time Gabby invited me in for a coffee before we began work, I had more or less decided I needed to spend more time on Jane's diaries. I had developed the notion that, after events at the garden party, Jane would have thoroughly investigated matters at home. Maybe what she found sealed Miss Parker's fate.

What was Miss Parker's fate? I knew nothing more of the woman following her sacking by Jane. Would what became of her be relevant to my current brief? Possibly… But it would depend on what that fate was. Despite my best efforts to avoid such thoughts, I suspected that Miss Lois Parker met with a similar fate to that of Jane's husband, George. That, in turn, begged the next question: Why? What would Jane have gained from it? Perhaps I do need to return to the diaries and devote more time to learning what they have to say – even if only cryptically.

Out of politeness rather than genuine interest, I asked Gabby what she planned to do today.

"Uhm… I'm hoping you don't want to read anything more aloud today. My throat is still raw. If you want to start on the next book, I'm sure I'll manage." I shook my head, and she continued. "Good. In that case, I'll return to reading the diaries. It's strange how fascinating they are, although there's nothing of any great import in Jane's entries."

"I'll be looking at diaries also today. It's probably wishful thinking, but I'm hoping for further comments somewhere about those pirated manuscripts. I find it hard to believe Jane did not follow up on the situation once she discovered what had happened, but so far, I've found no evidence of it. If you come across any mention of Miss Parker or Darcy Wilson in the diaries you read, please make a note of the date. I'm not looking for anything in particular, but something interesting might be lurking in Jane's entries."

With Gabby's day now sorted, I gave my own day further thought as I made my way to the study and the hidden space. It resulted in another decision. I was on a roll and in danger of surprising myself if I kept this up. I intended to work at home on the next two diaries, following the one in which Jane recorded finding her books on the stall at the garden party. Although I already had found entries relating to terminating Miss Parker and paying Darcy Wilson more money, I hoped Jane's subsequent entries might suggest she delved further into the matter of the pirated manuscripts.

My intention was to fetch the two diaries from the shelves and then head home, but I foolishly opened the first one and flicked through it. I don't know why I did. I wasn't looking for anything in particular, but it was my undoing. While riffling through the first few pages, an entry caught my eye. It was long and had nothing to do with Parker, Wilson, or manuscripts, but it provided a glimpse into Jane's everyday life. It was interesting. So, I dragged my chair closer and sat down to read it and the next few entries. That's where I was when Gabby announced it was time for morning coffee.

"Perhaps I'll take mine back to the study to keep working while I drink it," I suggested as I picked my mug up from the kitchen bench and started towards the door.

"You'll do no such thing. Coffee breaks are meant to be just that, a break from work. Sit down and relax while you drink your coffee… Or, have you found something so exciting, you can't wait to get back to it?"

"No such luck. If that were the case, I wouldn't have stopped for coffee. What about your morning so far? Have you found anything interesting?"

"Oh, it's all interesting, but none of it is relevant to the matters we are trying to sort out."

By the time lunchtime rolled around, I had waded through most of the first of the two diaries. I mentioned working from home for the rest of the day and having lunch there later. Gabby was having none of it. She insisted I stay for lunch and then go home if I really felt it necessary. I finally managed to implement an escape plan soon after lunch and left Ravenshead with the diary I worked on this morning, plus the next two in the series. My morning's efforts had produced nothing, and I had no confidence that whatever I did for the remainder of the day would prove any different.

As I felt I might be pushing my luck if I put Warren off again tonight, I hastily prepared a stew in the slow cooker for tonight's dinner and sent a text advising Warren accordingly. Then, anticipating a few hours of uninterrupted work, I settled behind the desk in my home office and opened the diary I started reading this morning. There wasn't too much left to read, so my afternoon coffee break was timed to slot between finishing that diary and starting the next one.

When Warren arrived just before seven o'clock, I was halfway through that second diary, still with no further mention of Miss Parker, Mr Wilson, or misappropriated manuscripts. It was sometime during dinner that a horrible thought arrived, and I found myself wishing Warren's phone would summon him back to work.

Warren's phone obstinately remained silent, but the exhausted detective inspector made his apologies and departed at about eight o'clock. I rushed back to my office to consider the troubling thought that arrived during dinner. That *thought* was a *memory*. I remembered that Jane's diary entries relating to buying the books at the garden party and paying Wilson more money were in the previous journal to the one I had finished this afternoon. And, they were early in the book, not at the end of it. I needed to return to that diary and to read all its entries.

Almost convinced that the remainder of the diaries I had brought home were too much later than the garden party entry, I decided to push on with them anyway, as I had nothing else to work on. Again, entries provided insight into what was happening at the time and how it was perceived to be impacting life at Ravenshead; all quite interesting, but not particularly useful. There was an upside to the situation. It allowed for an early night and the best night's sleep in a while.

The priority this morning was to return to the diary entries relating to buying the books from the stall at the garden party and then paying Darcy Wilson more money. With the relevant diary on the desk in front of me in the study, a new distraction slammed in and sent me hurrying back into the hidden space for the financial records for that period of time.

My earlier notes had recorded the appropriate page, so moments later, the ledger was open at Wilson's payment entry. Further reference to my earlier notes alerted me to the fact that the price for 'services rendered' had increased since Jane's previous large payment to Wilson. It didn't matter how many times I read the ledger or the journal entries, no further clues about the nature of the 'service' paid for could be extracted.

"Right...," I announced in disgust. "Let's see if there are any clues further on."

"Were you talking to me, or is there some other invisible form in this room you prefer to converse with?" I looked up to see a perplexed-looking Gabby hesitating in the study's doorway.

"Nothing so exciting. I was trying to ignite 'my other self' to think outside the box, and hopefully come up with some rational ideas I might explore. I keep coming up with ideas that seem promising but ultimately go nowhere. What about you? What are your plans for today? Your phone had your full attention when I arrived, so I didn't have a chance to ask you earlier."

"Reading more diaries was on the agenda, but now I have to go into town. I need to leave soon, and I doubt I'll be back until after lunch. Will you be okay to organise yourself something for lunch?"

"As I've told you before, you aren't supposed to be feeding me while I'm on this assignment. Anyway, that works out well for me. I am half inclined to take some stuff home to work on while I attend to some laundry that's been trying to gain my attention for a couple of days."

That wasn't quite true, but it wasn't a complete lie. I seem to think better, more creatively, at home… And I do have some laundry to attend to. So, the problem now is what to take home. Obviously, the two bundles on the desk in front of me were contenders, but what else might be useful? A few minutes later, I heard Gabby drive away. I quickly crossed to her apartment and made a coffee. When the grey cells are sluggish, feed them caffeine!

When I left Ravenshead about an hour later, I almost needed a trolley to take everything out to my car. Although I knew most, if not all, of it would be of no use at all, at least I would have proved that to be the case. Once I moved everything from the car into my home office and threw a load of washing into the machine, it was time for the hard question: Where to start? The decision wasn't so difficult; start with the two bundles initially drawn from the archives this morning. I opened both records at the entries regarding the payment to Wilson, and just prior to the journal entry about Miss Parker's termination.

About a month after her entry about paying the large sum to Wilson, another brief and obscure entry in Jane's diary caught my eye. In itself, it told me nothing when I skimmed it, but my gut told me otherwise and sent me back to study it: *Got it right this time. No loose ends to worry us.*

Does that mean what I think it might mean? Of course, I realised it could refer to anything happening in Jane's life at the time, but my gut kept telling me this was the clue I needed. What if my suspicions were right and the money paid to Wilson was for Miss Parker to meet with a similar fate to George's? Could a well-heeled woman of that time be so ruthless as to have those who displeased her permanently eliminated? Were those two people the victims of an overindulged woman's arrogance?

The questions were coming thick and fast, with each one more horrible than the previous. Am I concocting something out of nothing, something almost too horrendous to comprehend? Somehow, I didn't think so, but I needed to sit in solitude to contemplate the implications of such suspicions. I poured myself a large glass of red wine and took it out onto my back deck. The afternoon sounds of people returning home after a day at work had died away, and most of the neighbourhood had retreated indoors to prepare for their evening meal and the evening news broadcast on TV.

Soft, velvety shades of evening were descending as I collapsed into my favourite chair and took a long swig of my wine. The night seemed to cocoon me in its peace and silence, and yet it wasn't a complete silence. A lone cricket in a rosemary bush beside the deck played its monotonous solo recital, and a Willy Wagtail had its final few words to say for the day before disappearing into the jasmine along the fence. A few minutes later, I felt myself relaxing as my shoulders lowered from below my ears. Time to devote serious thought to those questions thundering about in my head.

If my interpretation of the various information gathered from Jane's documents is correct, how do I tell Gabby what I've discovered? It all happened a long time ago, but Jane was her grandmother. How would I react to discovering my grandmother had paid for the murder of not only her husband but also an employee who had robbed her? I giggled at the question. How would I know how I would react? I didn't know my grandmother. Obviously, I must have had one – two, in fact – but I never knew them. I was well into my teenage years before I realised they must exist out there – somewhere. But Gabby's situation was different.

Gabby did know about Jane and, as a child, had spent some time in the same house as her grandmother. Regardless of how she felt about her grandmother at that time, and what her memories of the woman are now, Jane was her grandmother, a part of who Gabby was and a part of the family legacy Gabby inherited. So, how do I tell her what I've discovered? And, when do I tell her? Is now the right time, or should I wait until my suspicions are confirmed?

I heard the little voice in my head demand there be no more questions, and I thought it wise to comply. So, slumped back in my chair, I focused on my wine and the descending night surrounding me. While I had been lost in thought, the moon had crept above the rooftops and begun bathing the area in a mix of dark shadows and silvery light. The evening star was already high in the sky when a group of six birds straggled past in front of it as they made a late trip home. A light breeze made an appearance. It rustled the jasmine hedge and wafted its sweet perfume over me. I felt myself relaxing and my eyelids growing heavy.

My doorbell made a rude intrusion into my solitude. My first thought was that Warren had managed to get away from work and had come for the evening. Then, I remembered that Warren had his own key and never used the doorbell. Besides, he would have called to say he was coming and not just arrived unannounced. The jangle of the doorbell again disturbed the silence of the night.

"Okay, okay, I'm coming," I muttered as I hauled myself upright and headed for the door.

"Gabby…! Has something happened? Come in. Come in and tell me what has happened." She hesitated on the doorstep and, for a moment, I thought she might turn on her heel and flee.

"Argh, hell… I shouldn't have come, not at this hour of the night and unannounced," she stammered as I caught her by the arm, reassured her she wasn't intruding, and guided her through to a lounge chair.

"Now, Gabby, what's this all about? What has upset you? Are you unhappy about the work I'm doing and the apparent lack of any real progress?"

"No, of course not. I've seen you working, and that's just the thing. You seem a bit like a dog on the scent of something. You're not just researching. It's as though you've found a clue, a hint of something, and you are trying to ferret out the whole story. Not knowing what you have found is killing me. Please put me out of my misery by sharing what you've learned so far. If I knew what you were working on, I might be able to help. Come on, Sophie, tell me. Are you on the scent of something, or not?"

Well, that tends to answer the question about when to share with Gabby what I've learned about her grandmother so far. I set us up with a platter of cheese and crackers and glasses of wine before taking a couple of deep breaths and launching into my confronting tale.

Chapter 13

Gabby was right. She was entitled to a progress report. There is no easy way to do it. It won't be easy for either of us, but the only way is to dive straight in and lay it all out for her, what I've discovered and my suspicions.

"I haven't been deliberately keeping anything from you, Gabby. It's more a case of not being sure about what I know, as opposed to what I *think* I know, but what I'm about to tell you will not be easy to hear."

"You are making it worse, Sophie. I knew something was wrong, and that's why you hadn't shared it with me. I assure you, I can handle whatever you have to tell me."

"Okay… Firstly, some things I need to tell you do not directly relate to your family's legend about Jane's pirated manuscripts, but they do have a connection (of sorts) that justifies researching them.

To begin, let's go back to that other family story about the Ravenshead homestead being haunted by your grandfather's ghost. Yes, there was an inquest into his death, but he did not die at the house. He supposedly came off his horse some distance away and wasn't found for a couple of days. The authorities apparently found something not quite right about his death. Their investigation culminated in an inquest. Ultimately, an accidental death was recorded. No charges were laid, but a certain 'smell' continued to surround his death."

"Ri-ight… But you had told me he didn't die in the house. That's why I've been able to overcome whatever prevented me from entering the main part of the house. Do you know anything more about his death and why suspicions surrounding it lingered after the inquest? If he came off his horse, I assume he was working somewhere out on the property at the time."

"That is the official story, but Jane's diary entries tend to tell a different story. Please understand that Jane's diary entries are not explicit. Anything extracted from them is obtained more by reading between the lines than from her actual words."

"Perhaps there is no surprise in that. Nothing about Ravenshead or its history seems to be straightforward or completely acceptable. What have you managed to extract from Jane's diaries about George's death?"

"While George supposedly was checking on a fencing team working some distance from the homestead, it is unclear whether he actually visited the team in question. Jane's take on the situation was that George wasn't going to visit the workers. He was going to visit a young widow living in a cottage close to the Ravenshead property boundary, and that is where he intended spending the night. I have found nothing to confirm Jane's version of the story, but if George had been playing away from home, it appears Jane was aware of it."

"Yeah… It wouldn't have made for a happy household if that were the case, but that has no bearing on George's death … Does it? He still died after coming off his horse."

"Taken at face value, the cause of his death remains the same, but other information raises questions about that."

I saw a stunned look sweep across Gabby's face, and I knew a torrent of questions would follow. So, to pre-empt some of them and help her to understand the situation more quickly, I rushed to tell her about my other suspicious findings.

"All the pieces of this story don't fit together like a Pulitzer-prizewinning novel. You will need to bear with me while I explain the next part of this particular story." Gabby looked unsure, but nodded and told me to continue.

"We have to refer to Jane's financial records to find the next vital bit of George's story … And it doesn't come after his death. This part of the story occurred a couple of days prior to it. At that time, Darcy Wilson, the delivery driver for Kennedy's General Store, regularly delivered to Ravenshead. Jane recorded that Wilson took morning tea with her a few days before George's fateful ride occurred. That same day, Jane visited her bank and paid a substantial sum of money from her personal account into Wilson's account.

A couple of days later, George died under what were considered suspicious circumstances at the time. Soon after that, and before the inquest, Wilson purchased a half share of Kennedy's General Store."

"Are you suggesting he used the money Jane paid him to buy into the store? Is there any evidence that was the case?"

"No, I don't have any hard evidence, but there was another interesting event that occurred on or about the day Wilson bought his share of the Store. Jane again transferred money to Wilson. On that occasion, it was only £500. While it doesn't sound like much today, it was a considerable amount back then. Now, I acknowledge the supposition might be that Wilson, finding himself a little short of the purchase price, asked his good friend Jane to help him out."

"Something along those lines might have happened, I suppose, but it doesn't fit with my picture of Jane. Although I have to admit, it seems as though she had a strange relationship with Mr Wilson. So, maybe she did lend him some extra money. Anything else you know about this?"

"Well, again, it might be coincidental, but after Wilson bought into the Store, Jane started receiving regular small payments from him."

"There you are, then. He was repaying her the extra money she lent him. You said small amounts. At that rate, how long was it going to take to repay all of the money?"

"Forever… But I don't think that was the intention. I think it is more likely that the extra bit Jane paid him secured her the equivalent of some shares in the business, shares that only she and Wilson knew about. The payments she received were the dividends on the shares she held."

"Sophie, this is becoming confusing. Are you suggesting that in return for her £500, Jane received a small number of shares in Wilson's half of the business?" I nodded. "But what about the significant sum she paid him earlier? What did she receive in return for that?"

"Good question, Gabby, but we need to dig a little deeper before we know more."

"If it's all the same to you, Sophie, I think I might go home now. I suspect you have more to tell me, but I've been in meetings for most of the afternoon. My brain is completely fogbound. It can't process what you've told me so far. Perhaps after some quiet time alone, things might start to fall into place. So, I'll leave now and will see you in the morning."

As I walked her to the door, a thought slammed in with such force it almost stunned me.

"Gabby, I might be a little late tomorrow. There are a couple of things I might do before I drive out to Ravenshead."

"Of course. See you whenever you arrive, but I'm half inclined to go into town myself again tomorrow."

After watching her taillights disappear down my driveway, I rushed to my office to scribble myself a note; a To-Do-Tomorrow note. Then, I was off to bed in the misguided hope that a sound night's sleep awaited. It didn't, and a whole flock of new thoughts, ideas, and questions regarding the Ravenshead project made sure I lay awake for what felt like hours.

Over breakfast, I reviewed all that had come to me last night and tried to decide where to start first this morning. Strangely enough, the majority of my thoughts had focused on the enigmatic Miss Lois Parker. By my second coffee, I had a rough idea of how my morning would progress. My first task was to put Google to work.

"So, there were elections that year," I muttered as I read Google's response to my search request, but there were some interesting footnotes attached.

As preparations for that year's Local Government elections began, it appeared there had been concern about exactly who now lived where and in which electorate they were eligible to vote. In some areas – and this electorate was one of them – the existing Shire Council employed what amounted to census takers to establish who was living in the area and if they were registered voters. According to the information Google provided, the 'head counting' process occurred while Jane still employed Miss Parker.

While it would be handy to access the outcome of those door-to-door interviews, I knew the best I could hope for was the local electoral roll that resulted from it. No, there wasn't an electronic copy online that I could access, so my only hope lay with the local library, or maybe the Council's records. I hoped the former, rather than the latter, would be the case as I imagined the hassle that would ensue if I asked to look at something in the Council's archives.

After making a few notes to guide my morning's research, I headed for the local library. My luck was in. A copy of the local electoral roll I wanted was on a shelf in the reference section. Its condition suggested it hadn't seen much use since that election. I told myself it would be too easy, and that I would be out at Ravenshead in time for morning coffee. That proved to be wishful thinking.

A scan of the Parker surnames on the roll drew a blank. There were more with that surname than I expected, but there was no listing for Lois Parker or anything similar. I sat stunned for a moment, pondering what to do next. Then, the little voice in my head kept repeating *the books*. What books? Whose books? Oh, *those* books. Worth a try, I suppose, I told myself as I flipped back a few pages of the electoral roll. If I was surprised by the number of Parkers on the roll, the number of McDonalds registered was stunning.

"Okay, let's see if any of those listed have the initials D M for their given names," I murmured as I ran my finger down the page to the first of the given names starting with D.

"Yes…," I hissed, then checked to see if anyone had heard me.

No one looked at me. The librarian on duty wasn't glaring at me… But I did have a problem. I had found a woman's name that fit my search parameters. Did that mean anything? It might be a coincidence. They were common enough given names, but her address showed she was living here in town. I scribbled down the address before heading to my car and to the place where Daphne Mary McDonald was supposedly living at the time of the local government election. The cute, old cottage I pulled up in front of gave me pause for thought. What do I say, without my sounding like a complete lunatic, when someone answers the door?

It stood to reason that the Daphne Mary McDonald of the electoral roll would no longer be living in the cottage. It was so long ago, even if she had been a young woman at the time, she was likely to be deceased by now. Still, whoever lived there now might know something about previous owners, I told myself, but it wasn't much of a confidence booster. A little old lady answered the door and stood there in the open doorway, blinking at me. There was no welcoming smile. I felt my confidence evaporate.

"I apologise for bothering you like this, but I wondered how long you've lived in this house and if you know anything of its history."

"Why would I want to answer that, and why do you want to know?"

"The question I should have asked is if you might know something of Daphne Mary McDonald, who once lived here?" My enquiry earned me a suspicious look.

"Who wants to know? I'm not sure why you're asking, but I don't think I can help you."

"Okay, it seems I'm not handling this well. What I intended to ask you is if you know anything about previous owners of this cottage, and if Daphne Mary McDonald was one of them?"

"Now, why would you be asking about someone who once lived here some time in the past?" she finally asked, her voice devoid of venom but oozing suspicion.

"My historical research indicated that a woman of that name once lived here, and I was interested in finding out a bit more about her. It would have been a long time ago that she lived here, and I realise she may be deceased by now. So, I wondered if you have lived here for long and if you know anything of the history of the house and its owners?"

She stood, looking me up and down for a few moments, as she appeared to consider my request before responding to it.

"Perhaps you had better come in and have a cup of tea while we talk this over." She stepped aside and gestured for me to enter.

Despite attempts to lighten and brighten the place, stepping from the bright sunlight into the darker interior of the cottage was like entering a dark cave. She indicated an overstuffed lounge chair, and I sat there obediently while she fussed about in the kitchen, before returning with a laden tea tray.

"Please don't think this indicates I'm about to answer any of your questions," she warned me as she thumped the tea tray on a small table in front of me. "Now, let's start with your name, shall we? And then you can tell me why you are so interested in all this historical stuff."

Giving her my name was the easy part, but explaining the rest of it was tricky and required a dash of creative thinking first.

"Right… Well, I understand your caution and confusion. I'll try to explain as best I can," I added after giving her my name and taking an extra moment or two to concoct my 'explanation'. She nodded, and I continued.

"In the course of some historical research I was doing, I discovered we had an author living in this area a few decades ago. The author had several books published under the name D M McDonald. A check on the electoral roll for around that time produced only one name that fitted my search criteria: Daphne Mary McDonald, whose address was listed as this cottage. I was intrigued and wanted to know more about this local author I previously knew nothing about, and whether the name I found on the roll was indeed the author's name."

"Ah, I see. Forgive me if I appeared less than hospitable, but you can't be too careful these days. To answer at least some of your questions, yes, Daphne McDonald did own this house and lived here quite some time ago. She was my mother, and I eventually inherited this place, but I don't know anything about any other owners prior to my mother."

"You say you *eventually* inherited the house. Was there something unusual in the way the property passed to you? Although I realised the author I was interested in would be deceased by now, I hadn't checked the cemetery or death records before coming here. So, I apologise if my questioning feels a bit insensitive. Was there a problem with probate or something that delayed ownership passing to you?"

"Well, if nothing else, I can probably save you some trouble. I doubt you will find my mother in the death indexes, and you definitely won't find her in the local cemetery."

She paused and seemed to retreat into her own thoughts for a moment. I didn't want to lose momentum, so I jumped in to query her comment.

"Oh, I see. Thank you for that. So, if she wasn't buried locally, where is she buried?" The moment I asked the question, I hated myself for being even more insensitive.

"Good question, but she isn't buried anywhere. Well, no, that's not true. As you say, obviously she is deceased. The problem is that we don't know where she died – or how. She just 'disappeared', and eventually was presumed dead. That process took years, and then it was a complicated and long process before probate was granted and this property passed to me."

"What an amazing story. No doubt there have been plenty of theories about what happened to your mother. Are there any you think might be correct?"

"No, not really. Our family isn't from around here, and I don't think she lived in the area for long before she disappeared. I don't think she became well-known during her time here."

"That's a poignant but intriguing story. Have you never been tempted to explore it, to dig into her time?"

"Not really. Argh, there was a time when I was much younger. When I was curious, but nothing came of it. I didn't know where to go or who to talk to for information. Anyway, I believe what happened to her remains a mystery. Maybe in the course of your research, you might uncover some clues, but I've learned to live with not knowing."

"Your mother was an author, so there must be some information about her around somewhere. How much do you know about that side of her life?"

"Nothing to speak of. My grandmother brought me up. I don't remember much about my mother, and I'm not sure how much of that is what I remember or if it was stuff I was told. I was a young child when she disappeared, and I had already been living with my grandmother for a while by then. Although I asked questions about her when I was a bit older, Grandma was reluctant to talk about her. I've always suspected there must have been some horrible secret in her past, but I never discovered anything.

Please, if you discover anything about her – anything at all – will you share it with me? I don't care whether it is good or bad. I would just like to know something of her before I die and, as I am now an old woman, that probably isn't too far away."

Of course, I agreed to share anything I discovered, but I wasn't sure I was being truthful when I did. Then, as she walked me to the door, something else occurred to me… and I just had to ask about it before I left.

"One last question before I leave you in peace. Did your family – your grandmother in particular – talk about your mother's career as an author? I mean, were they proud, or at least impressed, with the work she produced?"

"Goodness, no. After I kept pestering her for information, my grandmother did say that my mother was *a writer of some sort,* but that was all she would ever say. The family had money, so I assumed that being a writer was somehow considered below her station in life."

My mind was in turmoil as I drove away from the cottage, and my rumbling stomach wasn't helping me think clearly. I had intended to drive out to Ravenshead, but my stomach made me check the time. It was almost lunchtime. I needed time alone to think. That meant not being with Gabby. I drove to my favourite bistro, ordered, and parked myself at a table in a quiet corner.

Have I achieved anything this morning, apart from giving a little old lady false hope? I almost believed I had established the identity of the D M McDonald, whose name appears on the published pirated manuscripts. But have I established that she is the same person as the Lois Parker who reputedly pirated them? The short answer to that was a resounding NO. It is possible Parker passed the manuscripts to McDonald, who then published them under her name.

That realisation begged a new question. Who was the publisher? Was independent publishing possible back then? While it probably wasn't common, it was certainly possible, especially if you had the money to do it… And my new acquaintance suggested there was family money. Questions kept coming, while answers, informed answers, were in short supply. My way forward was clear: go to Ravenshead and check one of those books for the publisher's information.

All the way to Ravenshead, the tiny voice in my head kept telling me that I had solved the mystery. Although I didn't know what became of Miss Parker after her sacking, she certainly seemed to disappear from all records. Daphne Mary McDonald's disappearance fitted too neatly with Parker's to be a coincidence. So, where is the evidence to support that theory?

"No, no, no…," I hissed as I roared along the road to Ravenshead. "Don't go finding more questions. It's answers we need now, not more questions."

A bewildered-looking Gabby came out to meet me as soon as I pulled up out front. "I thought you must have become so involved in whatever you had to do that you decided not to come out here today. Nothing has gone wrong, has it?"

I gave a half-hearted laugh and shook my head.

"Good, come in and have a coffee before you do anything else. Even if you don't want one, come in and talk to me while I have one."

"Is everything all right with you? You sounded a bit desperate just now."

"It's that mob I work for. They...."

"Shouldn't that be past tense? I thought you had retired."

"Well, I had sort of, but I offered to continue to be available to work on the last project I was involved with until it was finally completed. All sorts of complications have arisen since then, and now they are begging me for help with problems on another project as well."

"You could always remind them of your retirement's agreed-upon arrangements."

"Oh, I know. But if my last project isn't completed successfully, it will be a permanent reflection on my abilities. I don't want to be remembered as someone who fell over at the last hurdle. It's a bad way to end a career … or a certain way of ending it, perhaps."

"To someone who knows nothing about your career, it sounds as though you are not yet ready to retire. Stop fighting it. Tell them you are prepared to continue working for them (in a limited way if that's what you would prefer), but that you will do it from here."

"Great thinking. Now, come inside for coffee and share some more of your sound wisdom with me."

"Okay. Go and make the coffee. I'll join you in a couple of minutes. There is something I want to check first," I called over my shoulder as I rushed to the study and that wall of bookshelves.

It doesn't take much time or energy to pull a couple of books from a shelf and check their title pages. What takes time is trying to work out what to do next, or at least, how to approach it. Those questions accompanied me for coffee.

Chapter 14

Gabby picked up on my preoccupation as soon as we sat down with our coffees.

"Is there somewhere else you should be, or something else you would rather be doing? Please, Sophie, don't feel you have to be here all day, every day. I'm beginning to understand how impossible this project really is."

"No, it's nothing like that. It's just that, when I'm researching, I tend to live in my head, and am not much of a conversationalist. I have some half-formed ideas I'm dealing with at the moment. They tend to block all other rational thought. By the way, I've taken a couple of books from Jane's bookshelves to spend a bit of time on them tonight. No, don't get excited. I'm just trying to get a feel for Jane's writing. Although the text has been altered here and there, the books are the easiest way of becoming familiar with her work."

As soon as we finished our coffee (and good manners permitted), I told Gabby I wasn't sure what time I would come out tomorrow or if I would come at all, and I headed home. Warren's message arrived as I was about to pull into my garage. He would be working late and would eat in town tonight.

"Perfect," I assured the universe, "an evening alone is what I need tonight."

Now I had the evening to myself, what was I going to do with it? With plenty of time before I needed to think about what to have for dinner, I settled down in my home office and waited for my computer to boot up. I didn't have a plan, but with my computer up and running, I knew what to do first. I typed the name of the publisher of the pirated books into Google's search bar and waited.

The bad news was that it had gone out of business, and a long time ago. I read the last of the few hits Google found for me before discovering anything further about the now defunct publisher. It appears to have been a small, independent operation that struggled to gain market share. It lost out to larger operators and was acquired by one of them a few years after publication of the pirated manuscripts.

Google's information was in keeping with the way this whole project was progressing. The moment I think I have a reasonable lead to help unravel some of the mystery, it turns into a dead end. I sat back to think about the now defunct publisher and whether there was anything more to be gained by pursuing it further. Almost as a last resort, I checked the list of books by D M McDonald that Google claimed were published. There were a couple of extra books on the list that I hadn't known about.

Checking the publication dates of all the books on Google's list revealed that the extra books were published after the 'garden party' at which Jane purchased the ones on her bookshelf. It appears Miss Parker had pirated two additional manuscripts that still awaited publication at that time – and before Jane terminated her services. Interesting information, I had to admit, but it didn't help solve the mystery. That gave me pause for thought.

What part of the mystery had I hoped information about the author and the publisher would solve? It took another long, strong coffee before the little grey cells sluggishly revived.

"Come on, Sophie Sinclair … Start thinking," I admonished myself aloud as I sat staring at my computer screen. "What are the connections? I have three names. How are they connected? Are any of them connected other than in a purely commercial sense?" I slumped back in my chair and stared at the ceiling.

"Aw, Hell! Can I really be so thick?" I demanded of the universe. Perhaps it's as well it didn't reply. "What was that little old lady's name who I spoke to this morning?"

I grabbed my notebook and turned to the scribbled notes I'd made over lunch. There it was, a serious connection. Gladys Tremaine shared a surname with Tremaine Publishing House.

After a couple of heartbeats, the other connection occurred to me. Gladys Tremaine was the daughter of Daphne Mary McDonald.

"Okay, now I have all three names connected. Where does that take me, if anywhere?" I sat back to ponder the question further.

The obvious answer was that all three might have been connected via a marriage between McDonald and the Mr Tremaine of Tremaine Publishing House, with Gladys the product of that union. It was a reasonable and tidy conclusion, but the little voice in my head kept telling me it was too tidy ... Too tidy to accept without further research.

Before embarking on any research, I needed a rough estimate of Gladys Tremaine's birth date. A precise date wasn't necessary. When she was born, if the parents were not married, the child was deemed illegitimate and would only be registered under the mother's name. Assuming all the legal formalities were met in this case, for Gladys to be Daphne and Tremaine's daughter and registered as Tremaine, her parents must have been married.

"Ah, perhaps not. For the baby to be deemed legitimate, they only had to claim to be married, and for Tremaine to agree to his name appearing as the child's father." No argument with my thinking was forthcoming from the universe or anywhere else, so I set about proving myself right.

Of course, if I could look up the birth and marriage indexes to confirm my assumption would be too easy. I planned to search for a marriage record first, but I needed to set a date range to search. I realised Miss Parker could, in fact, have been Mrs Tremaine long before Jane employed her. Any child of the couple could have been born early or late in the marriage. So, regardless of when it was, Gladys's birth was too recent to appear in the births index. I searched the marriage index for a Tremaine/McDonald marriage.

After several searches over an increasingly wide date range, no marriage was found. They might not have been married in this State. Fortunately, with all of the states' indexes online, it wasn't an impossible challenge. Nevertheless, in the end, the result was the same; no such marriage registered anywhere.

"Where to next? What else can I look at?" I hissed as I pushed myself away from the desk and turned to stare out the window.

Did it matter if my assumed connection existed or not? I managed to convince myself that not proving my assumption to be correct was just another hurdle I hadn't worked out how to climb over. I eventually persuaded myself to make a note of my assumptions and move on with my research... But move on to what? I was so fixated on proving the connection of those three names, my thinking hadn't progressed beyond that, and I now found myself up against that familiar brick wall. Still, it was dinnertime, and that was one way of removing myself from the frustration of negative research results.

The seven o'clock TV news dished up its usual serving of doom and gloom. Why did I allow myself to be so depressed by those broadcasts every night when I was already depressed enough by a lack of progress on Gabby's project? Back in my office, it took a few minutes before inspiration felt inclined to visit.

Time to forget about those three names and move on to something else. The 'something else' that came to mind was the winding up of Daphne Mary McDonald's estate. According to her daughter, there was some delay in processing her mother's estate due to no evidence of her mother's death. In such cases, I knew there was a period of some years (seven years in this State) before someone could be *declared* deceased, despite no evidence of death having been discovered. Would a coroner's inquest be needed for such a declaration? I told myself it was worth looking through the archives' records for an inquest or anything else that might be useful.

No record of an inquest was found. Further inspiration led me to search for probate records related to McDonald's estate. This time, luck was in my corner. I located an apparent relevant file and sent a request for a copy. I now have to endure a frustrating wait for the archives to send me a quote for the cost of the copy, and then a further wait until it finally arrives.

While I'm waiting, what do I do next? Is there anything more I can tackle tonight? I flipped through the pages of the pirated book I had brought home while I waited for inspiration to strike. My eyes became heavy, and I struggled to concentrate. I checked the time.

"My God, it's gone midnight already," I yelped. I had intended to have an early night.

As I crawled into bed, I realised the book I'd been reading had come with me. It had a haunting storyline, and I knew I would finish reading that book before I put it back on the shelf. It had become obvious to me that Jane was an excellent writer, and it generated a new respect for her. Although I knew some of her words had been 'adjusted' by Parker and the publisher before publication, it didn't mask Jane's ability as a storyteller. The one I read tonight was nothing short of enthralling. I realised how tempting it must have been for Miss Parker to capitalise on Jane's manuscripts she was typing.

I fell asleep last night with no clear thoughts about what I might do today. As I dawdled over breakfast, I wondered if it was worth going to Ravenshead today, given I had no idea what I might do there. After allowing the matter to rattle around in my mind for a while, I realised that, if I didn't go to Ravenshead today, I'd probably still be having this conversation with myself tomorrow. No new ideas about how to progress would be achieved by sitting draped over my breakfast bar. I dragged myself into my office and began packing my tote bag for the trip to Ravenshead.

Picking up my notebook, I flipped through the pages until one caught and held my attention. The name Darcy Wilson seemed to leap off the page at me. In my search for information about the books, I had forgotten about him, but he was a key player in all of this. Although not directly involved in the piracy of the manuscripts (of that, I felt sure), he was a major player in the saga. So, what did I know about him, and what more did I need to know?

The answer was not as straightforward as I expected. First, I had to distinguish between what I suspected and what was fact. I told myself that wouldn't be too hard, and reached for my notebook. The next challenge was to record it in a way that was clear and concise for future reference. After a couple of false starts, I gave up, booted up my computer, and opened a new document with two columns. One column would be for facts, while the other would record my suspicions.

Facts: Jane made two substantial payments to Wilson, as well as a smaller one. He was close to Jane, close enough to take tea with her whenever he delivered to Ravenshead. He bought a half share in Kennedy's General Store before later owning it outright. His business was significantly impacted by the arrival of major retail chains in the neighbouring town, ultimately forcing him out of business.

Suspicions: That he somehow was instrumental in Jane's husband's death and Miss Parker's disappearance, and was paid handsomely for his involvement. Did he vanish after his business closed, or where did he go? Was Jane at one time a minor shareholder in Wilson's business? What was the bond that appeared so strong between Wilson and Jane?

At that point, I stopped and read what I had recorded. The Facts column looked okay, but that wasn't the case with the other column. Instead of listing my suspicions as intended, it appeared to be filled with questions I had already asked myself many times without finding any answers.

"Well, that's what I should do next," I told my empty office. "Find out what happened to Darcy Wilson."

Of course, that prompted the next big question to ponder. *Does it matter?* Did it really matter what became of Wilson after he went out of business and appeared to have left the district? The initial answer was: no, of course not. My gut, however, kept insisting that was not the correct answer, or at least, not the whole answer. After a quick message to Gabby that I wouldn't arrive until later, I sat back to consider where to look for Darcy Wilson after he left here. A few seconds later, I realised I again had to visit the library to consult that electoral roll.

Yes, Darcy Wilson did appear on the same electoral roll as where I found Daphne Mary McDonald, but it didn't tell me anything I didn't already know. Replacing the electoral roll on the shelf, I stood back and scanned that shelf. It contained copies of both State and Local Government electoral rolls for a substantial period of years. Without too much thought, I selected one from closer to the start of the shelf and began working my way along the rolls. My pulse quickened as I checked the Wilsons listed in that next roll I selected.

A Thomas William Wilson was listed as living at Ravenshead Estate, but no others of that surname shared his address. The next randomly selected roll listed Thomas again, as well as Erin Wilson, also at Ravenshead. Excitement prickled me all over. Briefly, I felt sure I was closing in on the origins of Darcy Wilson and how he and Jane became acquainted. That was until I checked the next roll. Thomas Wilson was no longer listed. Only Erin remained on the roll. I immediately concluded that Thomas probably had died sometime during the intervening period.

While that might be the case, it didn't tell me anything I wanted to know about Darcy Wilson. Not if Darcy was Thomas and Erin's child, and if he was born at Ravenshead. That soon had me scurrying to one of the library's computers to talk to Google. Within minutes, I had found the death of a Thomas William Wilson listed in the correct time period on the death index and noted its details. I would order a copy of his death certificate later.

Next, a search of the marriage index revealed the entry for the marriage of Thomas and Erin. I was on a roll, and I could hardly believe my luck this morning. The little voice in my head urged me to keep going while I was on a winning streak. It was as I checked the dates involved that I realised how short-lived the marriage had been. They had been married for less than 18 months when Thomas died. I told myself that it was plenty of time for them to have produced at least one child, and switched my attention to the birth index.

Oh, this is almost too good to be true. There it was, an entry for the birth of Darcy Wilson. I hastily scribbled the relevant details in my notebook, but something didn't add up.

"Hang about. That can't be right," I thought aloud, startling the librarian on duty and earning me filthy glares from other nearby library patrons.

I offered them all a hastily murmured apology as I quickly checked my notes. Oh dear, it appeared Darcy Wilson was born about 13 months after his father's death. I had no further need of the library's computer. Now, I needed to sit at my own computer to order copies of the relevant birth, death, and marriage certificates. Quickly stuffing everything back into my tote bag, I left the library and rushed home. Minutes later, I ordered copies of the three certificates.

Why was I feeling so pleased with myself? I hadn't proved anything as far as Jane's pirated manuscripts were concerned. Aided by a fresh coffee, I reviewed the names and dates added to my notebook this morning. Some of the dates took on new meaning. I realised Darcy Wilson would have been about five years old when Jane was 18 and inherited Ravenshead on the death of her father. It was likely she had been familiar with the boy from soon after he was born … Was that enough to explain the strong bond that appeared to have existed between them in later years? I had difficulty accepting that to be the case.

God, I do make life difficult for myself. How will I control my curiosity until the copies of those certificates arrive? I decided the best way was to drive out to Ravenshead to search for other clues. Fortunately, there was little traffic on the road today. My mind was not on my driving. After parking out front of the house, I remained in the car for a couple of minutes. All sorts of 'what if' scenarios had built up in my mind during the drive to Ravenshead. I needed a moment to calm them down before meeting Gabby. It wasn't to be.

Gabby rushed out to the car almost as soon as I arrived. "I wasn't sure whether you were coming out here today, but your timing is excellent. I was about to make lunch. Are you all right, Sophie? You look a bit shattered. Has something happened?"

"Eh? No, I'm fine. That's apart from a late night again. I sat up reading Jane's book… well, the pirated version of it."

"Okay, come in, and tell me about it over lunch. I'm dying to read one of them, but I'm trying to go through the diaries first so that I'll have a bit of a feel for what she was like before I try reading one of her stories."

I had barely sat down before the interrogation began. What was Jane's story like? Was it worth reading? What genre was it? And so the questions continued with hardly a breath – or time for me to answer – between them.

"Damn, I wish I hadn't asked you about the book. Now, it's all I can do to stop myself from grabbing one of her books and reading it. I'm determined not to do that. Her diary entries are so fascinating, but often don't make any sense," and so continued her almost nonstop flow of words. Perhaps there was something of Jane in Gabby. She certainly loved words. Maybe she, too, would make a writer … Or maybe she was just lonely and welcomed the opportunity for conversation. Regardless, her endless stream of words allowed at least a part of my mind to devote itself to what I might do next. What it suggested came as a surprise.

At last, the flow of words came to a temporary halt when we sat down to eat, but it didn't last long.

"So, Sophie, what are you going to do today. If you are going to spend the day reading another of Jane's books, don't tell me about it."

"No, I won't be reading books today. Although I don't have any definite ideas, I will be spending some time in that hidden space. I have a couple of half-formed ideas I want to explore."

As soon as we had eaten, I rushed to the study. I hadn't been quite honest with Gabby. I did know exactly what I would look at today. Today's targets were a lot earlier than those examined in the past, and they would have me reaching for diaries well above my head on the shelves. As I let myself into the hidden space, I reminded myself that there was a real chance this could prove to be another exercise in frustration. But, as I had no other ideas, this was the best I could do for now.

Jane's 1912 diary looked much like all the others on the shelves. I hoped it might include some comment on the birth of Darcy Wilson. The next couple of hours were spent making copious notes of entries, none of which addressed my original interest in this particular diary. Not surprising, perhaps, there was no mention of the birth of Darcy Wilson. As it appears Darcy was illegitimate, it's likely the family's approach would have been to shield a vulnerable young girl from such matters.

With little confidence of achieving success, I replaced the 1912 diary on the shelf and selected the 1917 journal to read. This diary covered the period during which Jane's father died and she inherited Ravenshead. The first noticeable thing was the marked change in writing style since the 1912 diary. Jane now commented on almost everything, even the minutiae of everyday life, and she seemed to have developed a somewhat intuitive approach to her observations. It meant that I had to read this journal more carefully – and between its lines.

A few pages further on from entries relating to her father's death, I struck gold. There it was, the first mention I had seen of *the Wilson lad*. Jane also recorded how scullery maid, Erin Wilson, seemed still to struggle to come to terms with the death of Jane's father, Henry Finchley, even some weeks after the event. Having recorded the entry's relevant details in my notebook, I pondered whether to attach any significance to the entry or not. That's what I was doing when Gabby announced it was time for afternoon coffee.

Torn between continuing to work on the diary or joining Gabby for coffee, good manners won, and I went for coffee. Besides, once coffee was out of the way, I could leave early with that 1917 diary in my bag to work on it in the solitude of my home office this evening.

Chapter 15

Damn… I love his company, but tonight, I would be happier if Detective Inspector Warren Tyson were unable to come for dinner. He was bringing takeaways, so I didn't have to waste time cooking something for us. And, leaving Ravenshead early this afternoon had given me at least a couple of hours without interruptions to continue working on the 1917 diary.

Reading every word and consideration of every entry makes for slow going, but I've learned it's essential with Jane's diaries, essential to avoid missing the subtle nuances. After no further mention of 'the Wilson lad' for several pages, the next one appeared. A flip through the next few pages indicated he appeared frequently in the subsequent entries.

My notebook was ready for the notes I hoped to extract from the next few pages of the diary when I heard Warren's car arrive. I bumped the mouse as I stood up, filling my computer screen with my email inbox. Bugger! The Archives had sent me an email. Its attachments will be copies of the various certificates I ordered. Now, I'll have to wait until Warren leaves before I can read them.

Warren brought a selection of dishes from our favourite Chinese takeaway place, and we sat down to eat almost as soon as he arrived. It wasn't until we retired to the lounge with our coffee and port that the usual 'shop talk' began. The way Warren looked told me the locals were keeping the police service busy, but following our customary practice, I asked how his day had been.

"It's not full moon, is it? I don't know what else to blame, but the local bad guys have been running amok for about a week now. With so many open cases to work on, I hardly know what day it is. Tell me something interesting. How was your day, or perhaps the last few days, perhaps? It's so long since we've had a conversation."

While not intending to go into details, I found myself sharing with Warren all the questions regarding Gabby's project that were consuming my thoughts. At last, I came to the matter of what happened to Darcy Wilson.

Without lifting his eyes from the spot on the carpet he had focused on, Warren asked, "So, why does it matter? Unless I missed something you told me, I don't see how that bloke Wilson has any relevance to your project."

"Yeah, I'm not sure either."

I rolled out my suspicions about Wilson's connection to Jane, Ravenshead, a suspicious death, and a disappearance. Finally, I outlined my curiosity regarding Wilson's apparent close relationship with Jane and how that had come about. Warren remained silent. I wasn't sure how to interpret his silence, so I mentioned the certificates I had ordered.

"Did they tell you anything helpful, or are you still back where you started?"

"Well, the certificates arrived this afternoon, but I haven't had a chance to look at them yet. I suspect they will tell me exactly what I expect, and that will be of absolutely no use at all."

Mentioning the certificates seemed to energise Warren. He insisted we look at the certificates now, so I printed copies for both of us. On opposite sides of my desk, we studied them in silence for a few minutes. Warren was first to break the silence.

"Looks like there is a story about young Darcy Wilson. His illegitimacy appears definite and confirms your assumption. Anything else about his birth certificate that catches your eye? Anything look wrong or out of place? Back then, on the pretext of saving the child embarrassment in later life, people told blatant lies to avoid the illegitimate stigma."

"In this case, that didn't happen. No attempt was made to hide the young lad's status." I went to set the printout aside when something caught my eye. "Hang on a minute … Now, that is interesting," I chirped.

Warren scanned his copy of the certificate before waiting in obvious anticipation for my next revelation.

Erin Wilson, the widowed mother, was a scullery maid employed at Ravenshead, but the child wasn't born there."

"There might have been any number of reasons for that. Perhaps she went home to her family to have the child. Although it appears she didn't have the baby in a hospital. Maybe a home birth was preferable in those days."

"No, I think neither of those suggestions suits this situation. While the name of the place where he was born doesn't sound like a hospital, it does sound like an institution of some sort, perhaps a home for unmarried mothers."

"Babies born in those places were usually taken from their mothers and adopted out to other willing parents. From what you have told me so far, it appears Erin Wilson kept her child and brought it up back here at Ravenshead," Warren said, and continued after a moment's thought. "Is there evidence Erin Wilson was a widow, or is it speculation on your part?"

I directed his attention to the other two certificates. "This one relates to Erin's marriage to Wilson. This other one records that Thomas Wilson died, leaving a widow but no offspring."

"Hmm… Nothing to argue about there. Erin Wilson was widowed when Thomas died. I don't suppose you found that she married again?"

"If she had, she would no longer be Wilson. She would have taken her new husband's surname."

"Right. So what's your next move?" Warren asked as he cocked an eyebrow at me. "I admit, I don't see how any of this helps with Gabby's family legend of the pirated manuscripts, but good luck anyway."

Although there was no need to explain the twists and turns of this type of research to Warren, he wasn't the only one who struggled to see its relevance to my brief. Nevertheless, I wasn't disappointed when he opted for an early night and left about half an hour later. Alone in my office after he left, I had no difficulty working out what to do next. I asked Google to tell me everything it could about the place where Darcy Wilson was born.

Few hits resulted and most provided the same brief information. The length of the last one surprised me. My assumption had been correct. Darcy was born in an institution-type facility that had been founded many decades ago. Originally intended for the wives of men fighting, or who had lost their lives in the Boer War, who left a pregnant wife at home. It cared for the women during their pregnancy and childbirth, and then saw them well recovered before sending them home.

Of course, even back then, other women also needed such care. They had no husbands and often were shunned by their families. So, the institution also served as a home for unmarried mothers, and arranged through a church for those unwanted children to be adopted out by other couples. Over the years, operations expanded to include more lucrative services.

For a fee, well-to-do parents could have the unwanted offspring of their unmarried children taken care of as well, whether they be the result of a wayward daughter or a son sowing his wild oats. In the latter case, as well as a hefty donation to the institute for its care and confidentiality in the matter, the unfortunate girl also was paid for her silence. Almost as a footnote to the article, there was a final comment about prominent 'gentlemen' whose philandering ways landed them in difficult and embarrassing situations. They also availed themselves of the institute's services to deal with their problem, *one way or another,* to simply make it go away.

"Interesting… very interesting…," I murmured to my empty office as I considered possible 'what-if 'scenarios that occurred to me.

An interesting comment in the article claimed my attention. It said illegitimate children born to offspring of affluent parents sometimes were not handed over to the church to find homes for them, and that sometimes also applied to philandering gentlemen's unwanted offspring. In such cases, the child might be given to a married childless employee, whether a housekeeper or a farmhand, to raise as their own, although without the benefit of formal adoption processes and paperwork. Did some such scenario involve Darcy Wilson?

The flaw in such thinking was that, in Darcy Wilson's case, Erin Wilson, although a faithful employee of Ravenshead, was a widow. Would she have been considered suitable to bring up a child alone? And whose child? There was only the one Finchley offspring, Jane, and I had seen nothing to suggest there was anything 'wayward' about her behaviour… and she was only 13 when Darcy was born. I thought that then left only one other scenario to consider.

Was this then a classic example of the lord of the manor having his way with his lowly scullery maid? Was Darcy the result of Henry Finchley's playing away with Erin behind his wife, Martha's, back? It was not an uncommon practice. Back then, wives, although not so dull as to be unaware, were expected to accept the situation and maintain a dignified demeanour. Regardless of whether Henry's wife was aware of it or not, it did seem odd for Erin to bring her child back to Ravenshead and for him to grow up there. Was there some other plausible scenario that I hadn't thought of? Neither my gut nor the little voice in my head appeared too happy with anything I had come up with so far.

After staring off into the distance for a while, no new ideas had emerged, but I remained unconvinced about the veracity of all I'd managed to come up with. My next challenge was to prove my hypothesis by finding evidence to support or refute it. Then I remembered the 1917 diary I brought home and the string of entries relating to Darcy Wilson I had discovered just as Warren arrived. With nothing more productive to do, I decided to tackle the rest of that diary.

"Who knows what I might uncover?" I joked as I dragged the diary to me.

Within a few minutes, I was perched on the edge of my chair, trying to control my excitement.

"Oh, yes, reading the Darcy Wilson entries in this diary was a good idea," I murmured as I flipped back a few pages in order to reread some of those entries.

It didn't take long to realise a strong relationship between Jane and Darcy already existed prior to Jane's father's death. Did she know he was her half-brother? After reading and rereading the early entries relating to Darcy, I had to accept that there was no evidence she was aware. I sensed that something changed around the time of Henry's death and Jane inherited Ravenshead. Even my best efforts to read between the lines of her cryptic entries didn't yield any clues as to why there might have been a change.

After rereading the first three entries from the period after Jane's inheritance of the property was finalised, something did catch my attention. Among all the other comments about the legal process, it included a mention of a letter along with the other documents involved. Why would there be a letter, and why would Jane bother to mention it? Had Henry left her some final comforting words in a letter? Perhaps it reminded Jane that, along with the property, she had inherited the responsibility for her mother's care and upkeep as well as the standard that was to be maintained.

The little voice in my head kept insisting the letter was crucial to my research. My curiosity agreed. It was a possibility, but there was a problem: Where to find that letter after all these years? Was it a codicil to Henry's will, or a personal letter to his daughter? The answer to that might be a clue to where the letter might be now. Then it hit me… Henry's will… Did it reveal any well-kept secrets? Was there a codicil? After navigating my way through the Archives' website to the appropriate index, I found the listing for the probate of Henry's Will, and promptly ordered a copy. While I expected the usual frustrating wait for a copy to arrive, I secretly hoped that, somehow, this time, the process would be miraculously fast.

My mind returned to the letter mentioned in one of the diary entries that triggered my interest in Henry's will. I had no doubt Jane would not have destroyed it, but what would she have done with it? To keep it safe, was it likely to be with her solicitor, in a bank safety deposit box, or somewhere in her Ravenshead home? While all three options were possible, the latter held the greatest appeal to me.

If my assumption were correct, the most likely place for Jane to keep it was somewhere in that hidden space. I liked to think I had become quite familiar with the contents of the shelves in that space, but I hadn't encountered anything likely to hold that letter. At that point, the little voice in my head reminded me that, if I found the repository for the letter, it was likely I would find a copy of Henry's will there as well. Now I knew what I would be doing at Ravenshead tomorrow: turning the contents of that hidden space upside down to find a letter, and maybe a will as well.

While I knew I could continue reading Jane's 1917 diary entries, I lacked enthusiasm. Besides, while preoccupied with thoughts of what might prove to be critical documents, time had slipped away. I wanted to be alert and clear-headed when I began my quest for the letter tomorrow morning. About half an hour later, I lay in bed trying to shut down all thoughts of letters and wills.

The gods were in my corner this morning. On my early arrival at Ravenshead, I struggled not to grin when Gabby told me a Zoom session would occupy her for much of the morning. Depending on the outcome, she might have to go away for a few days. It was great news. Now I could conduct my search alone and not have to explain what I was doing and why. Foregoing a coffee with her, I headed directly to the study and its hidden space.

'Begin without assumptions,' I instructed myself as I entered the hidden space. 'The only assumption allowed is that what I am searching for is hidden in here somewhere.' That was the easy part. The hard part was where to start. Would Jane secrete the documents I sought amongst her financial records, on the shelves with her writing files, or with her diaries?

With each bundle of financial records labelled only with the date range it covered, it was impossible to know its contents without unwrapping it. That promised a lot of work for only frustration in return if the documents were not located. At least each bundle on the diaries' shelves contained only a diary for the period indicated on its label. I already had pulled the diary for the period in question (and hence the reason for my search) and knew it contained no extraneous documents.

After such a flimsy process of elimination, I announced to the space as I dragged over the ladder, "I'll start with the manuscript bundles' shelves, and I'll start at the top."

My delight at the way the morning was shaping up became somewhat clouded at that point. On the off chance it had more to say about the letter, I realised it might have been beneficial to have read more of the 1917 diary last night. Now, I wish I were more diligent when cataloguing the material on the top shelf. Starting at the left-hand end of the topmost shelf, I had catalogued the bundles according to their unenticing but now intriguing labels. These labels included, amongst others: Miscellaneous Rubbish, Detritus, Bits & Pieces, and Dead Ends. Six bundles had such unhelpful labels. There was nothing else for it. They all had to be unwrapped and examined.

One by one, and in correct order, I removed all six bundles and placed them on the huge desk in the study. Then the monumental task of examining every piece of paper in every bundle began. *Miscellaneous Rubbish* appeared accurately labelled. It held a couple of folders containing various loose pieces of paper. All were attempts at poetry or prose. Nothing in that bundle was of any interest to me.

The bundle labelled *Detritus* was another matter. As I went to unwrap the bundle, I discovered a second line on the label, but it was very pale and hidden in a crease of the brown paper wrapping. The whole label read: *Detritus of a Life*. If that didn't have me almost jumping out of my skin, nothing else would do it for me today. And, of course, the immediate big question was, *whose life?* But there was something else about this bundle that made it different from any of the others I'd handled. I wasn't sure what I might find. With something approaching reverence, I peeled back the brown paper wrapping.

"That's not what I expected," I yelped in surprise.

From the moment I lifted it off the shelf, I knew it felt different. Unlike the other bundles that were softer and somewhat flexible, this *Detritus* bundle was hard and rigid, and far too thick for a hardcovered journal. As I removed the last of the wrapping, my jaw almost hit the table in surprise. No books in that bundle.

It contained only one item, a small wooden box about the size of an old cigar box, but thicker. Gingerly, I picked it up and examined it. A lacquer work image was inset in the centre of the lid. The rest of the box was unadorned except for a clear, colourless varnish-like finish. It had no feet attached and sat squarely on its base. My pulse was racing along with my mounting excitement. Then, I turned the box around to face me.

A small brass lock on the front of the box seemed to wink at me. In the hope that it wasn't locked, I tried lifting the lid. My luck had run out. It was securely locked, and the lock held fast against my fairly determined efforts to force the lid to open. I soon discovered, fingers and brute strength were no substitute for a key. Setting the box aside, I searched the wrapping material for a key. I found none, not even a hint that a key had ever been wrapped in with the box. Of course not. That would have made it too easy for someone to access the box's contents – when the object of the exercise appeared to be to prevent just that from happening.

Frustration is not a pleasant emotion, nor one I handle well. I did not want to use a tool to open the box. Appropriate behaviour in such situations forbade it. I flopped onto my chair, placed my elbows on the table, rested my chin in my hands, and sat staring at the box. I don't know how long I sat like that, but no miracles occurred during that time. That's how Gabby found me when she came to call me to lunch and admonish me for not having come to her earlier apartment for coffee.

"I didn't want to be rattling around in your kitchen while your Zoom session was in progress," I explained.

Her eyes alighted on the box I had just discovered, and she visually examined it for a few moments.

"What have you there? That's a gorgeous-looking little box. Did it come out of that wrapping? Was it in the hidden space?" I nodded in response to both questions. She came and stood beside me. "Why would Jane keep such a box in there? What's in it?"

"Those questions I planned to ask you. Anyway, you said lunch was ready, and I'm more than ready for a coffee to go with it. Perhaps we might discuss the box over lunch?"

Needless to say, we had barely sat down to eat before Gabby went into interrogation mode.

"Come on, Sophie, tell me about the box. Where was it? How did you come to find it? I want to know everything about how you discovered it and what you think it might contain."

"Well, I could say it was by sheer luck that I found it, but it wouldn't be quite true. A logical process led to its discovery, but that now seems somewhat vague even to me. As for what the box contains, I was hoping you might have some ideas about that."

"Me… Not a clue, I'm sorry, Sophie. I'm still trying to make sense of the fact that she saw fit to wrap that box like the rest of her manuscripts and store it in that hidden space. I can only assume that it must hold something important or perhaps embarrassing"

"…Or even details of a crime, I suppose. We could continue speculating about it forever, unless we manage to open the box. Gabby, this will sound absurd, but do you know of any small keys lying around anywhere in this house? Is there such a thing as a key locker somewhere, although I'm not sure the tiny key for that lock would be in a key locker."

"No-o, I shouldn't think so. Somehow, the box reminds me of a trinket box, or a woman's jewellery box, perhaps. In that case, its owner wouldn't have put the key in a key locker."

"Yeah, if that were its intended use, the woman would have kept the key in her possession. So, where might we find such a key now?"

Chapter 16

"How soon do you want an answer to that question?" Gabby asked. A serious expression occupied her face.

"What question are you talking about?"

"Your question about where we might find a small key for that box."

I shook my head to signify I didn't know what she meant. She laughed before pausing in thought for a moment. When Gabby spoke again, she was concerned and apologetic.

"This might take a while, Sophie. I know there is something about a key hiding in my memory banks. If only I could drag it out…."

"Don't try to force it. Go and do other things that take your mind off it. Maybe then it will come to you," I suggested and hoped I sounded genuine.

After leaving her to clean up after lunch, I rushed back to the study. Was it possible that Gabby might know something about the key? I doubted it, but she appeared quite certain she might know something. Now back in the study, what was I going to do? I was so excited after finding the box, I couldn't wait to return. Now I was back at the desk, I realised there was nothing more I could do with the box until we found a key. I was loathe to even contemplate busting it open. After loosely wrapping the box in its brown paper again, I set it aside and dragged the remaining two bundles to me.

Bits & Pieces and *Dead Ends* were not the most exciting labels. I thought it unlikely I would find anything of interest in either of those bundles. In the interests of thoroughness, I would subject their contents to the same degree of attention as I would any other file – or so I told myself before I began. Selecting *Bits & Pieces*, I carefully unwrapped it and extracted two hefty folders. For a moment, I wondered if perhaps I had misjudged the importance of that bundle.

A moment was about as long as it took to realise the contents were true to label. Both folders contained scraps of poetry, quatrains, and short pieces of prose, all of which appeared rejected by their author. There was no consistent theme or intended outcome for the writing. In frustration, I pushed the open bundle aside and dragged over the one labelled *Dead Ends*.

The label itself suggested there was unlikely to be anything of interest in it, and it was right. Its contents closely resembled those in the previous bundle. The exception in this case was that none of the works had been completed.

"Well, now what am I going to do for the remainder of the day?" I asked myself aloud.

Although I was tempted to believe the documents I searched for were in that locked box, in reality, there was nothing to support such thinking. Because of such uncertainty, there was nothing for it but to continue my search in the off chance that those documents might reside in some other obscure file. I returned to my catalogue of all the bundles on the manuscript shelves. All the bundles on these shelves (and there were plenty of them) had appeared faithfully labelled when I checked each one as I catalogued it.

If I were honest, I'd admit that such checking involved nothing more than ensuring the title of the manuscript in the bundle agreed with the label on the outside. What if other material had been secreted along with the manuscript in some of those bundles? A glance over my shoulder at the bundles on the shelves along the back wall of the hidden space made me groan. Conducting a thorough check on each of them would be a hell of a job, especially since I wasn't convinced that's where I would find the documents I wanted.

Any hope of finding a clue drained from me as I ran my eye over the catalogue for each shelf. It was the list of contents on the bottom shelf that triggered something. A little bell ringing softly in the back of my mind caught my attention.

"Oh, yes, now I remember," I whispered as an image flashed through my mind.

At the left-hand end of the bottom shelf, the first bundle was somewhat unusual. At first, I thought it might be empty, but I decided to unwrap it anyway. After all, it must contain something. Nobody would go to the trouble of wrapping a neat brown paper bundle around nothing. It didn't contain much, just a small folder labelled 'Notes'. When I opened the folder, its first item was a couple of lines of poetry scribbled on the back of a used envelope. I decided it contained rubbish and didn't explore it further.

Slumped back in my chair, I took a few moments to consider how to proceed. If I went ahead and explored that bundle of 'Notes', shouldn't I also more fully investigate every bundle on the manuscripts shelves? I was still pondering my dilemma when Gabby's voice cut through my thinking.

"Sophie, I remembered. Sophie, are you listening?"

"Eh? Yes, of course, I'm listening. Now, what's this all about?" I asked cautiously.

"I've remembered about the key. At least, I think it could be the key we need for that little box. You have to remember it was a long time ago, when I was only about four years old."

I nodded and asked her to tell me about the key. After all, listening to Gabby's story delayed having to work out what to do next. Gabby sat across the desk from me, folded her arms on the desk, and leaned onto them.

"As I said, it was a long time ago, but my memory is pretty clear now. It was when Mum and I returned to Ravenshead after we had received word that Jane was not well. The day after we arrived, Mum took me to meet Jane. That was the first time I'd met my grandmother. She was in one of the rooms downstairs. I think it was across the entrance hall from the study. She wasn't welcoming, not of me anyway. She glared at me the whole time we were with her. I had to sit there, completely silent, while Mum and Grandma talked about something that seemed to upset my mother.

It doesn't take a child long to become bored, but I found Jane fascinating in a strange sort of way, and I remember not being able to take my eyes off her. Maybe that's why she kept glaring at me… didn't like me staring at her."

"Fascinating story, I'm sure, Gabby, but what does it have to do with a key?"

"Oh, yeah, the key. Well, I discovered Jane wore a small key on a gold chain around her neck. It became the thing I focused on when I stared at her. My mother had never worn a necklace, and I had only ever seen one other person with a string of glass beads hanging around their neck. So, to that small child, the key around Jane's neck was entrancing."

"Okay, I suppose I can understand its attraction, but do you know what happened to it? Do you know what happened to the key? I hope you're not going to tell me she was still wearing it when they buried her."

"No… Well, no, I don't know, but I don't think so. I recall being taken to see Jane again a day or so later. As usual, I was expected to say and do nothing while I stood in the background during our visit. The thing I remember most about that visit was seeing a gold chain with the little key attached lying on a bedside table. In my mind, it was the same key I had seen previously hanging around her neck.

At that time, I believe Jane was still capable of getting around in short bursts, but was unable to climb the stairs. Then, some people arrived – probably the ambulance – and they helped move Jane to a bedroom upstairs. A while after that, when I think they were preparing to move her into care, I was taken upstairs to see her for one last time. It was a brief visit, probably no more than a couple of minutes, but long enough for me to notice that she wasn't wearing the chain with the key, and it wasn't anywhere else that I could see."

"So, what are you saying? Are you suggesting that the key had been put away somewhere safely, and that she probably was wearing it when she was buried?"

"That's exactly what I am suggesting. Of course, I could be wrong, way off track in fact. After all, the memories I'm recounting are those of a young child."

"Still, it does shed an interesting light on things, doesn't it? I suppose she might have insisted on it being buried with her, but somehow, I'm more inclined to think she secreted it somewhere here in the house, or had someone else do it for her. Do you think that might have been something she would have asked your mother to do for her?"

"Anything is possible, I suppose, but no, I don't think she would have entrusted something like that to my mother to do. Mother and daughter were not close. Now, in the light of old age, I believe that both women viewed their relationship as something not of their choosing, yet something that had to be endured. Given the lack of affection, and probably trust as well, between them, I doubt Jane would have entrusted such a 'secret mission' to my mother."

"Unfortunately, I'm inclined to agree … And that does not make our task any easier. We still have to find that key or wreck the box to access its contents…."

"…And may find it empty when we do open it," Gabby reminded me.

We sat in silence for a few moments, no doubt both of us considering our options regarding the box, until Gabby checked her watch.

"Argh, I have to go. I have a meeting in town late this afternoon. I'll probably spend the night in town. So, you will have the place to yourself in the morning. I should be back by lunchtime, if all goes well."

"You won't be missing much. I intend to start a systematic search for the key this afternoon, and I have no doubt it will remain ongoing tomorrow."

It was a relief when she rushed off and I was alone again in the study. "Now for deep and logical thinking about where to find a key," I murmured as I tidied the desk before slumping back in my chair to ponder the almost imponderable task ahead of me.

After a few moments of staring off into the distance, I felt my eyes drawn to my catalogue of the various shelves in the hidden space. Had I catalogued any other strange bundles anywhere in there? I chose to focus on the shelves holding the manuscript bundles and started working my way through those catalogue entries. There were numerous bundles on numerous shelves, resulting in a large number of entries to consider. The exercise seemed to progress at a snail's pace, but at last, I had reached the list of entries for items on the bottom shelf.

While nothing jumped out at me from those entries, the little voice in my head kept urging me to look at them again. Well, what else did I have to do? I had no other idea where to start looking for a tiny key in this huge house. So, I returned to the start of the list for the bottom shelf. Again, nothing immediately jumped out at me… Then, something drew me back to the first entry for that shelf.

The entry for the first item at the left-hand end of the shelf was another 'strange bundle'. There was no label on the outside of the package. I had listed it in the catalogue as 'Miscellaneous'. Perhaps it would be worth my while to find out more precisely what was in it. Before retrieving anything else from the shelves, I again wrapped the bundles I had looked at earlier and stacked them tidily out of the way on a corner of the desk. Then I went to fetch the 'Miscellaneous' package.

Again, this was a thin bundle containing only one folder. A faded label on the folder, which I hadn't noticed before, read 'Lost & Found.' Should I take that as a clue? I doubted Jane had such generous and accommodating intentions. A flip through the first few pages in the folder suggested it had been the start of a story that hit a wall quite early in its development. After the first three pages of the abandoned story, the contents of the folder became a jumbled mess of scraps of paper and used envelopes that appeared to have been used to jot down ideas for the story. Amid that rubbish was a small pocket-sized notebook.

A list of names chosen for (presumably) the characters in the abandoned story filled the first page of the notebook. The next page appeared to be a rough timeline of events to occur in the story. Rather than look through the notebook page by page, I opted to riffle through it… Except it would not be 'riffled'. The notebook was too stiff for me to bend it enough for the pages to flip past. That wasn't right. Such notebooks usually were of flimsy construction, but something was making this one quite rigid. It didn't take long to find out why.

"Bloody hell!" I yelped as I sat staring at the notebook lying open on the palm of my hand. "That looks about the right size. As if I could be so lucky…." I reminded myself.

For a few moments, I was unable to do more than just stare at my find. After the first several pages, a small recess had been carved out of the remaining pages to leave only the last half a dozen pages intact. While holding the notebook open, I carefully flipped it over. Its hidden treasure tumbled into the palm of my hand. Again, I was shocked into an apparent inability to move, and I sat there staring at my hand for some moments before my brain resumed normal function.

Of course, it had to be the missing key for the lock in the little wooden box. What else would the key belong to? And, why else would anyone go to such trouble to hide the key? The small brass key sat in the palm of my hand and almost winked at me. It seemed Jane had intended whatever was in that box should remain a secret. With something akin to reverence, I picked up the key and examined it. There was no chain hidden with the key. No jump ring was attached to it, but the hole where a jump ring might have been attached to hang the key from a chain showed signs of wear. This had to be the key we needed.

"So, why are you still sitting here admiring it?" I demanded of myself. "Fetch the box and let's see if this key fits its lock." That had me up off my chair and sprinting into the hidden space.

My hands trembled with excitement as I placed the small wooden box on the desk in front of me. A couple of deep breaths, and I picked up the key and tried to insert it into the lock. My hands were trembling so much, it didn't go in. For a moment, I wondered whether my excitement was in vain… That this wasn't the correct key for the box. After another couple of deep breaths, I tried again to insert the key. This time, it went in. That's when it occurred to me. The lock had remained hidden and unmolested for many decades. The crud of ages might have accumulated in its workings over that time. The last thing I needed to do now was to break the key off in the lock.

Gently, ever so gently, I wriggled the key in the lock. That told me nothing. So, just as gently, and as I held my breath, I tried turning the key… And immediately encountered resistance.

"No, no, no… Don't do this to me now. Come on, you can do it. Just try to release a little," I hissed at the box as I psyched myself up for another attempt at turning the key.

"Yes…!" I yelped, but I was a bit premature.

I had felt the key turn ever so slightly – and then stop as the lock refused further cooperation. I knew I needed to spray the internal workings of the lock to help ease it open. For a few moments, weighed down by the agony of disappointment, I sat glaring at the lock. Then, clear thinking resumed.

"Okay, it needs a good spray of lubricant to loosen it. So why am I still sitting here when I have a can of just what I need in my car?" I sprang up and dashed out to the car.

After a frenzied scrabble around in the toolbox I carry in my car, I was galloping back to the study, brandishing the can of spray in the air like some triumphant trophy. While patience might not be my strong suit, in this case, there was no alternative but to find some. After inserting the little plastic tube into the lock and hosing its internals with the lubricant spray, it was necessary to leave it for a while to allow the lubricant to penetrate.

"Coffee… Go and have a coffee while you wait," I told myself, and headed for Gabby's apartment.

A coffee alone doesn't take nearly as long as coffee with someone else to talk to, so the lubricant I sprayed into the lock hadn't had much time to do its work when I returned. Regardless, I had to give it another try. This time, the key turned a little further. After wriggling the key in the lock a few times and then turning backward and forward as far as it would go freely several times, I decided to try using a little more force. I took a couple of deep breaths to steady myself, then held my breath as I made a more determined attempt. After turning the key as far as it would go, I applied a bit more pressure.

Victory was mine. There was an initial hesitation before the key finally turned all the way. I heard the lock release… At least, that's what I thought I heard. What if it wasn't the lock letting go, but something more disastrous that I had heard? I remained with the key still firmly gripped between my thumb and forefinger. Gingerly, I tried turning the key again. This time, it went all the way around to the unlock position without any resistance. Leaving the key still in the lock, I sat back to review the situation for a moment.

"Okay, so I've unlocked it. Now what happens?" I asked the universe before heeding the little voice in my head that demanded I stop messing around and open the thing. So, with a fairly unsteady hand, I slowly lifted the lid.

The musty smell of old paper and mould assaulted my nostrils. Suddenly, I felt guilty. Gabby should be here for this moment. After accepting that some things just can't be helped, I grabbed my phone and took several shots of the open box before I disturbed any of its contents. My level of self-control amazed me, but I knew I had to accurately record everything that happened.

While inclined to dive into the box and start pulling out its contents, I also experienced a hesitancy, much as one might feel before handling a sacred icon. However, the sight of the uppermost item in the box helped banish that hesitancy. As soon as the images of the opened box had been recorded, I reached for the first item.

It was a large document, folded in half and tied with pink legal tape. To me, it screamed 'legal document'. I gently flipped it over to read the front of it, and caught my breath. There it was: The Last Will and Testament of Henry Finchley. For a moment, it beggared belief that I had found it after such a short time spent searching for it. Again, my self-control was amazing. Instead of untying the tape and flattening it out to read it, I placed the will aside and focused my attention on the rest of the box's contents.

After flipping through the next few items and discovering they were envelopes with no visible indication on any of them as to who they were meant for, or what they were about, I dropped them back into the box. There is only so much self-control available in such situations. I pushed the box away from me and dragged the will to me. It was time to see what Henry Finchley's intentions had been.

There was nothing new or particularly exciting to be gained from the will. As I already knew, he left everything to his only child, his daughter, Jane, on the proviso that, if her mother was still alive after her father's death, Jane should establish some form of allowance or annuity to support her mother for the rest of her mother's life. No other beneficiaries were mentioned, and no grants or donations to any organisations. I felt let down. The whole exercise had been a major anti-climax after the excitement and expectations felt on opening the box. The only thing that I learned from Henry's will that I hadn't known before was that Henry had instructed Jane to decide whether her mother should continue to reside at Ravenshead, or if Jane wanted to turf her out to find somewhere else to live.

For a few moments, I pondered how Jane might have reacted to that, and how she had reached the decision to allow her mother to continue living at Ravenshead. Regardless of what influenced the decision-making process, according to Gabby, family legend suggests it didn't result in happy days for either of the women.

At that point, my phone demanded my attention. Warren wouldn't be joining me this evening. Somehow, that wasn't disappointing. Tonight, I wanted to be alone to reflect on what I had learned from the contents of the box.

Chapter 17

"What did I have to reflect on?" I murmured as I sat slumped in my chair.

Apart from the fact that Henry's will confirmed what I'd already been told, I had nothing new, except that it was Jane's decision where her mother resided after Henry died. However, I still had the rest of the box's contents to examine. Whatever it contained must be of some importance, or Jane wouldn't have gone to the bother of stashing it in the box and secreting it in the hidden space.

The temptation was to put the will back in the box and put the box in my tote bag to take home with me. I felt uneasy about doing that. Somehow, it didn't seem the right thing to do. On the other hand, if I started going through the other contents, I could find something interesting, and wouldn't be able to tear myself away to go home. Temptation won the battle. I gave in, put the will back in the box, and shoved the box into my bag. A couple of minutes later, I was on my way home.

Exploration of the box's contents resumed almost the moment I arrived home. After clearing everything off the surface of my desk, I placed the box there and once again removed Henry's will. Then, a couple of deep breaths to steady my emotions before removing the next item from the box.

It was an envelope devoid of any identification or inscription, except for the name 'Jane Finchley' scrawled in a firm hand across the front of it. In the decades since it was last opened, the glue had reattached the flap. I gently inserted a letter opener under one corner of the flap and was relieved to find it came away cleanly and easily. As I slid about a centimetre of its contents out of the envelope, there appeared to be only a single sheet of paper.

After sliding it out onto the desk and gently unfolding and flattening it out, I discovered it was a brief handwritten note on a single sheet of expensive-looking writing paper. The signature at the foot of the note made me catch my breath, and my pulse stepped up a notch. Was this Henry's parting words to his daughter?

A brief note, covering about two-thirds of the page in clear, well-spaced handwriting, did not waste words in conveying its message. In a serious, no-nonsense tone, it was nothing more than a stern instruction to his daughter:

Erin Wilson, currently a domestic staff member employed at Ravenshead Estate, must remain at Ravenshead and be afforded every support she requires for the rest of her life, or until such time as she remarries, or chooses to relocate from Ravenshead Estate. Her child must be provided with every opportunity to gain a sound education. She has been granted life tenancy free of charge in the cottage in which she currently resides, and this situation must remain in place.

The foot of the note was signed simply 'Henry Finchley'. Nothing surprising about the signature, but the date underneath it was. I checked my notes.

"Yes…!" I yelped, "There it is. That says it all."

Well, it told me all I needed to know, although it might not have provided sufficient evidence for anyone else. Contrary to what I had expected, while this might have been Henry Finchley's last words to his daughter, they were penned a long time before his death. The date on the note suggested it had been written not long after Erin Wilson had given birth to her illegitimate son, Darcy Wilson. Why would Henry Finchley be so concerned about the future welfare of his scullery maid and her bastard son, unless he was directly involved…? *Unless he was the child's father.*

Jane and the young Darcy appear to have developed a friendship long before Henry's death, so the note he left her had the potential to either make or break that friendship. It seems Jane rose to the occasion. If anything, the note only served to strengthen their relationship. For no apparent reason, I suddenly found myself wondering what became of Erin Wilson. Did she remarry at some point? When she became too old to work, did she spend the rest of her days at Ravenshead?

"Stop! Stop… What does it matter what happened to her?" I admonished myself. "Focus on the issue you're supposed to be investigating." Of course, that led back to that earlier question: what happened to Darcy Wilson?

I managed to convince myself that Darcy Wilson's life after his days at Kennedy's General Store was an important part of Jane's story. While it had nothing to do with her pirated manuscripts, perhaps, in some still unclear way, it was important. The only way to know for sure was to find out what happened to Darcy Wilson … And maybe his mother as well.

'Back to the box,' I told myself as I set aside Henry's note to his daughter. A stray thought slammed in from nowhere. I found myself wondering if Henry had left other notes to be distributed following his death. Had he left similar 'last words' for Darcy Wilson? If Darcy were his son, might he want to acknowledge the lad? And what about Erin Wilson? Did he have any 'last words' for her?

"For God's sake, just concentrate on what's in the box," I snarled.

Had I heeded such advice at least half an hour earlier, I would have saved myself a great deal of effort in developing 'what if' scenarios. The box proved something of a minuscule Aladdin's Cave. Every document or envelope I examined proved to be another gem, a gem that answered at least some of the questions I had asked myself at some point during this project.

Probably of greatest interest were a couple of documents (contracts, really, I suppose) relating to Jane's relationship with Kennedy's General Store, or more precisely, with Darcy Wilson. While not referencing those substantial sums of money paid to Wilson, they referred to the other, smaller amounts that I already knew he had received. They spoke volumes about the depth of the relationship between Jane and Darcy Wilson.

It occurred to me that nowhere, except in Henry's note to his daughter, had Erin Wilson's name appeared. Was that significant? I managed to tell myself it wasn't, and returned my attention to the two documents lying on the desk in front of me. They laid out the conditions attached to 'loans' to Wilson. Only one of them, the first of the small payments, referred specifically to acquiring shares in Kennedy's Store in return for the cash dividends. Neither of the documents made any mention of repayment of the 'loans'.

After rereading the two documents several times, I sat back to consider their contents. It wasn't so much that I had learned anything new; it was a case of previous speculations confirmed. The small sum of money Jane paid Wilson after she had paid him the first substantial amount was to help him purchase a half share in Kennedy's Store. That next small 'loan' (as they were always described) was to result in Jane's owning a few shares in Wilson's half of the business. Those small cash payments she received after that 'loan' were the 'dividends' paid by Wilson from his proceeds from the business. It had me feeling quite chuffed about my intuitive skills. I guessed that those small cash receipts might be from some similar arrangement.

"Right… now what about this second 'loan' document?" I murmured as I laid aside the first document.

The second document related to the small sum of money Jane paid Wilson shortly after paying him the second substantial sum of money. Again, my guesswork had been right. Wilson needed that small amount of money to have sufficient funds to purchase the remaining half of the business when Kennedy wanted to retire. The document was far less informative, and therefore far less helpful, than the information provided about the other 'loan'. It made no mention of repayment. So, it probably wasn't a loan in the strictest sense of the word. It also didn't refer to shares or dividends. So, was this a loan, or was it some form of payment for other consideration received from Wilson?

With nothing further to be gained about that payment, I grudgingly looked at what else the box had to offer… And promptly recovered my sense of excitement when I opened the next envelope. It was a copy of a legal-looking document, but it wasn't a will. At first glance, I could see it had something to do with a coroner's inquest.

"Not another one," I murmured, "Or is it the same one again?"

I was inclined to believe it was something further to do with the inquest into George Creighton's death, although it was strange to find it here and not with the other documents from his inquest. Once it was unfolded and flattened out on my desk, I could see that it comprised only two pages. Further investigation revealed it was only the coroner's verdict on the investigation into the death of Thomas William Wilson.

"Oh, God, there had been another one," I yelped, and took a moment to calm myself before reading the coroner's verdict.

Yes, it was another death that happened on Ravenshead. Wilson was working away from home on the property at the time and was found dead when he failed to return home as expected. With no other information attached, it was impossible to know how long the hearing had taken or what had been said at it, but the coroner took two pages to deliver his open verdict. I caught my breath. If what I think I know about George Creighton's death is correct, was his death and the subsequent inquest a case of history repeating itself? Without other documentation, it was impossible to know what was said and by whom at the inquest hearing into Wilson's death. That both of those inquests resulted in accidental death outcomes almost beggared belief. I sat back to think on it for a while.

If, as I suspected, Jane had arranged her husband's death via the services of Darcy Wilson, was she merely replicating something that had happened a generation previously on Ravenshead? It was hard to believe anything else. By the time she was ready to get rid of her husband, was Jane aware of the details surrounding Wilson's death? She would have been a child at the time Wilson died. In the subsequent decades, did

Jane discover the truth about Wilson and come to see how a similar application might be useful in her own situation?

"Christ, how do I tell Gabby about this?" I asked the universe, but received no useful response.

One thing was clear. All I had was speculation on my part. Before mentioning anything about this to Gabby, I need proof. There was only one thing for it. The contents of the box would have to wait. I needed to search the Archives' index for coroners' inquests. About 20 minutes later, I had requested a quote for a copy of the coroner's inquest hearing into the death of Thomas William Wilson. Again, I would have to curb my impatience until I received a quote, and then the copy to arrive. Regardless of what I discovered, the conversation I would have with Gabby would not be an easy one.

"Right, what's next? Come on. What other surprises do you hold for me?" I demanded of the box.

A quick flip through its contents was surprising enough. It held considerably more than I expected and much more than I imagined such a small box could hold. There were several plain envelopes, none labelled, and they all had resided in the box for some time. Towards the bottom of the box were newspaper cuttings yellowed with age. Jane hadn't noted the date on any of them, and nothing was written on them. They were quite delicate, possibly due to a combination of age and the effects of the wood of the box. Despite my careful and reverent handling, a couple of the clippings almost disintegrated at my first touch.

For the next half hour, I was so anxious, I don't think I even breathed. But at last, when I finally sucked in a lungful of air again, all of the clippings had been removed from the box and each one placed in a separate protective plastic sleeve.

As they were on the desk in front of me, it seemed logical to look at them next, now that it was safe to do so. All the clippings were taken from copies of the then local newspaper. The size of their headlines suggested a couple of them had been front page news. My excitement level soared when I saw that one of them related to Thomas William Wilson's *apparent mysterious death,* as quoted in the article.

It didn't tell me more than I already knew from the coroner's verdict on Wilson's death, but it provided some interesting background information. It confirmed that Wilson had been employed at Ravenshead for decades. A long-time single man, he had recently married the much younger Erin Wilson, who also was employed at Ravenshead. He was survived only by his wife, there being no surviving children or other close family.

The article almost mirrored the details of George Creighton's death, right down to the fact that both men were much older than their wives. For a moment, I wondered whether that was an important detail, then dismissed it. Most of the men employed on properties such as Ravenshead tended to be single and stayed that way for many years, probably due to a shortage of easily accessible, suitable brides. Perhaps the transcript of the coroner's inquest hearing will tell me more about whether Wilson's marriage was significant to my project or not.

I set that clipping aside and turned my attention to the next one. This one's headline also suggested it had been front page news. Supposedly about the retirement of 'old man Kennedy' of General Store fame, only its first paragraph dealt with that man, his long association with the town, and his retirement on the sale of his remaining share of the General Store. The remainder of the lengthy article focused on the store's new owner, Darcy Wilson... And that part was interesting.

It provided me, via what amounted to an abridged history of the man's life, with a little more insight into the relationship between Darcy Wilson and Jane. According to the article, Darcy's early life had not been easy, due in part to the stigma of illegitimacy, and despite receiving a sound education courtesy of the Finchley family. It hinted that the lad had 'gone off the rails' for a brief period before the new owner of Ravenshead took him in hand and helped turn his life around.

In my mind, the new owner referred to was Jane. If that were the case, the period referred to would have to be after Jane inherited the place and during Wilson's early teenage years. Although lacking definite information, the article did suggest (at least, it did to me) that getting Wilson's life back on track somehow involved his employment at the General Store. In closing, the article waxed lyrical about how diligently Wilson had saved and worked his way up through the business to finally become the owner.

"Interesting…," I muttered as I sat staring at the old newspaper clipping. "But is it relevant?"

After turning it over in my mind for a few moments, I decided it might be, but it would depend on whether Jane had any part in the lad turning his life around. Her diaries from that time might shed some light on what was happening, and perhaps, if young Darcy was getting into trouble, the local paper might have commented on his activities. If the latter were the case, Jane obviously didn't see fit to keep any such newspaper clippings, at least not in the box with the others.

"Well, the diaries are a job for another day. So, what other gems does the box have to offer?" I set aside that clipping and dragged the last of the three sleeves to me. I let out a low whistle. "Ah hah… Jane did think a clipping about the disappearance of Miss Daphne Mary McDonald was worth ferreting away in her secret hidey hole."

The article didn't tell me anything new. It simply reported that the police were concerned about the apparent disappearance of a Miss Daphne Mary McDonald, who had recently been employed in the area for some weeks. A neighbour reported the disappearance to the police after Miss McDonald hadn't been seen about her cottage for a couple of days. Then, when Miss McDonald hadn't come to tea as arranged, the neighbour contacted the police. Later, using the spare key McDonald had given the neighbour, when the police checked the cottage, they found all McDonald's belongings were still there. The police requested that anyone with information regarding McDonald's current whereabouts come forward.

"Now that is disappointing," I muttered. Some follow-up clippings would have been nice, but there was nothing more.

Okay… Again, it appears that the 'key player' was missing for 'a couple of days' before anyone thought to become concerned about her absence. It would be unusual for the newspaper not to follow up on the article, even if the police had no further comment. My mind immediately turned to Jane and her former employee. Had Jane become embroiled in the police investigation into the disappearance of Miss McDonald? Was there a police investigation? For that matter, was Jane aware of the connection between Lois Parker and Daphne McDonald? It stands to reason that, having been made aware of the possible disappearance of the woman, the police would have been obliged to investigate … Unless something happened to eliminate the need. Surely, there would have been some further comment in the newspaper about the woman's disappearance.

It was all I could do to prevent myself from abandoning the box's contents in favour of searching the archives of the then local newspaper. Somehow, I managed to stop myself and contented myself with making notes about tomorrow's research targets: Jane's diaries and the newspaper archive. Actually, quite a bit of research involving Jane's diaries is needed prior to gathering more information about the various things I've discovered tonight. To begin with, if Jane were aware that Parker and McDonald were the same person, as I now believe them to be, did she refer to that discovery in her diaries?

For the first time in a couple of days, I found myself wishing Warren were here tonight. If the police had become involved in Miss Parker's disappearance, perhaps there is more information in their ancient files. Argh, it was just another possibility that would have to be explored another day – like when I next see Warren.

My stomach growled. Although it wasn't late, perhaps it wouldn't hurt to take a break before tackling the rest of the box's contents. It doesn't take long to slap some cold chicken and a leaf of lettuce on a bread roll and make yet another cup of coffee to add to today's total. I carried it all out onto the back deck, where I intended to indulge in food and creative thinking for a while. *A while* didn't last long enough for me to finish eating the roll before I picked up what was left of it and the coffee and carted it back to my office. I had barely settled in behind my desk when my phone played its tune: Warren.

"Oh, God, please don't let him want to come to dinner at this time of the night," I murmured, hoping the intended recipient would hear my plea.

No, he wasn't interested in dinner, he assured me when I asked. I felt a surge of relief flood through me.

"I was passing your house on my way back to the precinct and saw the light was on in your office. Are you too busy for a nightcap or a coffee?"

"Either one or both of those would be welcome, as would you be, if you felt inclined to turn around and come back here."

About five minutes later, Detective Inspector Warren Tyson, while sitting draped over my kitchen bench, watched me make coffee, pour a couple of glasses of port, and arrange a platter of cheese and crackers before we took our feast through to the lounge. Although I wasn't investigating the box's contents, I told myself that sitting with Warren wasn't wasting time. Now, I could tell him about Miss McDonald's disappearance and try to persuade him to check the police archives for a file on the matter.

Warren wasn't in any hurry to leave, and was more than a little interested in what little I knew about the disappearance of Daphne McDonald – or should that possibly be Miss Lois Parker? It was while I considered how to explain the situation I needed to unravel, another thought slammed in from nowhere. Might Daphne Mary McDonald also have been known as Mrs Tremaine?

It took some time and a couple of roughly drawn possible family trees before Warren grasped the intricacy of the problem

I wanted him to help sort out. Once he understood the problem, he was off and running with it, and came up with a couple more even more far-fetched possible scenarios to consider.

When he left, I was totally confused and mentally exhausted. I was fit for nothing more than a shower and bed, although I doubted sleep would soon arrive.

Chapter 18

A poor night's sleep had me conflicted this morning. My body wanted to go back to bed for a few hours, while my mind was eager to attack Jane's diaries to pursue the research ideas that came to me last night. So, although dragging myself through my normal morning routine felt like swimming through treacle, I managed my usual early morning departure for Ravenshead.

Thankfully, and as expected, Gabby did not rush out to me. It would be too easy to linger over coffee and conversation instead of getting on with the job. The moment I pulled up, I grabbed my bag and headed for the study. The process of transferring items from my bag to the desk and opening the hidden space took the usual few minutes, but still, there was no sign of Gabby.

"Okay," I said as I opened the list of notes I made last night. "Where to start? What is likely to provide the most useful information?"

I found my eyes constantly drawn to notes I made regarding the clipping about the disappearance of Daphne Mary McDonald. As it seemed as good a place as any to start, I went in search of the appropriate diary for more information. Although the clipping was undated, it mentioned a delay of a couple of days before the police were notified of her possible disappearance, and it might have been a couple of days later before the newspaper learned of the situation. So, my starting point in the diaries probably should be immediately following Miss Parker's termination.

While I knew that line of thinking depended on Parker and McDonald being the same person, with no better alternatives, I stuck with the assumption and went in search of the appropriate diary. Having previously reviewed relevant comments in Jane's diaries, I was able to select the ones I needed and make a start quickly.

Shortly after discovering the entry about the book stall at the garden party, I found where Jane terminated Miss Parker's employment as her typist. Skimming subsequent entries, I worked through the diaries until I reached the entry that suggested 'the deed had been done right this time'. Nothing… I read all the same entries carefully again. Still nothing. There had to be something, I told myself. After all, why would Jane keep that clipping about McDonald's disappearance if she hadn't discovered the connection? Now convinced I hadn't missed any important clues, I moved to entries after the one about the deed having been done right this time.

Initially, after reading entries that went way beyond the possible dates for the newspaper clipping, rather than continuing further, I decided to reread those pages – carefully.

"Yes, there it is," I yelped, and then added, "Maybe…" As with all of Jane's entries, it was cryptic and somewhat difficult to decipher.

The entry that held my interest referred to a meeting between Jane and her solicitor. She recorded the meeting as 'satisfying' and that they had 'devised a plan'. Although it told me nothing, the entry sparked my interest. It appeared around the right date for it to have followed the article in the newspaper.

"So tantalisingly close, but no prize," I murmured. "I don't like my chances of discovering details of 'the plan'."

Since it was the only clue I had, I opted to read on in the hope that something else might emerge. And it did…. About a fortnight later, another entry caught my eye. Almost buried in a rambling entry about something else, I discovered one brief comment that set my pulse racing: *Parker/McDonald confirmation.*

"Jesus, would it have hurt you to be just a little more enlightening?" I growled.

How was that confirmation achieved, and exactly what was confirmed? Of course, I wanted it to be that Jane then knew that Parker and McDonald were the same person, but was that really the case? I reminded myself that just because I wanted something doesn't mean it actually happened. If my assumption were correct, how would Jane achieve such confirmation? Would her solicitor tell her face-to-face at a meeting, or would he send her a letter? A phone call, maybe…? Did Jane have a phone back then?

I was good at coming up with questions, but absolutely rubbish at finding answers. Lacking any better idea on how to progress, I continued reading diary entries. After more than another month's worth of entries, I accepted that nothing more was to be gained from the diary and laid it aside. Slowly, another disappointing realisation sank in. Perhaps, having gained the information she sought, Jane felt no need to comment further on the matter … And I now had to turn to some of the other questions I came up with last night.

What about Darcy Wilson's youthful misbehaviour as alluded to in that other newspaper clipping? Was Jane sufficiently concerned about it to have noted it in her diary? I believed she would have been. Their close relationship appears well developed by then. So, when might that have been? The phrase 'teenage years' suggests the time period 1925 to 1931.

"Ooh…Now, that is interesting," I murmured as I looked at the time period I scribbled in my notebook.

Jane married George Creighton in 1925. Was there a correlation between that event and Darcy going off the rails? Was Jane's marriage the trigger that sent the young lad into a downward spiral? It seemed probable that, for Darcy to turn his life around so effectively, he needed solid, ongoing support. Support from someone like Jane. Is she likely to have recorded anything about this episode in her diaries? The six-year period in question involves numerous diaries. It would be handy to know which one to read first.

Adhering to the principle of 'start at the beginning', I retrieved Jane's diary that covered the start of 1925. The question I faced was whether to read it here in the study or to select an extra couple as well and take them all home to read. The latter option won out, and I returned to the hidden space to fetch the next two of Jane's diaries. Would that be enough to keep me busy for the rest of the day and into this evening? As I packed my bag to go home, I added one more diary to the pile. Just in case….

I was about halfway home when I passed Gabby heading back to Ravenshead after spending the night in town. We exchanged a wave as we passed, but neither of us showed any interest in stopping for a chat. That was a good thing. It meant that once I was at home and had made a coffee, I could get stuck into the diaries without fear of interruption. While the coffee machine did its thing, I placed the 1925 diary on my desk, ready to begin my research.

By lunchtime, I had read about half of that first diary and found nothing useful. While I munched on a sandwich, I pondered my morning's results. I found no mention of Darcy or of any misbehaviour on his part. Thinking about it, I realised there had been comments that suggested things were not quite normal. When I went back and reviewed those comments, I developed the distinct impression that Jane's life was a bit stressful at that time. It might have been when Darcy first started playing up, but I found nothing to support that supposition.

The most notable thing I had gained by the time I finished reading the 1925 entries was that Jane was extremely unhappy and stressed, but I was no wiser about the cause. As with everything in Jane's diaries, nothing was ever straightforward. Her entries were cryptic, some more difficult to decipher than others, and occasionally, a secondary matter was introduced midway through an entry.

It was a great manoeuvre if she intended to prevent everybody from understanding her entries while also obscuring her thoughts. I wondered why she had adopted such an approach and whether it stemmed from when her father forbade her to write. If he read her diaries, it allowed her to make adverse comments about her father without him realising it.

Darcy Wilson had not been mentioned in any diary entry for that year. That seemed strange. If she were so close to him and something was askew in his life, I expected at least some reference to it. There was none. Was that because the rot had not yet set in, and his name wouldn't start making appearances in her diaries until the following year at the earliest? I looked at the two remaining unread diaries on my desk and thought I should have brought more home with me, but there was nothing for it but to move on to the journal for the next year..

"That's more like it," I murmured as I reread an entry from early 1926. Jane recorded having had an 'earnest' conversation with the lad. There was no indication of the topics or why.

Over the ensuing months, it appeared Jane had a number of such conversations with 'the lad' without Darcy Wilson's name appearing in any such entries. Had I not been seeking specific information about a supposedly known problem, I might have overlooked those comments relating to an unnamed lad. Without any other information, it could be inferred that those conversations were with one of the workmen on the property, or possibly a gardener. Either of those might have been a genuine possibility. Despite no other information, I was convinced they related to Darcy.

Overall, her diary for 1926 painted a picture of a troubling year for Jane. One particular entry in the closing stages of the year piqued my curiosity. Again, although frustratingly obtuse, Jane recorded having had a conversation regarding a possible position in the New Year that she hoped might rectify the problem. She also added the comment that *it had not been an easy sell*. Although I tried to convince myself it could have referred to any number of things relating to running the property, the tiny voice in my head kept telling me it was about Darcy Wilson. If my thinking was correct, Darcy Wilson's behaviour had caused concern for much of 1926, and possibly from some time in the previous year.

Was the 'possible position' Jane mentioned about a deal she struck with Kennedy's General Store for the employment of Darcy Wilson? If my interpretation were correct, it would suggest Jane held some bargaining power over the store's owner. It was an interesting extension of my thinking, but not impossible to accept. If young Wilson had gone off the rails in a big way, surely it would take considerable bargaining power to persuade Mr Kennedy to employ the lad. It gave me food for thought, so I made a coffee to help me ponder it.

As I leaned against the kitchen bench, waiting for the coffee machine to do its thing, a flash of inspiration arrived. What sort of 'gone off the rails' type activities had young Wilson been involved in? If they had been significant misdemeanours, some reference to them probably appeared in the local newspaper. Jane's diaries had given me some indication of a date range for such activities, so it shouldn't be too difficult to locate mentions in archival copies of the paper.

With the diaries pushed to one corner of the desk, I turned to Google for its wisdom. After careful consideration, I decided upon fairly specific search criteria: the newspaper name, the date range, and Darcy Wilson's name. While Google went off to search for the information I wanted, I opened my notebook to a new page and headed it 'Darcy Wilson'.

Google churned away for an extraordinarily long time before presenting me with a list of hits. It wasn't a comprehensive list, but six were more than I expected. With some degree of hesitancy and trepidation, I clicked on the first (the earliest) hit that met my criteria… And there it was, Darcy Wilson had fallen foul of the local police for a relatively minor misdemeanour. Encouraged by this, I moved on to the other hits with enthusiasm.

While he hadn't joined some major criminal mob of the day, he apparently had thrown his lot in with a gang of young ruffians who seemed to progress from just making a nuisance of themselves around town to petty larceny. Their last efforts, which Google found mention of, resulted in the ringleaders of the gang being incarcerated for a few months. Wilson escaped with a 12-month good behaviour order imposed. As part of that, he was to return to Ravenshead and remain there, except for attending his place of employment.

At first glance, it seemed a big ask of a fourteen year old. Then I reminded myself that things were different back then. Except in upper-crust families, in those days, most lads of Darcy's age would have swapped education for earning a living – and maybe helping support the rest of their family. It's doubtful Darcy was in the latter category, given his mother's continued employment at Ravenshead and their grace-and-favour cottage on the property. I checked the dates of the newspaper articles Google had found.

Darcy's court appearance was some time after the gang first rated a mention in the paper. If Jane were responsible for arranging meaningful employment for the lad, she had a little time in which to achieve it before his hearing, but not much. Still, her comment in her diary about it being a 'hard sell' might well have been an understatement. I can't imagine anyone in the community being too keen to take on an apparent tearaway lad awaiting a court appearance. To secure his employment at Kennedy's General Store, she must have been a persuasive talker... Or was there some other influence involved?

That last thought arrived half-formed and took its time maturing into a well-developed possibility. Did she hold some leverage that she applied to pressure Kennedy into employing Wilson? It sounded far-fetched even as an idea. What possible leverage could Jane have over the store's proprietor? I had seen nothing to suggest there had been much involvement between Jane and Kennedy's General Store other than regular supply orders for Ravenshead House. Speculation is a waste of time. I needed evidence. Back to the diaries....

Armed with the (approximate) date of Darcy Wilson's court appearance as reported in the newspaper, I turned to entries from around that time in Jane's diaries. Surely, if this were as important to Jane as I believed it was, she would have recorded something about it. Every entry from the relevant date range was read and reread. Yes, there were hints about heavy negotiations occurring, but they were couched in such an obscure way as to provide me with no clear answers. Nevertheless, I was inclined to believe these entries related to Jane's efforts to secure employment for Wilson.

Wilson's court appearance probably didn't provide a happy start to the new year. From the newspaper reports, I determined that Darcy Wilson appeared in court on Thursday, December 30, 1926. As his sentence allowed him to leave Ravenshead to attend his place of employment, it indicated that such employment had already been arranged. Further perusal of Jane's diary revealed that Darcy started work (or was to commence working) in the stock room of Kennedy's General Store on Monday, January 03, 1927.

Okay, progress at last. While not the most significant discovery, it was progress, and that's more than I've managed to achieve in other matters. Any elation I felt was short-lived, nudged aside by the recurring question of how Jane managed to secure Wilson's employment. I was even more convinced she had applied leverage to make it happen, but what kind of leverage? Although Ravenshead was one of the few major properties in the area and would have been a valued customer of the Store, would the threatened loss of such custom be enough to influence Kennedy to employ Wilson? Somehow, I doubted it would be. Anyway, threatening to boycott Kennedy's Store, the only such store in town, would have been more of an inconvenience for Ravenshead than a worry for Kennedy.

'Sometimes you just have to cut your losses and move on,' I counselled myself as I checked all the notes I had made regarding Darcy Wilson.

Heeding my own advice, I returned my attention to Daphne Mary McDonald. Having already established that Jane had become aware that Miss Parker and McDonald were the same person, what else relevant to the project was there to discover? I already knew that, at some point in the future, I would be delving into the life of D M McDonald, as I felt sure there was much more to discover about the woman… And another visit to her daughter was not out of the question.

So, having finished with Darcy Wilson for the moment and relegated further McDonald research to 'another time', what else was there to go on with? In essence, the question on which the project was based had been answered. That answer was, yes, some of Jane's manuscripts had been stolen and illegally published by Tremaine Publishing House, under the author's name of D M McDonald. So, the family legend was based on truth and fact.

Perhaps it is time I spoke to Gabby about wrapping up the project, but I'm not sure she will agree. She seems to be enjoying searching Jane's diaries for snippets of family history, and I think she looks forward to the company I provide. Still, the project has been completed and needs to be signed off. With that thinking firmly in place, I went in search of leftovers in the fridge that I could reheat for dinner.

Warren's earlier text suggested that, although we wouldn't be dining together this evening, he might call in later if I was still up. I had no argument with those arrangements. Besides, reheating leftover pasta had more appeal than cooking a meal for two. After returning to my office, I checked my emails. My earlier quest for information had borne fruit.

Copies of the certificates I had requested had arrived, as well as the transcript of the coronial inquest hearing into the death of Thomas William Wilson. While the printer busied itself printing out all I had queued up, I dealt with the dilemma of what to look at first. Common sense quickly answered that question. It would take no time to study the certificates before beginning the major undertaking of reading the transcript of the hearing into Thomas Wilson's death.

I began with the certificate relating to Daphne Mary McDonald's death. It wasn't so much a death certificate as a declaration of death document. While it told me nothing much more than I already knew, it did contain a couple of gems. According to the certificate, Daphne Mary McDonald had married one Randolph Tremaine in London, and the marriage had produced one child about a year later, a daughter named Gladys Tremaine. It then confirmed details of McDonald's disappearance, and stated that nothing had been seen of or heard about her since then. Despite strenuous efforts to locate the woman over the ensuing years, nothing more was known of her following her disappearance. Finally, the document declared that, under the circumstances, it was reasonable to presume the woman was deceased.

Okay… So, the McDonald/Tremaine connection is now confirmed, as is that of the little old lady, Gladys Tremaine. The one piece of information in the document that made me catch my breath related to McDonald's parentage. It stated that McDonald was the daughter of the Earl of Northumberland and that, in the absence of a male heir, Daphne, as the oldest child, was in line to inherit the title.

"Phew," I whistled. "What the hell was she doing working as a typist in out of the way places in Australia, especially given she had married into the wealthy Tremaine family? Perhaps Randolph was a second or lesser son, and as such, wouldn't inherit the family's money. Was his position in the family important, or not? While it wasn't related to Gabby's project, it certainly sparked my curiosity. I knew the Tremaine family history and Daphne Mary McDonald's role in it would be my consuming interest as soon as Gabby's project was wrapped up.

"What about Gladys Tremaine?" I murmured. "How much does she really know of her family's history?"

When I visited her, she claimed not to know much about it, telling me she had been brought up by her grandmother, who was tight-lipped whenever she was questioned about any of it. Perhaps another visit to Gladys might be in order once Gabby's project is finished. Now that I know more about her parents, I might ask more pointed questions next time to elicit more information. Of course, if she doesn't know anything but is interested, I could share with her whatever I manage to dig up in the meantime.

With nothing further to be gained from the certificate, I put it aside and turned my attention to the other printouts. I was just about to succumb to temptation and start on the transcript of the coroner's inquest hearing into the death of Thomas William Wilson when my phone interrupted me. It was Warren. I remembered his earlier message about maybe dropping by later. I didn't need to guess what his call was about.

"Good evening. I see you are still up, so how about a coffee and port?" he chirped. How could I refuse?

Chapter 19

Warren didn't stay long last night. After he left, the lure of the coroner's hearing transcript rapidly faded. It was too late to start such a big job. Besides, the transcript would still be waiting on my desk in the morning.

This morning, despite a relatively early night, I struggled to get started, let alone find top gear. As I dawdled over my coffee, I pondered what to do today. Although that transcript topped the list, I was concerned that it might not be relevant to Gabby's project. Should I tie up any loose ends before calling time on the project? Indecision at this hour is not advisable. It always results in no start on anything until after a significant portion of the morning has been wasted.

Finally, parked at my desk in my home office, I dragged over the transcript of the coroner's inquest into the death of Thomas William Wilson. The list of people called to give evidence was daunting. Even if none of them had much to say, it would take some time to read everything. Without much enthusiasm, I launched into the task and was soon lost in the story of Wilson's last days.

I finished reading the transcript at about eleven o'clock and took a coffee break. My mind was reeling in disbelief. I knew I had to reread much of it. The similarities between Wilson's death and that of Jane's husband, George Creighton, went way beyond coincidental. They were almost identical, except for some details in Wilson's story. I knew that both men were considerably older than their wives, and I was aware that was not uncommon back then. But the information revealed in the course of Wilson's hearing stunned me. The hearing appeared to loosen previously 'tight lips'.

Testimony given by more than one person confirmed the significant age difference between Wilson and his wife, Erin. It also emerged that the young domestic servant, Erin O'Malley, towards the end of her first year of employment at Ravenshead, found herself unmarried and pregnant. At the time, Thomas Wilson was a longtime employee who resided in the barracks with the other men employed on Ravenshead. As an inducement to marry Erin, Wilson was offered a free cottage and elevation to a leading hand position. That left few questions about the likely father of Erin's child. Why else would Henry Finchley become involved?

The 'arrangement' and subsequent marriage were confirmed by more than one of those giving evidence prior to Erin taking the stand. Then the story took a dark turn. After being questioned about the events immediately preceding her husband's disappearance, Erin was questioned about the state of her marriage, the coroner having picked up on the fact that it was an arrangement rather than a romance.

Deeply embarrassed and fighting back tears, Erin told a dark tale of cruelty and abuse. She had been subjected to severe beatings almost from the day they were married. She blamed such treatment for the loss of her unborn child in the sixth month of her pregnancy. Her account of the marriage continued with the revelation that there were no further pregnancies because the couple never slept together; never even shared the same bed. The physical abuse continued anyway.

Shocked by her forthright account of the state of her marriage, the transcript suggested that the coroner appeared at a loss as to how to proceed with her questioning. Then, regaining his composure (supposedly), he asked Erin how she felt when her husband didn't come home when expected. She claimed she wasn't concerned. When he was checking on the men, unexpected incidents often delayed his return. It wasn't until he was a couple of days overdue that she became concerned and raised the alarm.

Erin must have cringed and found the coroner's next two rapid-fire questions difficult to answer:

Did you think it possible that he might have met with an accident? How did you feel when you learned your husband had indeed met with an accident and was dead?

Well, of course, I was aware he might have had an accident and might be lying out there somewhere seriously hurt, but my main concern was about what my life would be like if he were left incapacitated by his accident and I had to care for him for the rest of his life.

The transcript recorded that the coroner allowed Erin a few moments to compose herself before resuming his questioning.

So, you were relieved when you learned your husband was dead?

No. No, of course not.

What did you feel when they brought you the news that they had found his body?

Shock, I suppose. Yes, it was shock. I guessed he might be hurt, but never thought he might be dead.

And following his death, you then returned to your former employment at the big house on Ravenshead?

I never stopped being employed at Ravenshead. Even after my marriage, I never stopped working there. I still live in the cottage on the property and still work at the big house.

My dislike of the coroner grew with each question he asked Erin. Then, as I wondered how much more upsetting he could become, he ended his questioning of the young widow. The next two Ravenshead employees questioned also were asked about the state of the Wilsons' marriage. Both expressed their disgust at the way Wilson had treated his wife and labelled him a 'brutal wife beater'. The second man added the remark that Erin *was much better off without the mongrel.*

That echoed more veiled comments by others about his treatment of his wife. So, his behaviour was no secret and had caused him to be despised by at least some of his coworkers.

However, was that enough for Wilson's death to be anything but a workplace accident? The transcript certainly cast doubts about it. Although the coroner alluded to the strong possibility of accidental death, the evidence was inconclusive. Ultimately, the coroner deemed it appropriate to deliver an open verdict.

After pondering the coroner's apparent mental deficiencies for a few moments, I turned to the testimonies given by those involved in the search for and discovery of Wilson's body. Again, I sat shaking my head in disbelief as I had the first time I read their statements. Everything about Wilson, from when he left home until his body was discovered, almost replicated what I had read recently in another coroner's report. George Creighton's apparent accidental death some decades later was almost a carbon copy of that of Thomas William Wilson. Coincidence…? I don't think so. To me, both 'accidents' smelled of having been orchestrated by others with (perhaps justifiable) motives.

George Creighton's 'playing away' with the young widow in the cottage near the Ravenshead boundary might have been sufficient reason for Jane to want rid of him. Wilson's case was a little different in that it might have been Henry Finchley who saw fit to have him eliminated, and not Wilson's wife, Erin. After all, it appeared that Finchley might have orchestrated the Wilson marriage that brought nothing but misery and pain for Erin… And it all probably stemmed from Finchley's guilt and efforts to cover up having got Erin pregnant in the first place.

Finally, I finished the transcript and put it aside. As I cast my eyes over my notes, I couldn't help but wonder how Gabby might react to all of this. The similarities between the deaths of Wilson and Creighton beggared belief that they were mere coincidences. That then begged the question: Was Jane familiar with the investigation into Thomas Wilson's death? I found it difficult to believe she wasn't, even though she wasn't yet a teenager when it happened. And, despite my best efforts, I could not persuade myself that she hadn't paid Darcy Wilson to organise George Creighton's 'accident', and probably provided him with the blueprint from the Wilson case.

That then left the real object of Gabby's project to consider. Had I verified the family legend as required? The answer to that had to be yes, but would that satisfy Gabby? It wasn't enough to satisfy me, so it was unlikely to answer all Gabby's questions. What more is there to know, or still needs to be uncovered?

It is confirmed that Jane was a writer and that a number of her manuscripts were pirated –the exact number is unknown. Subsequently, some of her manuscripts were illegally published. Whether that was all of the pirated manuscripts or not remains unclear. Jane blamed the typist, Miss Lois Parker, whom she had employed to transcribe her handwritten manuscripts, and promptly dismissed her after discovering that her work had been illegally published. While it might have been obvious that the only access to her work was via the typist, the author's name that appeared on the books wouldn't confirm her suspicions.

Two unanswered questions remained. Was Jane aware that Parker and McDonald were the same person? If she was, when did she learn of it? That then leaves the question of the Parker/McDonald disappearance. Although not physically involved (perhaps), did Jane play a part in what happened? Again, the question of significance arises. Were answers to any of those questions important to closing the project? Much as I wanted to say no, I knew that wasn't the case. If I were Gabby, I definitely would want to know… and I'm sure that will be her response.

Establishing what Jane knew when was not going to be easy. The entries in her diaries are the only record of her thoughts at the time. Before embarking on more cryptic puzzle solving, I needed to revisit everything I knew, or thought I knew, about Daphne Mary McDonald. The little I've discovered so far just renders her enigmatic. Where might I find further information about the woman and her life? The little voice in my head was shrieking the answer at me: Another visit to Gladys Tremaine.

Why not? Thanks to my curiosity, it was on my list to do, so why not see if it provided something useful in relation to

Gabby's project? After a quick search of the local phone book, I was soon listening to Gladys' phone ringing in her cottage. She took a while to answer, and I was about to end the call when she did.

"I'm sorry," she wheezed. "I'm not as nimble as I used to be, and I was outside filling the bird feeder when I heard the phone ringing. Now, who am I speaking to and how can I help you?"

When my name didn't precipitate a meltdown, I felt it was safe to ask for a meeting. She seemed genuinely surprised.

"Goodness, I hadn't expected to hear from you again. Yes, of course, you're welcome to visit me. When would you like to come, and is there anything in particular you wish to discuss? As you are aware, I'm a bit long in the tooth these days, and like the rest of me, my memory is a bit slow to react. If there is something specific you want to talk about, I could give it some thought before you arrive."

Now, what do I say to that? Of course, I wanted to talk about her mother, but she had already told me she didn't know much about her. I made the quick decision to suggest something more nebulous and to do so in a circuitous manner.

"As I told you previously, I was surprised to learn that a well-published author had been living in our community, and I felt her story should be documented. I suppose some of her story is integral to the Tremaine family history, and I would like to learn a little more about that… If you might be prepared to discuss it with me."

"Well, I'd be happy to tell you what I know, but I'm not sure I'll be able to give you much information or answer your questions."

Good … she hadn't thrown up her defences the moment I told her what I wanted to discuss. She told me she was available all day today. We agreed I would be there in about an hour. Taking her to lunch somewhere meant we could begin our discussions while we were out. She excitedly agreed, and I realised that she probably doesn't get taken out to lunch too often. I felt a mix of sadness and guilt, and decided that investigating her family tree could wait until after she had enjoyed eating out.

She was dressed and ready to go when I arrived. I sensed an excitement in her that I hadn't noticed before. I took her to a little bistro in the city centre that's become a favourite of mine. It's one of those places that offers international cuisine, but dishes as common as bangers and mash and shepherd's pie are also on the menu. As I ordered my seafood omelette, I wondered what she might finally choose. It took her ages to select something, and then surprised me by asking for a Caesar salad with calamari. As soon as the waiter moved away from our table, she leaned over to whisper to me.

"I don't get to eat much seafood these days; too expensive. The menu here is wonderful. It's a bit like an Aladdin's cave. I would have been happy to just sit here drooling over it."

So far, so good, I told myself. Let's see if I can get the next bit right as well. After waiting until we had dispatched a significant portion of our meals, I eased gently into her family history.

"Gladys, I still find it hard to believe that your mother, a published author, who lived here in this community, has so little recorded about her. You and the Tremaine family must be proud of what she achieved, and it must be a bit galling that so little is known about her locally. I know you said you don't remember much about your mother, but what do you know about her life? And what about your father? Was he proud of her achievements?"

"When I said I didn't remember my mother, it was true. The last time I saw her, I would have been four or maybe five years old. After that, I was brought up by my grandmother."

"Was that your Grandmother Tremaine, or your Grandmother McDonald? I assume McDonald was her maiden name."

"Yes, McDonald was her maiden name, but I never knew… never met any of her family. Not as far as I am aware, anyway. I believe they all stayed in England. None came to Australia. Well, I don't suppose there was any motivation to come here.

They were reputedly a very well-to-do family back in the UK, with considerable landholdings and involved in various other ventures. The Tremaine story bears a certain resemblance inasmuch as they were 'upper crust' back there, and the Tremaines also had a title of some sort.

My Grandfather Tremaine was the second son in the family and, therefore, stood to inherit nothing. He married well, and they immediately immigrated to Australia, with no real plans or prospects awaiting them here. As I understand it, my grandfather took advantage of various employment opportunities until he had saved enough capital to establish his own business. They went from strength to strength after that, and the family continued to do very well."

"Did none of the Australian branch of the Tremaine family ever return to England? With two such well-set-up families on opposite sides of the world, I imagine there would be close communication between them, either for the sake of their business operations or just for family reasons."

"No, not really. Well, that's not strictly true. My grandfather's older brother, who was my Great-Uncle and inherited everything as the oldest son, married well but only managed to produce one daughter. She died in childbirth when she was quite young. So, in effect, the UK branch of the family had no heir to carry on after my Great-Uncle. When he died, the family were desperate for an heir. My grandfather reminded them that his eldest child was a son and, therefore, was the legal heir. So, my uncle was shipped back to England to pick up the reins over there."

"It sounds like he landed on his feet all right, but what about what was left of the family here in Australia?"

"Oh, I think the family here were happy that the eldest son was gone. Over the years, I gathered that my uncle had been… uhmm, 'difficult' probably describes it, and appears to have been a constant source of tension within the family. No one ever openly admitted that, you understand. It's only the impression I gained growing up in the big house with all the family.

"What about your father? How did he cope with being a bit 'second prize' when the family's fortune was being doled out and his brother had done so well out of it?"

"He didn't have any such problem, I don't think. My father remained in Australia and eventually inherited everything the family had established here. I think my father caused my grandparents some concern earlier in his life. He dabbled in various ventures, including some get-rich-quick schemes. It ended up all right, though. When Grandpa became ill, my father took over running the business, and it seems he did well at it."

"Was Tremaine Publishing House a part of the family's business operations, or was it your father's business? It must have been a relatively sound operation for one of the big publishing houses to want to buy him out."

"I'm not so sure about that. I don't remember how old I was when I overheard a conversation – a row, really – between my father and his mother. They were discussing my father's publishing business, and it must have been around the time it was sold. Grandma accused him of being stupid and having no head for business, and that he had kept the publishing going just for 'her'. I realised that the 'her' she was talking about was my mother. Grandma said he should have closed it down long ago instead of persevering with a 'dead horse' for so long. At the time, I didn't understand what some of it meant or what it had to do with my mother, but the words stayed with me. It wasn't until I was much older that I remembered them, and I understood what it was about."

"Perhaps not the nicest words a young child should hear about her mother… Would I be correct in assuming your grandparents were not happy about your father's choice of a wife?"

"Well, I don't know about Grandpa because he died while I was still quite young. I think he was careful about what he said when I was around. On the other hand, Grandma made no secret of her feelings about my mother."

"Your grandmother brought you up when, for whatever reason, your mother was no longer on the scene. Perhaps at her stage of life, Grandma resented finding herself having to care for a young child. I can't help but wonder how your parents ever managed to get married in the first place, given your grandparents' unhappiness about the relationship. Was there something in your mother's background that they considered unsuitable or concerned them?"

"Possibly, but I don't know what it could have been. Since I had never been told anything about my mother, I did some research when I was a bit older to learn more about her. Grandma was still alive then, so I had to do it covertly or there would have been a row about it."

"Surely, it wouldn't have been so bad as to upset your grandmother so much."

"Mother came from a titled family with lots of land and pots of money. She appears to have been well-educated. I don't know why, but I suspect she might have been a rebel, rather than maintaining the image of Lady something or other, the debutante. Anyway, maybe they were right to be concerned about her. After all, she did disappear, leaving them to raise me. My father was never much involved in my upbringing. Somehow, I don't think he ever got over my mother, and he never remarried, even after my mother was declared dead."

"Just out of curiosity, what happened to the family line back in England. Does the line continue, or has it died out for want of a male heir again?"

"Hah, ha… No such problems occurred. My Uncle Barrington married well – twice – adding lands and money to the family's wealth on both occasions. His first marriage produced a son and two daughters, and his second marriage gave him two sons and a daughter. So, the Tremaine family line remains strong in England, and the family's male line of inheritance continues through Barrington's son and, in future, through his grandson."

"What about here in Australia? What is the family's situation now?"

"Aah, well, the line has all but died out. I am the last of the Australian branch of the Tremaine family, and my age suggests the family's days are numbered. I probably won't be around much longer. Oh, don't get me wrong. I have no regrets about my life. I was well provided for and was left comfortably situated after all of the Tremaine interests were sold off. Funnily enough, towards the end of my father's life, his brother, Barrington, wanted to send over one of his sons (his second son, I think) to take over the family's operations here after my father. My father refused and assured his brother that there would be nothing to take over after his death, as he already was in the throes of selling off the last of the family's holdings. If I'm honest, I did quite well out of the sale. As the sole remaining member of the family, what else was he going to do with the proceeds?

No, as I said, I have no regrets about the life I've had. My one regret is that I did not get to know my mother better. Despite my efforts over many years, I still don't know much about her. I will be ecstatic if you manage to uncover anything at all about her life."

What more encouragement could I need to continue digging into the life of Daphne Mary McDonald, author and absentee mother?

Chapter 20

We both appeared lost in our own thoughts on the trip back to Gladys' cottage until I shattered the silence.

"What a sad story. While she was brave to give up her life in England to start a new life here, things appear not to have worked out as she might have hoped. Do you think your grandmother's feelings towards her were unpleasant from when she arrived, or did they change after she abandoned you with your father and your grandparents?"

"Oh, I'm fairly sure Grandma resented my mother, and my father to some extent, from the moment they were married. My mother was not the wife my grandmother wanted in the family. She had her eye on another woman for my father. Someone with family connections that could benefit Tremaine's business operations. When I was a teenager, I overheard Grandma telling my father that they would have a vast, successful operation now if he had married the right woman."

"It must have been difficult for your mother to settle into a new life where she knew she wasn't wanted. Your grandmother's refusal to discuss your mother intrigues me. Do you think that was out of resentment, or because she wanted to withhold the truth about something regarding your mother?"

"A bit of both, I think. I've asked myself that same question many times, but I don't know enough about my mother to form an opinion. That's why I'm keen for you to document my mother's life. Well, that's part of it. Yes, I want to know everything about my mother, but I would also love to see some recognition of her life's accomplishments. Until you came asking about her, it was as if my mother had never existed – except, perhaps, in my memories. And those memories are so fragmented and coloured by other people's opinions and prejudices, it's impossible to know what she really was like."

I eased to a stop in front of her cottage. She invited me in. I declined. She looked a little weary, and I suspected she routinely had an afternoon nap. I think a hint of relief flashed across her face when I declined to go in with her. She thanked me for what I was doing and asked to be kept informed about anything I discovered about her mother. She undid her seatbelt and was about to get out when another question flashed across my mind.

"Gladys, how did you learn about this cottage having belonged to your mother?"

"Are you sure you wouldn't like a cup of tea while I tell you the story?"

How could I refuse such bait? I sat patiently while she bustled about making the tea. When we were both seated at the table, Gladys seemed to spend a few moments working out how to tell her story. Finally, she took a deep breath and launched into it.

"My grandfather died before my mother was declared deceased. As expected, upon Grandpa's death, my father inherited everything: the business, the money, the house; everything. Grandma received a small annuity and continued to live in the big house. She was concerned that, now that my father had inherited everything, my mother would return and could inherit everything if anything happened to my father. When my Uncle Barrington wanted to 'lend' us one of his sons to ensure inheritance continued down the male line, Grandma supported the idea. Several serious arguments occurred within the family before Grandpa and my father convinced her that it wouldn't happen.

Once my father had inherited everything, I was next in line and stood to inhWhat derit whatever was left when he died. Somehow, that did not sit well with my grandmother. She resented my existence from then until she passed away. I wasn't living at home at the time, so I don't really know the details. After she died, I moved back to live with my father, but he suffered a severe stroke a couple of years later and died."

"Goodness, that must've been overwhelming for you. Not only had you lost your father, but you then had the family's business interests to look after. How on earth did you manage?"

"No, it wasn't as bad as that. As soon as Grandma died, my father started disposing of the family's assets. Just about everything was sold off by the time he died. The only outstanding matters were the sale of a couple of properties, but they already had been contracted to buyers. Nevertheless, I still spent a lot of time in our solicitor's office, tying everything up and dealing with loose ends. To complicate matters, old man Whitson, the family's solicitor forever, passed away a couple of weeks after my father's death."

"Your life was difficult enough without that happening. Were there still matters to be tidied up when he died?"

"Yes, but it wasn't so bad. Old Mr Whitson's son, who was also a solicitor, had come back to work with his father a short time before my father passed away. The young Mr Whitson took over his father's clients, and that included me. With all his father's files and notes to guide him, the transition was relatively smooth. Anyway, after we dealt with everything else, all that was left of the family's estate was the big house. Mr Whitson asked about my intentions regarding that, and I told him I intended to continue living there, at least for the foreseeable future. Although I knew I wouldn't spend the rest of my life living there, I had no other ideas or inclinations about where else I might live."

"So, when did you find out about this place, your mother's house?"

"When you think you know all there is to know, you find you don't. The day the solicitor asked me what I was going to do about the big house, he checked what still needed to be addressed in the Tremaine family files. He came across a thick file that he hadn't seen before. It was about this house.

When my mother disappeared, Old Man Whitson applied to the court to administer her estate, as her husband had already expressed his reluctance to do so. It was granted, and Whitson rented out this cottage and kept it that way. The money was used to pay rates and utility bills. After a while, the rental income covered some minor maintenance as well."

"I suppose your father didn't want to administer your mother's estate if he believed she would return one day. Do you think he knew about this cottage?"

"Neither my father nor my grandmother had ever mentioned it when I was around. So I didn't know about it either until young Mr Whitson told me about it. The file contained Old Whitson's notes, including one to the effect that he had spoken to my father about the cottage that he, Whitson, had helped my mother purchase. My father supposedly said he wasn't interested and didn't want to know about it. That's when Whitson decided to approach the court about administering her affairs. Apparently, once my mother was declared deceased, Whitson again asked my father about it and received the same response. According to Whitson's notes, my father insisted his wife was not dead and she would return in her own good time."

"So, as the next of kin, the only surviving next of kin, you inherited the cottage?"

"Yeah… but it was a while later before I decided to sell the big house and move here to live."

"Didn't it strike you as strange that your mother purchased a property so far away from the family, without telling anyone about it? Wouldn't she have needed to ask your father for money to purchase the place?"

"Sophie, what is there about my family that isn't strange? If not strange, everything about them and their lives is unfathomable, even to me. She wouldn't have had to ask anyone for money.

That was the other thing I discovered during my meeting with young Mr Whitson. My mother was wealthy in her own right. She inherited a significant amount of money from her family connections – some before her marriage and more later. Old Man Whitson had helped her invest and manage it without my father's knowledge. It amounted to quite a tidy sum by the time it came to me."

My mind was in hyperdrive as I drove home. Gladys was right about her family. There was nothing conventional about it. While it was a most interesting episode, did I learn anything today to help me complete Gabby's project? The short answer was no, but my gut was telling me I had learned something that might be important. Now, if I could work out what that was, who knows what I might achieve?

As I drove into my garage, Warren messaged me that he would be coming this evening and would bring something for dinner. I had planned to cook a roast, but takeaways tonight were fine instead. The little voice in my head questioned whether I really wanted company this evening. I would have preferred to be alone to mull over all I had learned from my meeting with Gladys. In the end, I resigned myself to the fact that Warren was coming, and some company might be nice.

Warren arrived as I finished typing up my notes from my meeting with Gladys. He rushed in, waving a carry bag at me.

"It's Chinese, so we should eat straight away before it starts to go cold. What have you got to drink with it?"

"Good question," I said as I bounded to the fridge. "Ah, we are in luck. There is a neglected-looking bottle of Chardonnay biding its time in here."

While Warren organised the table, I dealt with the wine, and moments later, we were tucking into Chinese takeaways.

"Did you think we might be particularly hungry tonight?" I asked, eyeing off the collection of containers in the centre of the table.

"Not exactly. You know how they tell you not to shop for groceries when you are hungry…? Well, it also applies to buying takeaways. I was hungry. It all smelled so good, and I couldn't make up my mind about what to order. So, we now have a varied selection to enjoy."

Later, carrying our coffees, as I trailed Warren, laden with our bowls of gelato, into the lounge room, I once again realised how much I enjoyed his company. He was easy to be around. He had a keen sense of humour, but knew instinctively when a quiet time was required.

With the first sips of coffee, the companionable silence that accompanied dessert gave way to lively conversation. He asked how my day had been and if I had done anything interesting. I told him of my lunch with Gladys and reminded him about who she was.

"Oh, yes… D M McDonald's daughter. I thought you'd lost interest in the McDonald woman when you hadn't mentioned her until now. I take it that your lunchtime outing was in aid of your investigation into the woman's disappearance?"

"Yeah. I'm trying to keep an open mind, but my suspicions are mighty powerful."

"You haven't asked me if I managed to dig up anything in our archives."

"Well, no. You've been so busy, I knew you wouldn't have had time for 'extracurricular' activities."

"For you, I'm never too busy. I mean that, and yes, I did have a fossick in the archives… And I found the file of the investigation into her disappearance."

I caught my breath and sat forward in my chair. All the while, the little voice in my head chanted 'don't get your hopes up'. I was so surprised, it took me a few moments to respond.

"Ri-ight… maybe give me the punch line first so I can decide whether it's worth asking any further questions. I don't doubt that file told you nothing more than we already know, that she disappeared without a trace."

"Aah, it doesn't work that way. You will just have to suffer all of the preliminary info before the punch line is delivered."

What a tease…! I grimaced and emphasised that I only needed information relevant to my investigation. He laughed, ignored my plea, and continued as he had intended.

"Okay, I can confirm that it was McDonald's neighbour who raised the alarm about her nextdoor neighbour. It appears she had invited McDonald to join her for tea. The two women had tea together on a fairly regular basis, with the venue alternating between their two homes.

"Wait, wait…."

"What? I thought you wanted to hear what I had discovered."

"I do… I do… But just hang on for a minute before you tell me anymore. There's so much going on in my mind at the moment, I'm in danger of forgetting what you tell me, or remembering it wrongly." I sprinted to my office and returned with my digital recorder. "Right, now I'm ready. So, McDonald's neighbour was expecting her to come for tea, but McDonald failed to arrive. Have I got it right so far?"

"Yep, that's the story as far as we've gone. Moving on… When McDonald didn't show up as arranged, the neighbour went over and knocked on her door. There was no answer, so she prowled around the yard looking for anything that might be out of place. It was then she realised that she hadn't seen McDonald since she had agreed to come for tea. The neighbour told the police that McDonald had come home from work during the day. That was unusual as she normally worked long days. The neighbour thought McDonald might've been ill. Knowing McDonald lived alone, the neighbour went to see if she needed anything. McDonald said she was fine and rejected her offer of help.

It was obvious to the neighbour that McDonald was upset. Although McDonald didn't want to talk about it, the neighbour persuaded her to open up a bit. McDonald told the neighbour she had just been sacked. When the neighbour asked if there was anything she could do to help, even lend her some money if she needed it, McDonald said she was all right and then clammed up and wouldn't talk about it any further.

Later that evening, the neighbour again went next door to check on McDonald, and that's when she invited McDonald to tea, but she had suggested the next day. McDonald said the next day didn't suit, and they then agreed to have tea together the day after that. That was the last time they spoke, and the fact that

McDonald had been so upset at the time alarmed the neighbour when McDonald failed to come to tea as arranged."

"Hmm… She was fortunate to have had such a caring neighbour. I wonder why tea 'the next day' didn't suit McDonald, but the day after that did."

"Probably doesn't mean anything. McDonald probably just wanted some time alone to weigh up her options, and didn't need her neighbour, no matter how well-intentioned, fussing over her."

"So, after the neighbour became concerned and contacted the police, what happened? Did the police immediately assume McDonald had disappeared and begin an investigation?"

Warren chuckled and gave me an 'aw, come on' look before resuming his story.

"Things weren't all that different back then. Of course, they didn't immediately start an investigation. The file indicates that an officer visited McDonald's house to assess the situation and reported finding no one at home. A couple of days later, the police again visited McDonald's house and, still finding no one at home, went next door to talk to the neighbour, who assured them she had not seen or heard anything of McDonald since she had first raised her concerns with the police.

When questioned, the neighbour confirmed that the last time they spoke, McDonald had been upset, but it wasn't as though she was angry about losing her job. She claimed that McDonald behaved more as though whatever had happened was more of an upheaval, something to be worked around, rather than being concerned about her financial future."

"Did the report contain any comment by the neighbour regarding McDonald's employment? I mean, any comment that indicated the neighbour was aware of the nature of McDonald's employment?" Warren stared off into the distance and thought for a moment before replying.

"Not exactly… As you might expect, the neighbour was asked if she knew what work McDonald had been engaged in prior to her being sacked. The only comment the neighbour had to offer was that she believed McDonald was involved in office work of some sort somewhere in the district."

"As you suggested, not exactly helpful. I imagine McDonald might've been a bit tight-lipped about what she was doing, although maybe not when initially engaged as a typist. She certainly would become cautious once her work expanded into more lucrative endeavours."

I sat bolt upright and stared off into the distance. That half-formed question that had been bothering me ever since I left Gladys finally developed.

"What? What just happened? Was it something I said?" Warren's rapid-fire questioning had me shaking my head.

"No. No, it's just that something that's bothered me all afternoon suddenly became clear. I'll tell you about it after we finish your story."

He gave me a sceptical look before returning to his notes in his small notebook.

"There's not much else to tell you. A full-scale investigation into the woman's disappearance was instigated. By then, it had been several days since her disappearance was reported. What followed was much as you might expect. Every available resource was thrown into the search for the missing woman. No trace of her was found. The search continued for several days before being called off. The surprising aspect to all this was that, apart from the neighbour, no one knew she had been sacked on the same day she was last seen. Even more surprising, perhaps, was the fact that no one knew her or where she had been working immediately prior to her disappearance."

"Were the police aware of her use of two different names? It wouldn't have helped their investigation if they weren't aware."

"I don't think so. It appeared as though they were unaware of the Parker name the woman had used. From the file, I could see that the search was for a missing Daphne McDonald. I didn't come across any mention of a Miss Lois Parker. At first, I thought that was too strange to be believed. After thinking about it for a while, I came to accept that it might have been possible that the woman had been living two separate lives."

"Hmm… I suppose that could be true. McDonald might not have told her neighbour where she was working because of the side hustle she was running with the manuscripts, and Jane had no reason to know about the woman's life away from Ravenshead. It seems the police were on a hiding to nothing before they even started their search."

"Maybe… But I would have thought that Darcy Wilson's involvement with Kennedy's General Store might have at least alerted him to the connections of the two names."

"The few things the woman would have bought at the Store probably would have been cash purchases. If she ran any accounts around town, they were likely in her McDonald name to avoid concern if she paid them by cheque bearing that name. Whether Wilson might have worked out the connection or not is another matter, and could depend on whether he had any involvement in her disappearance.

I've no doubt news of the police investigation into McDonald's disappearance spread rapidly through the community. Wilson wouldn't have to belong to Mensa to work out that it was too much of a coincidence for a woman to go missing at the same time as another one had been 'dispatched'. I have no doubts that Jane would have informed him of the pirated manuscripts saga and her actions in that regard. Then, if my suspicions are correct and Jane paid him a substantial sum of money to wreak her revenge on the perpetrator, it would have been wise for Wilson not to know anything about the connection between the two names."

"Are you suggesting there was calculated collusion to obstruct the police investigation?"

"Well, now, wherever did you get that idea? I don't remember using any such words." I gave him a wide-eyed, innocent look and giggled at his discomfort.

"As I have nothing more from the police files to tell you, perhaps it's your turn to share with me. Earlier, you mentioned that something that bothered you all afternoon suddenly became clear. What was it?"

"Saying it had become clear might have been a bit misleading. I knew there was something that didn't make sense, but I couldn't work out what it was. I've now worked out what doesn't make sense, but I still don't know why it happened."

"Would you like to try explaining that in language I can understand?"

"Okay… During today's lunch with Gladys Tremaine, she gave me an insight into what life was like in the Tremaine household before her mother left home. Gladys was barely school-aged when her mother left her in the care of her father and her grandparents. She painted a picture of her father as a man who never stopped loving his wife and always believed she would return one day… And, yes, I know there is nothing unique about that.

What intrigues me is that Jane's manuscripts were pirated and illegally published after Tremaine's wife apparently abandoned her home and family. Tremaine Publishing House published those manuscripts for her using her maiden name as the author."

"So, you're saying that the lines of communication, for want of a better way of putting it, between husband and wife remained open for some time after the wife supposedly left the marriage?"

"That's exactly what I'm saying… Additionally, as the last couple of manuscripts were published after her disappearance, it suggests that communication between the husband and wife continued at least until her disappearance. Tremaine's publishing enterprise was a small show that was eventually acquired by one of the big players. I'm wondering if it had been in financial trouble prior to the takeover, and if Tremaine and McDonald had colluded in the pirating of Jane's manuscripts in a desperate bid to keep the business afloat."

A few minutes later, after he received a phone call, Warren was on his way out the door to attend a new crime scene, leaving me with possibly more questions than I had before he arrived this evening.

Chapter 21

A call from Gabby this morning, as I sat toying with my breakfast, brought on a major dose of guilt. She hadn't seen me for a couple of days and was concerned that I was ill or something had gone awry with the project.

"Thanks, Gabby, but everything is fine. In fact, I was hoping to review a few things with you over the next day or so. How are you situated?"

She would be at Ravenshead for at least the next week – she hoped. I told her I would see her for mid-morning coffee and went to my home office to work out what I wanted to say to Gabby about her project. I was convinced the desired project result had been achieved some days ago. I wasn't sure Gabby would see it that way.

Yes, we had proved the veracity of the family legend regarding Jane's manuscripts being stolen, but in doing so, we had uncovered so many unanswered questions about Gabby's family. The question now was whether she wanted to pursue those answers or not. For me, some of the most interesting aspects of this project are the unanswered questions; questions about goings-on at Ravenshead so many decades ago. I knew that, if Gabby decided she had learned all she wanted to know, I would seek her approval to continue researching her Ravenshead family's life.

Freshly baked scones awaited me at Ravenshead. We wasted no time sitting down with coffee to do them justice. Then, it was time to initiate what I thought would be a tough discussion.

"Gabby, the reason I wanted to catch up with you is to review your project. Is now a good time for you to do this?"

"I hope you are not going to pull the pin on it. There is just so much I want to know, need to know, but I do understand that you have another life and work to do away from Ravenshead."

"That's an interesting statement. Perhaps you might outline some of those things you still want to know about. I assume the scope goes well beyond the family legend of the stolen manuscripts."

"Of course it does, and, yes, I realise the original scope of the project has been achieved. There are other things you've discovered along the way, significant stories that I know nothing about. If I am to live here and run this place, I want to know everything about it and the people who have lived here… No, I *need* to know what happened back then and who was pulling the strings at the time. I know none of that impacts me or my running this place today, but there are so many ghosts hanging about."

"Are those ghosts the material of other family legends?"

"No, that's not what I mean. The bit you've uncovered about this property's past has me almost feeling as though I'm living in a foreign land. I know so little about the place and the people who inhabited it over so many years and so many lifetimes. I'm probably not making any sense, but I feel a sort of unsettled uneasiness exists here. Whenever I'm in the house, it's as though I can feel people – or vibes, or spirits or something – following me around and peering over my shoulder."

"You have been going into the house for a while now. I thought those problems had disappeared." Gabby shook her head in response. "Does that problem exist here in your apartment?"

"No. As I said, it doesn't make any sense, but that's how it is. I hope that, if I know the whole story of what has gone before, the 'ghosts' might disappear. I attribute it to the fact that I know nothing of my past or my family's history, except for a few names and a couple of family legends. No one ever talked about the family's history. I'm not sure my mother even knew anything about it to be able to pass it on to me."

"So, I take it that you want me to continue delving into the history of Ravenshead and the people who have owned it over the generations. Is my interpretation correct?"

"Quite correct… I want to know all there is to know about this place and its people. What do you say, are you up for it?"

"What do you plan to do with whatever information we uncover?"

"Do with it…? I don't know. Do I have to do anything with it? Is that some sort of condition you're imposing for you to continue researching?"

"God, no, nothing like that. Look, Gabby, I wanted to talk to you because the project you engaged me to work on is well and truly completed. We proved the family legend was accurate. Jane was a prolific writer, some of whose work was pirated by the typist she employed, who later published those works under her name. We also know that Jane discovered the theft and promptly sacked the typist.

There you are. Legend confirmed. I felt guilty about still ferreting around in Jane's archives and other places for more information when I knew the project had been completed. The problem is that, along the way, so many mysteries were uncovered and so many questions left unanswered – none of which was covered by my initial brief. Those mysteries have hooked me thoroughly. Today, I intended to ask if, despite having completed my brief, I could continue my research. Of course, at no ongoing expense to you."

"Oh, please, please continue. Don't worry about the expense or what happens afterwards to whatever we discover. Please just continue your research. If you need help, just tell me what to do.

Argh, I do have a major concern about that, though. I'm concerned that the time you are spending on Ravenshead research is impacting your real work. I won't allow that to happen. I need your assurance that you will not allow it to become a problem – if it hasn't already become one."

"You have my assurance that it will not be a problem. For example, I have an article to submit next week. I have already created a rough outline for it. By the end of the weekend, it will be ready to be sent off."

"Okay, but only if you are sure." I nodded emphatically.

"Right, so what comes next, and what do you want me to do?"

They were good questions, but ones I couldn't answer. I told Gabby that, before I could answer, I needed to check on a couple of things I had parked until after I spoke to her. Now, I had her okay to keep going, I needed to figure out what to do next.

"Gabby, I'm going to work in the study for a while. I don't know how long I will be there, but I might take some stuff home to work on tonight. Are you going to be around?"

"So far, I'll be spending today here at home. I've taken your earlier advice and will continue working part-time for my former employers. It will mean spending time in town sometimes, and out of town on occasions."

"What about the big house, Gabby? What are your thoughts on that?"

"Don't have any thoughts, not yet, anyway. I guess I'll see if we lay any of the 'ghosts' to rest before wasting thought on what to do about the house."

I returned to the study. The question of what to do remained. Perhaps a list of all the questions and anomalies would be the best first step. I opened my notebook, turned to a new page, and ruled it into two columns. Why…? I had no idea why two columns were necessary, but it seemed like the right thing to do while I tried to decide what to start working on. I headed one column *Questions and Anomalies to Research,* and the second column was simply headed *Outcome.*

About an hour later, the first column was well populated with issues to explore, although some were no more than half-formed ideas. As I reread the list, a thought slammed in from nowhere. It seemed to have nothing to do with anything I had listed, but demanded my attention: *What about the relationship between Jane and Darcy Wilson?* The question looped through my mind without providing even a clue as to what it really meant.

My research already had established the connection between Jane and Wilson and the origins of their relationship. After a few moments of confusion, the little voice in my head changed its message. It now insisted I consider all the ways in which Jane appeared to support or assist Wilson. My mind immediately flew to the money Jane had paid him, which he ultimately used to buy Kennedy's General Store, and my suspicions about why she paid him that money.

My mind drifted to Darcy Wilson's employment as a teenager at Kennedy's General Store, the employment reputedly instrumental in turning his life around. I did not doubt that it was only through Jane's efforts that it happened. Her help didn't seem out of place given the relationship between Jane and Wilson, but how she managed to achieve it posed a question.

It wasn't a new question. I had wondered if Jane had some sort of hold over Kennedy that allowed her to pressure him into employing Wilson, but I had no idea what that might have been. The two obvious possibilities were dodgy dealings or something financial. If Jane had evidence that Kennedy had been involved in some form of illegal dealings in the past, would that provide sufficient leverage? I didn't think so, and left only some form of financial leverage to consider.

Perhaps Kennedy obtained a loan from Jane, and she might have threatened to demand immediate repayment. Possible, I suppose, but it wasn't a good fit with the people or the situation as I knew it. The other financial scenario I thought of was that Jane was an investor, a shareholder, in Kennedy's Store. Hmm... Possible, I suppose, but Jane would need a significant shareholding to be able to bring pressure to bear. Were there any records of dividends or loan repayments anywhere? ... And would any financial involvement be by Ravenshead or Jane personally?

Any Ravenshead financial involvement would be almost impossible to explore. But, if the money had been from Jane's personal account, some record of it might be in the material in her archives.

"Yeah... Worth a thought," I murmured as I scrambled up off my chair and rushed to open the hidden space. "There will be something in her financial records," I told the universe and reassured myself.

I came to a sudden stop in front of the shelves holding Jane's financial records. Where to start? Wilson was getting himself into trouble around the time of Jane's marriage. Whatever she had in place must date from earlier than that.

"Great…! How much earlier?" I demanded in a flash of temper.

With no answer or inspiration forthcoming, I pondered the problem for a few moments before speaking to myself. 'Stop stuffing around. Pick a year, any one that is a few years before she was married.' The year 1920 seemed as good a year as any, so I selected it and took it to my desk in the study.

"Now, what do I look for?" I murmured as I fanned a handful of sheets from the file.

As the papers flick past my eyes, I thought I caught a glimpse of something that resembled a bank statement. I doubted it was a statement. I had not come across a bank statement previously, but that is what it looked like. So, I carefully leafed back through the sheaf of papers… And there it was, a bank statement. I savoured the moment. I hadn't had too many lucky breaks to date.

It was a typical bank statement. Money went in, money went out, and the end balance was either black or red. In this case, at the end of the period, the balance was black. Somehow, that felt reassuring. I took a deep breath and began reading each of the transaction entries, paying particular attention to any deposits to the account. It didn't take long to identify income of the same amount arriving at regular intervals. I assumed it might be some sort of allowance. That's what it looked like, and I decided Jane must have arranged an allowance for herself so she could keep her private life separate from that of the property.

Of course, there were other deposits as well, so I focused my attention on them. Almost immediately, I realised another relatively regular payment had been made to Jane's account. The amounts varied, but not by much. Initially, the source of the payment didn't make much sense until I realised the payments were transfers from another bank account.

"Okay, so someone paid her some money every month," I murmured as I scanned the statement.

The payments were only relatively small amounts, and I wondered about their frequency. Surely, if the payments were from another business, instead of making a transfer every week or so, it would have been more efficient to combine the amounts into a single payment every month. I found myself wishing there was a way to identify that other bank account after all these years. A quick riffle through the rest of the file did not produce any other bank statements.

"Damn...," I growled and slammed the file shut.

From the start, this whole project had progressed at the rate of 'one step forward and two steps back'. Just when I think I've discovered a vital lead, it turns out to be a dead end. After a few moments of seething and sulking, I again opened the file. It made sense to at least look at everything in it, even though I knew there weren't further bank statements. I started reading each sheet, and it didn't take me long to realise that most of the documents in the file were transaction reports.

"Could be useful," I told myself, and settled back to examine each sheet in the thick file.

I realised it would take me longer, much longer, to go through the complete file than I initially thought. A few minutes later, I gathered up the file I had been working on and those for the two subsequent years and was on my way out to my car. I didn't see Gabby, and if I'm honest, I don't think I gave her a thought. I was so focused on going home to work on the files.

After a quick sandwich to ward off starvation, I settled into my home office with yet another mug of coffee at my elbow. Then, with the same file open on my desk, I again examined its contents one page at a time. Most of the sheets were records of outgoing transactions, interspersed randomly with receipts of monies paid in from various other accounts. Identifying payments from the Ravenshead account to Jane was straightforward, but most others provided little information about the source or reason for the payment.

I was more than a quarter of the way through the file before I realised that, apart from the regular Ravenshead payments, there was also another regular payment. A quick check on the only bank statement I had found so far confirmed those extra receipts were for deposits I had noted earlier on the bank statement. The frustrating thing was that neither the receipts nor the bank statement told me where the money came from or why it was paid to Jane. Something told me those payments were important enough for me to keep track of them.

"Back to the start of the file again," I growled and heaved a sigh as I opened my notebook to a new page.

My list of dates and amounts for those unknown regular payments soon snaked its way down the page. It was a long, slow process. While my main interest was in those receipts, I knew that to avoid having to do it later, I had to examine every page as I came to it, regardless of its purpose. After an hour, I was fast losing interest and concentration, and was seriously considering more coffee and a few minutes away from the file.

"What the…?" I yelped and flipped back a couple of pages to reread something that now seemed possibly important.

Although it was a receipt, it wasn't one of those I had noted as I worked through the file. There was something different about it. I caught my breath. It looked different because it was a more detailed record of the payment. As with other receipts, it displayed the account number from which the payment originated, but it also included the account holder's name and the reason for the payment.

A quick check on the notes I had made confirmed that the 'different' payment also came from the same account as all the other receipts recorded on my list. I double-checked the account numbers. Yes, they were the same. All those on my list, plus the 'different' one, had been paid from the same account. Now, thanks to the overzealous efforts of a clerk somewhere, I knew whose account the payments were from… And I knew what it was for. At least, I knew what that particular payment was for, but how did it compare to the others on my list?

There was little room for doubt. The amount of the payment fell within the range of other payments from the same account, and the timing was approximately right for when the next payment would have been due. Therefore, all the payments I had recorded were made from an account in the name of R L Kennedy. A quick review of my other notes confirmed that the Kennedy associated with Kennedy's General Store was Richard Louis Kennedy. I was prepared to accept that the R L Kennedy who owned the account was the Richard Louis Kennedy of Kennedy's Store.

"Okay, Kennedy is paying Jane a small sum of money on a regular basis. Interesting…." I murmured.

Checking the dates against a calendar suggested the payments were made every four weeks, not monthly, as I had expected. The word 'dividend' on the receipt struck me as odd. Surely, a dividend would be paid out only once or twice a year, not monthly. Might it be interest on a loan, or even some repayment arrangement for a loan? Was a loan involved at all? Perhaps Jane had purchased shares in the business. If Kennedy had been going through a lean patch at some time previous to 1920, perhaps Jane helped him out by buying shares in the Store. For some reason, that alternative sat most comfortably with me.

If I accepted the shares scenario, it gave me something else to consider. The purchase of shares or a loan to Kennedy should have been formalised in a contract of some sort, if not in a formal legal contract, then at least in a simple document signed by both parties. Where would Jane have kept her copy of such a document? While I knew I hadn't gone through everything in Jane's archives, and there were plenty of places in the house that I hadn't searched too thoroughly, I had seen no trace of any such document. If not at Ravenshead, where else might she keep such things as legal documents?

The only possibilities that came to mind readily were in a bank safety deposit box or with her solicitor. Neither of those options thrilled me. I felt sure any bank safety deposit box Jane had would have been cleaned out when her estate was being processed. If it remained with her solicitor, logically it also would have been dealt with at the time of her death. If it hadn't come to light and been dealt with then, God knows where it might be after so many decades.

Having slammed hard up against that brick wall, I took myself off to sit on my back deck and sulk for a while. When my thought processes returned to normal, the question that floated in to torment me was whether finding a document that formalised Jane's arrangement with R L Kennedy was of any importance at all. Weren't the regular payments to Jane sufficient evidence that some such arrangement existed? On any other day, I would have agreed, but today was not one of those days. As there was nothing I could do about it, I decided to put it aside and concentrate on something else – anything else that looked interesting in the financial files. I failed.

Every time I tried to think about something else, a question – the same question – kept intruding: *When and why did the arrangement start, and when did it end?*

Finding an answer to the first part of that question would take time and hours poring over financial records. That would be something for another day, if it proved to be of any real importance. Several possible answers to the latter part of the question immediately came to mind.

Perhaps it ended when one or other of the parties to the arrangement died. I suspected that might be Kennedy, but I had seen nothing to substantiate the notion. An alternative possibility was that the arrangement was finalised when Kennedy disposed of his remaining share in the business to Darcy Wilson. I was convinced that either of those scenarios was possible. I attempted to determine whether it was worthwhile to invest time and effort in establishing the facts of the matter, considering there might be more important and interesting aspects to explore. A new thought slammed in to ruin that line of thinking.

What if Jane had used her loan to Kennedy, or her shares in some way, to apply pressure on Kennedy to employ Darcy Wilson? Although unconfirmed by any evidence, I estimated that Wilson had commenced employment at Kennedy's General Store when he was about 14 years old in about 1926. I groaned. All I could see ahead of me were hours of poring through God knows how many of Jane's financial files to find answers.

Regardless of how I looked at it, just to get from where I was in the 1920 file to at least the end of the 1927 file would require a lot of time and effort.

Chapter 22

The thought of what it might require to overcome the current brick wall I had encountered was too depressing. I took myself out onto my back deck to sit and review my situation.

Did I really want to know what Jane's financial arrangements with Richard Kennedy were, or how she managed to persuade Kennedy to employ young Darcy Wilson in his store? For that matter, did I need to know anything further about Jane (Finchley) Creighton's life or the goings on at Ravenshead? If I continued pursuing this 'rabbit back to its burrow', what would I do with the resultant information? And, realistically, how much of it can I charge to Gabby? Perhaps Gabby and I do need another conversation about her expectations and envisaged outcomes.

As I sat watching a couple of hawks floating in circles riding the thermal currents high above me, I relaxed, and the noise in my mind abated. After about half an hour, I felt drowsy. The temptation was to indulge in a nap, but I reminded myself that I didn't nap during the day. Instead, I remained steadfastly in my chair. As I felt my eyelids starting to droop, a vague memory flashed in from nowhere and had me wide awake again.

"Wasn't Darcy Wilson paying Jane some money on a regular basis after he bought into Kennedy's Store?" I asked the willy wagtail perched on the railing in front of me.

While I couldn't recall the specifics, I was curious about money deposited into Jane's account from what looked like Wilson's private account. That recollection had me up off my chair and heading to my office… via the kitchen for a coffee. A search of my notes soon located the details I had recorded. It now felt like so long ago. As I studied my notes, something else came to mind. I recalled wondering whether Wilson was paying off a debt to Jane, or if Jane had somehow acquired a minor shareholding in Wilson's share of the Store.

Some form of shareholding kept coming up as the favoured explanation, but the exact nature of such a situation continued to elude me. A tug-of-war between what I knew and what I suspected clarified how to progress my research. Yes, I still needed to check Jane's financial records, but I had narrowed the period to investigate.

First, I needed to see what happened to Kennedy's payments to Jane around the time Kennedy employed Wilson. Any changes found might be indicative of some form of financial pressure having been applied. That would involve examining Jane's financial files for the years 1925, 1926, and maybe 1927. It still looked like a lot of work, but I felt it might be easier than I imagined.

Then, secondly, I would need to look at Jane's financial files for the period immediately after Darcy Wilson purchased a half share in Kennedy's Store… And that was not long after the disappearance of Miss Parker.

Now I had a plan. The only immediate problem was that I did not have any of the relevant files at home. Was it worth a drive out to Ravenshead to fetch them at this hour of the day? I decided it wasn't, and that I would survive without them until tomorrow. About then, a message from Warren said he would be coming this evening. That sent me scurrying to the kitchen to put the roast, which had been languishing in the fridge, into the oven for dinner.

When Warren arrived earlier than expected, I had just put the vegetables into the oven, so we had plenty of time to chat over a drink while waiting for dinner to be ready. While we went through the usual 'how was your day' routine, I detected that Warren seemed keen to get it over and done with as soon as possible. I sensed a hint of excitement about him, and it stirred my interest. As soon as the routine stuff was out of the way, I sat back, sipped my drink and left the conversation to him.

"Are you still interested in that Daphne McDonald stuff? I know I didn't give you much the last time I was here, but I wasn't sure how important she was to whatever you're working on. Anyway, I had a bit more of a dig around in the archives and dredged up a few more bits and pieces. I don't know that they'll tell you much more, or even if you will find it interesting."

"Aw, just stop stuffing around and tell me what you've found… please. I don't know yet how important she is to what I'm doing. I suspect she might be a significant part of the Ravenshead story, but until I know more about her disappearance, I can't be sure. I suppose, even if she wasn't important in the context of Ravenshead, she has captured my interest. I suspect that I will be writing something in the near future that focuses on her. Apart from the intrigue of her disappearance, what I've already learned of her life is so interesting.

Anyway, come on. Tell me what you've found today."

"Well, I'm not sure how useful it will be, but another file I found contained details of the search for the missing woman. No, they didn't find her, but the file does contain information about where they looked and why they searched those places."

"While it might not be of relevance to the Ravenshead story, I suspect it would be of significance to the Daphne McDonald story I want to write. So, let's have it. What have you found?"

"I'm just going to fetch something. I'll be back in a moment."

He sprang off his chair, marched out to his car, and returned, carrying a large folder that appeared to be fairly empty. He carefully placed it on the table. It seemed to take him forever to settle at the table again, all the while keeping one hand firmly on the folder. Patience is not my strong suit. It was all I could do not to demand that he give me the folder. When he finally stopped faffing about, he clasped both hands on top of the folder and appeared lost in thought for a few moments. That did it for me. I had humoured his antics long enough.

"For God's sake, are you going to tell me what's in that folder, or should I allow you a bit more time to meditate about it first?"

"Eh? What are you on about? I wouldn't have gone out to my car for the folder if I didn't want you to know what was in it. And, for your information, I wasn't meditating. Thinking of all the rules I'd broken today gave me pause for thought for a few moments.

My initial intention was to make notes of anything interesting I came across in this file. Then, once I got started, I realised that wasn't going to work. By the time I read it and worked out what was important and what wasn't worth noting, it would have taken at least a month. So, I decided it was much easier to copy the contents. You have more time and interest in all of this, so you can labour over the copy of the file for however long it takes you."

"Oh, gee… Thanks. No, seriously, I mean that. Thanks for copying it. I know it won't tell me where to find the body, but I suspect it will provide invaluable insight into what went on at the time."

"Yeah, it does, but in most instances, it also provides information about why searches were carried out in certain areas."

"Do you mean after information was received from the public, or whatever?"

"That sort of thing, yes. Some of it seemed a bit spurious to me, but I suppose they were desperate enough to follow up on anything and everything. Anyway, in those days, they probably weren't trying to cope with a serious crime wave while searching for a missing woman. Searching for the woman might have provided a welcome relief from the daily monotony of policing in a small town."

The oven timer ended further discussion of the file, and we relocated to the kitchen for dinner. Great conversation accompanied dinner before continuing in the lounge, accompanied by coffee and glasses of port. The 'natives' had been up to all sorts of high jinks in the community over the last couple of weeks, with the prevalence of serious crime the highest in months. Listening to his accounts of it made me realise how busy Warren had been and how little sleep he managed in recent days. I felt a heightened sense of gratitude for the work he had done in retrieving information from the police archives for me.

I looked over at him. He looked wrung out and on the verge of nodding off. Such a surge of care and concern flooded through me.

"Warren, I'm not sure you are in a fit state to drive home tonight. You're just about out on your feet. If you think you are safe to drive home, go now. Otherwise, the bed in my spare room is made up, and you should make its acquaintance."

Of course, he insisted he was fine, as I expected he would, but agreed an early night might be nice. I watched him haul himself out of his lounge chair like a man twice his age, and slowly ease himself upright. I walked him to his car and held the door open while he slid into the driver's seat.

"Go straight to bed," I barked. "Do not go via your office, the police precinct in general, or any crime scenes. Go straight home. I do not want to hear tomorrow morning about your fatal accident on your way home tonight." He gave me a lopsided grin as I closed the car door, and moments later, I watched his taillights disappear down the driveway and out onto the street.

With remarkable self-control, I resisted the temptation to rush back inside and open the folder until I had cleaned up the kitchen and taken a shower. Although it wasn't late, I felt a little weary, which isn't ideal when you're researching; vital clues are missed. Although my shower didn't work any miracles, I returned to my office anyway. As I plonked down on my chair, I realised I hadn't checked my emails today. I wasn't expecting anything urgent or important, but I do like to stay on top of my emails, just in case....

Among the usual pile of rubbish that always arrives was a reminder that I had an article due in days. The only other thing that caught my attention was a State Archives' email with a large attachment. I couldn't recall any outstanding orders, but it had to be related to the Ravenshead work I was doing. When the printer whirred into life to print out the attachment, I turned my attention to fossicking through my various notes for those that I'd made in relation to my article that now loomed large on my calendar.

By the time I found my notes, read through them, and devoted a few tired thoughts to how to start the article, I realised my eyelids were heavy and my mind was working at about half speed. I cast a longing look at Warren's folder. "Not tonight," I admitted to the universe before heading for bed.

Barely out of bed and dragging myself around the kitchen, I was making breakfast when Gabby called. Was there anything I needed to discuss with her before she left for the next few days? A former work colleague had passed away. She would attend his funeral and use the opportunity to catch up with a few other old friends she hadn't seen for a while. I assured her there was nothing urgent I needed to discuss and advised her that I probably would visit Ravenshead while she was away.

For some reason, it felt like a relief not having Gabby around for a few days. I couldn't think why, because we didn't have much to do with one another when she was at home. When she wasn't there, I found it a little easier to do whatever I wanted whenever it suited me … Like bringing home a pile of material to work on at home. While sometimes inconvenient to find that I hadn't brought home the very thing I needed, I found it easier to work at home. I didn't feel as though I had to keep an eye on the time, didn't have to drop everything to have coffee or lunch with Gabby, and didn't feel obliged to give her regular progress reports.

Following Gabby's phone call, I relaxed into the day. When should I start? What should I do first today? It was a no-brainer. That article, due next week, isn't going to write itself, and it will be a distraction until I deal with it. I told myself I could probably knock it over in a morning if I didn't procrastinate too much. So much for confident thinking….

The article took all day and remained in a fairly rough state when Warren called at about six o'clock to say he was on his way to a crime scene and wouldn't be coming tonight. I hoped my response didn't sound as relieved as I felt. My article still needed quite a bit of work, and I needed to finish it tonight. If I didn't, I would end up wasting a hefty slice of tomorrow faffing about with it. Midnight was knocking on my door by the time I attached the article to an email and dispatched it to my editor.

All day, I had felt a bit peeved about producing the article, as it had interfered with my progress on the Ravenshead research. As I climbed into bed, I reminded myself that the regular articles I'm contracted to write are my 'bread and butter' now that I've decided to become semi-retired. Anyway, now the damned thing is done and won't be hanging about distracting me. Tomorrow is another day, and it's one I can devote entirely to Ravenshead – or more precisely, to Daphne Mary McDonald.

Although I still didn't know how much significance to attach to McDonald regarding the Ravenshead story, the woman had a firm hold on me. It was the mystery of her disappearance that held my interest, but my gut told me there was more to the story, apart from the fact that she went missing and what happened to her remains unresolved. The only definite thing about today was that I would be driving out to Ravenshead this morning to ferret around in Jane's archives. I attempted to map out a plan of action for my day over breakfast.

"Right… So, where shall I start?" I asked my empty kitchen as I munched my toast. "Do I start with Daphne, or something else?" The lack of a response simply prolonged my time spent perched at the breakfast bar.

It wasn't until I was halfway to Ravenshead that the day took on any real direction. My main task today was to look through Jane's financial records. I wanted to clarify what eventuated with those small, regular transfers from Kennedy's account to Jane's, and then, whether there was any correlation between Kennedy's payments and those later payments from Darcy Wilson. To avoid wasting hours poring through the relevant files, I needed a timeline that would lead me directly to the appropriate years or a specific range of years.

When I arrived at Ravenshead, I was relieved not to have Gabby rush out to meet me. It's not that I don't like Gabby's company. I know she is probably lonely. It's just that socialising wastes a lot of my time. Anyway, today, I had no excuse for not getting on with it, and that's exactly what I did.

First things first: when did Kennedy's payments end? Realistically, that was at about the time Kennedy was 'persuaded' to employ Darcy Wilson. It would have been around 1926 or 1927. With Kennedy's payments made on a fairly regular basis, finding the transaction records in the file was a relatively simple matter once I had located the first payment in 1926.

Kennedy's payments continued through to December of that year. My calculations suggested the final payment for the year should have been made on or bout the last day of the year. I found no such transaction record.

'Not surprising,' I told myself before setting the 1926 file aside. 'A payment due on the last day of the year was more likely to be carried over to early in the new year.'

Leaving the 1926 file on my desk, I fetched to folder for 1927 and began examining every transaction record from the start of the file. I reached the first of the February transaction records without finding any further transfer of funds from Kennedy.

"Okay… Does it mean I've established the answer to that part of the question?" I murmured. "Looks like my hunch was right." I allowed myself to feel a bit chuffed.

It wasn't exactly irrefutable proof, but it lent some credence to my assumption that some form of financial inducement had brought about Kennedy's employment of young Darcy Wilson. Although relatively pleased with myself, I knew that feeling would be short-lived. I still didn't know the exact nature of the financial leverage Jane had used, and I'm already wondering again why Kennedy was paying her money in the first place.

"Move on…," I growled aloud. "There is still the second part of the problem to solve."

The second part of the problem was to determine when Wilson started making regular payments to Jane, and also to establish if there was any correlation between his payments and Kennedy's. The big question was, how soon after he was employed did Wilson begin making payments? I returned to the first sheet in the file for 1927 and carefully examined every page. Although I'd searched through all the January transactions for payments from Kennedy, I hadn't looked for payments from anyone else. It did occur to me that, if Wilson only started work in January, it would be unrealistic to expect him to start making payments immediately. A more realistic approach would have been to wait until Wilson had received a few pays before expecting him to start paying Jane.

My search of the file had reached the beginning of June when I decided it was time for a coffee break. Any feeling of elation I felt earlier had disappeared by then. The coffee break wasn't so much about the coffee as it was about giving myself time away from my desk to ponder the situation. It was a good forty minutes later before any glimmer of intelligent thinking made an appearance.

Of course, Jane wouldn't expect Wilson to pay her anything so early in his employment. They were close. I felt she would have wanted him to be well settled in at his new job before she expected him to part with some of his earnings. As a youngster working in the storeroom, Wilson would have been making barely enough to exist on and was unlikely to have sufficient left over to pay Jane. No, it can only mean that my assumption is fundamentally flawed. In the absence of bright ideas about what I should do about it, I returned to the 1927 financial file and continued from where I had left off.

The first transaction in July of that year caused me to yelp. There it was. And no, it wasn't what I expected. I reread the transaction details several times before slumping back in my chair to consider it. My shock was that the payment wasn't from Wilson as I'd expected. It was yet another transfer from R L Kennedy's account. Why…? Why, after six months, would Kennedy start paying her again?

Once I recovered sufficiently from the shock to regain rational thought, I reached for a calculator and a pad. The payment was an unusual amount compared to what Jane had been paid previously. I didn't need to be a mathematical genius to determine that it was approximately half of what Jane would have been paid over a six-month period previously. The other change was that, instead of a small amount being paid every four weeks as in the past, it seemed payments had become six-monthly.

Given the small monthly payments, it wasn't surprising that the payment schedule had changed, but the altered amounts were intriguing. Did the new reduced amounts reflect the changed financial arrangement Jane entered into in order to secure Wilson's employment? While it seemed highly likely, details of the changed circumstances were nowhere to be found. I resolved to comb through Jane's diaries, both at the time she probably was negotiating Wilson's employment and around the time of the first six-monthly payment.

"Well, that sort of answered that question," I told the universe as I snapped the folder closed. "All that remains now is to investigate when Wilson began payments to Jane – and why."

Realising I might have been a bit hasty in closing the file so soon, I opened it again and flicked through to the mid-year payment by Kennedy. A careful check on transactions through to the end of the year produced nothing of relevance until the last days of December, when Kennedy made another small payment. No payments by Wilson were discovered.

"Where to now?" I asked the universe as I again closed the 1927 financial folder.

Chapter 23

Thank God, it was an appropriate time for a lunch break. Removing myself from the study and everything I had been working on allowed the fog built up in my mind to dissipate and clear before I returned to work. I hoped that would be the case today. I had no clue where else to find the information I needed.

My sandwich long since dispatched, I dawdled over a coffee as I waited for inspiration to come. While slow coming, it finally arrived as I rinsed my mug and added it to the dishwasher. But it only reiterated one simple question: *When would Darcy Wilson be in a position to start paying Jane?*

The answer was a no-brainer. It's likely Wilson wasn't earning enough to pay Jane anything until he bought into the business. Until he bought the half share in Kennedy's General Store (with Jane's money), he would have been on a very low basic wage. After some consideration, I decided it was a reasonable assumption. I hurried back to the study to test it. My notes provided an approximate starting date for any payments Wilson might make.

"Right… Wilson was paid a huge sum of money by Jane in 1934, with which he appears to have bought his half share in the Store soon after," I mused aloud. "Would Jane expect payments to begin immediately, or would she allow Wilson some period to find his feet first? And, what was he paying her for?"

After all this time, that last question continued to haunt me, I mused as I again entered the hidden space. A quick trip, just long enough to locate and collect the financial folders for 1934 and 1935. Then, with everything else pushed well out of the way, I placed the 1934 folder squarely on the desk in front of me. I flicked through its contents until I reached what I believed was an approximate date for when Wilson became a partner in Kennedy's Store. It was some time after that before I came across the first transfer of funds from his account to Jane's.

Reference to my earlier notes confirmed that Wilson's payments closely mirrored the monthly amounts originally paid to Jane by Kennedy before those amounts were reduced.

"Interesting…." Regardless of why she saw fit to reduce Kennedy's payments, Jane obviously didn't find it necessary to extend the same degree of largess to Wilson. "So much for close relationships and mates' rates," I murmured.

A short time later, I questioned my earlier thinking. Those payments from Wilson to Jane, made every four weeks, suddenly stopped. A couple of months of no payments had me wondering whether some critical event had caused the cessation. I shook my head. No, Google hadn't found anything like that when I had sent it off to search for information about the store and Wilson's involvement with it. Anyway, the Store continued trading after that, so they hadn't gone broke or gone out of business.

Since I had no other thoughts on what else to do or where else to go, I returned to perusing the transaction sheets in the folder. My mind was so preoccupied with trying to come up with plausible scenarios to explain the cessation of payments that I almost missed it.

"That was one," I yelped, with my hand poised ready to flick to the next document.

I had to turn back a couple of pages for the required sheet. As my mind had belatedly noted, it was a transfer of funds from Wilson's account to Jane's, but the amount paid suggested that payments had become quarterly.

"Not surprising perhaps… Simply a case of a change for efficiency and expediency," I suggested to the universe. But was it, or was it triggered by something else?

Nothing was forthcoming to change my original thoughts about the change. Quarterly payments continued through to the end of 1934 and then to the end of the 1935 folder. Should I continue checking each of the subsequent folders or skip ahead to around the time Wilson became the Store's sole owner? The latter option prevailed, and I returned all the folders on my desk to their designated places on shelves in the hidden space.

Where to begin the next phase of my research required further consultation with my earlier notes. Logically, if there were to be a change, it would have occurred sometime after the disappearance of Miss Lois Parker…If my suspicions about Wilson's involvement in her disappearance are correct. My gut kept insisting that it was too much of a coincidence for Parker to disappear and Jane, yet again, to pay Wilson another significant sum of money… for Wilson to purchase the remaining half of Kennedy's Store after such a relatively short time. There had to be a connection, but I had discovered in the last day or so that payments to Jane made a mockery of some of my original thinking.

Earlier, I had thought that, following Parker's disappearance, Jane's extra payment of £500 to help finance Wilson's purchase of the remaining half of the Store was by way of securing a small amount of shares in the business. Now, research thoroughly dispelled that idea. Whatever was going on between Jane and Kennedy's Store, it had happened long before Wilson was involved with the business. Although the notion of shares in the Store still appealed, was it worth pursuing?

If there had been a share arrangement with Kennedy, and then later with Wilson, surely contracts containing the terms and conditions of the shareholding would have been necessary. Where are those contracts now? The only place that came to mind was the small wooden box, and that's when I realised I still hadn't finished inspecting its contents. Checking the box would have to wait until I was home. In the meantime, how could I determine the duration of the payments from Wilson to Jane?

For lack of a better idea, I randomly selected financial folders from over the years after Wilson became the sole owner of the Store. It was a slow and confidence-destroying process. Although the same degree of diligence was not applied to those subsequent folders, even a quick check was sufficient to confirm the payments had continued.

"Now, when did Kennedy's General Store finally go out of business?" I asked the empty study as I returned to my notes.

I turned my attention to the financial folder for the last couple of years the Store was still in business. Payments to Jane had continued up to about six months before the Store closed, but over the final couple of years of its operation, the amount of each payment slowly decreased. It wasn't too difficult to assume that, as the Store's trade dropped away, diminished payments to Jane reflected that loss of business.

"Okay...," I murmured. "So, the Store closed while Jane was still alive. So, what about her relationship with Wilson? More important, perhaps, is what became of Wilson after the Store's closure?" As usual, I had plenty of good questions, but no idea where to find the answers.

After reflecting on the period following the store's closure, what became of Wilson took on increased importance. He was younger than Jane and possibly was still alive when she died. While that mightn't be important, where he went and if they kept in touch might be. That led to the inevitable question: when and where did Darcy Wilson die?

I had previously devoted some research to his death, but found nothing. What other resources might shed some light on his death? Probate and inquests immediately came to mind … along with the question: *where?* He could have moved away from here and died anywhere in the country. In that case, any probate or inquest files would be held by the state archives of the state in which he died. I groaned at the thought of the hard slog that might involve, but resolved to start with a search of this state's archives.

The day was fast disappearing, and I had quite a bit of computer work to undertake before I could progress much further. Although I could work on my laptop in the study, I preferred using the computer in my office at home. Folders were returned to the hidden space, 'homework' was packed into my tote bag, and I was on my way home. A text from Warren told me he would not be coming for dinner, but might drop by later if he could escape at a reasonable hour. Sometimes luck is in your corner, and this was one of them. I could spend the rest of the day and into the evening immersed in the research I had set myself to do.

It was as I drove up my driveway that yet another question slammed in from out of nowhere. I parked in my garage and sat there stunned for a few moments. Why hadn't that question ever occurred to me before? Was it important? Did it matter where Darcy Wilson had lived when he owned the Kennedy's Store? Why am I worrying about where he lived after the Store closed if I don't know where he lived while he was in business here? I dismissed the possibility that he continued to live in his mother's former cottage on Ravenshead. The daily commute to work would have negated such an arrangement. No, he had to have lived somewhere in or near town.

Although it was almost four o'clock, it was Thursday, and the library remained open until seven o'clock on Thursday evenings. I detoured into the city and parked at the library. As I walked through to the section along the back wall where the copies of the electoral rolls were shelved, I tried to establish which years interested me. By the time I was standing in front of all the electoral rolls, I had decided that the roll for any election after Darcy Wilson first bought into the Store should be useful.

"So any time after 1935," I whispered as I ran my eyes over the volumes. "Oh, good…." There had been a local council election the following year.

My excitement was short-lived. Finding the entry on the roll for Darcy Wilson didn't require too much time, but it was disappointing. He supposedly was residing in a boarding house in town. After a moment's thought, I searched for an entry for Richard Louis Kennedy. His address was the same as Kennedy's

Store. I accepted that made sense. As in many cases back then, the store probably had living quarters above it. As the owner, it wasn't surprising to find Kennedy living above the store. That meant Wilson had to find somewhere else to live. A boarding house was an obvious choice. But what happened after Kennedy was no longer involved in the business?

After several failed attempts, I eventually found a state electoral roll from the period. It showed that, at the time, Darcy Wilson resided above the Store. So, up to that point, things were much as I had expected. I told myself there was little point in checking Wilson's address on any further rolls until around the time or soon after the business ceased trading. It then occurred to me that, although the store had closed, it was still there. Wilson could have continued to live upstairs in the building that he still owned – presumably.

Did he sell the building, or was it allowed to just sit there and rot? At some point, the building was removed. The building that now stands on the site of the old store dates to around the same time as the store closed. Perhaps, with the closure of the store or soon after, Wilson was forced to find new accommodation. The next roll I looked at was for a local council election held approximately 12 months after the store's closure.

Darcy Wilson's name did not appear on the roll, suggesting that he had left the district. I searched along the shelf until I came to the roll for a state election 18 months later and two and a half years after the store closed. Again, I struck out. There was no Darcy Wilson registered as a voter anywhere in the state. I was ready to give up and go home when I saw the electoral roll for a Federal election. That election was held about a year after our state election.

"One last try before I buy fish and chips for dinner and go home," I murmured as I carried the Federal roll to the table I was using. That's when I realised the roll comprised three volumes. Returning that one to the shelf, and on the assumption that surnames beginning with W would be near the end of the roll, I selected the third volume of the set.

I had used up my quota of luck for the day. No one named Darcy Wilson appeared on the roll. Disappointed and frustrated, I returned the roll to the shelf and marched out of the library. All the way home, I reminded myself that checking the rolls had been a long shot from the outset, and despite that, I now had further information on Wilson's whereabouts for at least some of the time I was interested in.

Fish and chips don't improve when left sitting around for long, so as soon as I was home, my priority was dispatching the fish and chips, quickly followed by a shower to wake me up a bit before I went to my office. Although Warren wasn't coming for dinner, I didn't know when or if he would appear. It made sense to complete as much research as soon as possible. However, given my current run of luck, I wasn't confident of success.

Although indexes of marriages and deaths across the country had been explored previously, I decided another quick check probably wouldn't hurt. It proved a waste of time and produced the same result.

"Fancy that," I exclaimed in frustration. "Darcy Wilson must now be the world's oldest bachelor. He never married and still hasn't died."

That's when the little voice in my head reminded me, 'Ah, yes, but he might have married and died somewhere overseas.'

Bugger! I'm on a hiding to nothing tonight. For a few moments, I considered abandoning further research. That was until common sense told me that tomorrow's results would still be the same as tonight's, so I might as well get on with what I planned to do this evening. The last items on my list of resources to check tonight were the wills and probate indexes in the various state archives.

For no definite reason, I decided to concentrate on the wills indexes first. My search had been in progress for slightly more than half an hour when something caught my eye as I scrolled down alphabetical entries in an index.

"Whoa! Hang on… What was that?" I yelped and slowly scrolled back up through the list to what had caught my eye on the way past. "That's it… What the…? That's got to be significant…."

No, I wasn't anywhere near the W section of the index when a name almost leapt off the screen at me as I sped past it. While I knew it wasn't the Wilson surname that had caught my eye, I did wonder if my mind was playing tricks on me. Maybe I am tired and should call it a night. I can try again in the morning when I'm fresh. Inching my way back up the list entry by entry, I finally came to the one that had set my pulse racing.

It was only the surname that had caught my eye as it flew past, but now the whole name had me perched on the front of my chair in excitement. There it was: *FINCHLEY, Darcy Henry*.

Finchley wasn't a common surname. At least, I didn't think it was. In all the research I did for Gabby's project, I had only come across that surname associated with Jane's family. Could Darcy Finchley be my missing Darcy Wilson? … And, if it were, when did he acquire the middle name of Henry? It didn't matter. I needed a copy of that will, and immediately completed the request form. I froze before I clicked the SEND button.

How was I going to endure the usual delay that would follow? The archives would take at least a couple of days to send me a quote for a copy, and then another couple of days at least before the copy was emailed to me. Damn! I don't want to have to wait that long.

I slumped back in my chair to sulk for a while. The completed request form still filling the screen continued blinking at me. After a few moments, rational thought had me rummaging in my desk drawer for an address book. Years ago, I became friends with a genealogist who seemed to spend half her life in that state's archives.

"Let's hope she hasn't changed her phone number," I murmured as I keyed the number I had in my book.

Yes, it was late, but not so late that I should postpone calling her until tomorrow. I listened to the number dialling for quite a while, and was on the verge of ending the call when she answered.

"Sophie, great to hear from you. It's been a while. How are things with you? Apologies for taking so long to answer. I stayed on at the archives until they closed this evening."

"Good to hear you're still spending time in those archives. Kath, I know you probably are flat out with clients' requests, but I was hoping you might be able to fit in a spot of work for me. It's just that it is fairly urgent, and you know how long it takes to get anything out of the archives."

Kath would be at the archives all day tomorrow and was only too happy to help. She listened patiently as I gave her a story (some of which was true) about how I needed a copy of that will urgently. I gave her the file details, she checked my email address hadn't changed before promising to email me a copy in the morning. She had done similar work for me previously when I needed information urgently for an article that was nearing its deadline. I knew she would photograph every page of the file (and pay the appropriate copy price) and then compile all the images into one document to email to me. It required a chunk of her time and wasn't cheap, but I probably would have my copy by lunchtime tomorrow.

Pleased with my efforts, I gave my pulse rate and blood pressure a chance to return to normal before heading to the kitchen to reward my quick thinking with a glass of wine. While still standing at the kitchen bench, I realised finding the entry for that will was only half the job done. Glass in hand, I hurried back to my desk.

If Darcy Henry Finchley, in another life, had been Darcy Wilson, he would be well and truly dead by now. If not, his name would be known by many as the oldest man alive… And if he were dead, there would be a probate file from when the deceased's estate was processed. Dare I call Kath again tonight? No, I couldn't bring myself to do that … But I could email her, and I did.

As I sat wondering if there was something else I might work on tonight, Warren arrived. He looked haggard, and I noted that it was becoming his regular appearance. I happily abandoned my office in favour of spending time listening to Detective Inspector Warren Tyson recounting snippets from his harrowing day.

Chapter 24

There is probably no end to the research I could do this morning, but it would be a waste of time to try. I wouldn't be able to concentrate. All I'd been able to think about since I climbed out of bed was what surprises might lie in the material Kath would send me sometime today.

As I'm unlikely to receive anything before lunchtime, I have several hours to fill in before then. To keep busy and help the time pass more quickly, I resorted to throwing myself into domestic chores. By the time I stopped for a mid-morning coffee, the laundry was done and the house positively sparkled.

'But once I finish this, then what?' I asked myself as I sat sipping my coffee.

A mug of coffee occupies you for only so long, no matter how much you dawdle. By the time I finished mine, I knew how to spend the next part of my day: grocery shopping. That was a neglected task of late, and my fridge and pantry were starting to resemble Mother Hubbard's. After dashing off a quick shopping list, I headed for the supermarket. Half the town must have had the same idea. The supermarket was crowded, and only two checkouts were operating. Every machine in the DIY section was in use. There was nothing for it but to cool my heels in the queue – and watch my tub of ice cream slowly come to room temperature.

I had just started transferring items from my trolley to the checkout counter when my phone demanded attention. It was Kath. I felt my pulse rate step up a notch, and the sound quickly moved to something resembling jungle drums in my ears.

"Have I interrupted something?" she asked as the sounds around me filtered through to her phone.

"Not at all. I'm just going through a supermarket checkout, so you have my undivided attention. Is there a problem? I mean, are you having trouble with the stuff I asked you to obtain for me?"

"Eh? No, not at all. I just called to let you know I just emailed the files you asked for."

"Fantastic! I can't thank you enough. Oh, and I hope you sent your invoice along with all the other stuff."

"Give me a break. I'll get around to that sometime either tonight or tomorrow at the earliest. Those files have my antennae twitching. I'll look forward to hearing what it's all about."

By the time the call ended, I had reached the stage of the process at the checkout when I had to produce my credit card. After swapping my phone for my wallet, I was soon on my way to my car and heading home. I carried a couple of bags of groceries inside with me and left the rest in the car until I had fired up my computer and sent it to check for emails. While it was doing that, I returned to the garage and brought in the rest of the groceries. The ice cream went straight into the freezer, but I told the rest of the bags of groceries that they would just have to wait a bit before I unpacked them.

Kath had sent two files, one much larger than the other. The huge one, I soon discovered, was the probate file. The other was a copy of Darcy Henry Finchley's will. With the will file first, both went to the printer. While they printed, I returned to the kitchen and attended to the other cold items among the groceries. Then, with nothing else 'domestic' to distract me, I grabbed the pile of printouts and settled at my desk. A couple of minutes later, the printouts of the files had been sorted into two piles and placed loosely into separate folders. My stomach grumbled loudly, reminding me that it was now lunchtime. It would just have to wait a bit longer.

My priority was the folder containing the copy of the will. It was a slender file. In a standard format, it didn't involve a long list of beneficiaries, just one. It had been made several decades ago and simply bequeathed everything to Mary. It didn't even bother to tell me anything about Mary. But did the fact that there was a wife mean that this Darcy wasn't Darcy Wilson, as I had suspected?

It didn't matter how many times I read those pages, they refused to offer any further insight into the man whose will this was… or Mary. In fact, the only thing I learned from the document was that the solicitor who had drawn up the will was a member of a law firm in Sydney. The Sydney address of the law firm wasn't encouraging either. Disappointment flooded through me. I had been so sure that the Finchley name was the vital connection to Darcy Wilson I needed. A lunch break before perusing the probate file seemed a good idea. If nothing else, it would allow me time to prepare for further disappointment.

With an almost overwhelming feeling of dread, I opened the probate file. I took little comfort from the fact that it referred to the estate of the late Darcy Henry Finchley, but nothing more. I started reading and soon found myself totally engrossed in the document. I didn't have to read too far to learn that Mary was Finchley's wife and that it was she who sought probate of his estate. Although her address was given as Brisbane, the probate work was handled by a firm of solicitors based in Sydney. I moved on to the section that detailed the bequest.

The extent of the estate was stunning. Even by today's standards, it was a monumental bequest. "Lucky Mary…," I murmured as I returned to the start of the list of properties and began slowly reading each entry. Shaking my head in disbelief, I looked for the section that gave the value of the estate. "Crikey! I definitely need to know more about that Mary person. His death left her almost a millionaire."

Most of the afternoon had disappeared by the time I had read every word in both documents. It made for fascinating reading, but it hadn't confirmed my suspicion about the real identity of Darcy Henry Finchley.

Taking a coffee and the two folders out onto the back deck, I sat staring off into the distance, allowing my mind to wander through everything contained in the folders. My coffee was cold when I heard the little voice in my head suggesting I knew Mary.

"No, I don't. I don't know any Marys," I growled, "not in terms of this project anyway."

Although it took a while, the fog clouding my thinking eventually rose. I fetched my notebook and turned to the list I had made of every name encountered during Gabby's project.

"See… No Marys…," I murmured. "Oh, hang on… Could that be….? Surely, not." But my gut demanded to know *why not*?

What to do next proved to be a relatively straightforward task. All I had to do was prove the connection beyond the fact that the names involved so closely reflected other people I had encountered in the project. The little voice in my head was screaming encouragement. "Find the marriage."

Of course, I was sceptical. I had checked all of the country's online marriage indexes and found nothing. "Ah, but I had looked for Wilson marriages. What if Wilson had changed his name after he left this district?"

Why he would do that was a mystery to me, and whether he changed his name legally or simply started using a different one was another question. Perhaps it all stemmed from some long-held hangup about his illegitimacy. I couldn't help but wonder what Jane would have made of the situation. Regardless, my task for the moment was to find if and when Darcy Finchley was married. I began by asking my co-conspirator, Google, to find me this state's marriage index.

It took mere moments to confirm that no Finchley marriages had occurred in this state within a realistic range of years. As his will had been drawn up in Sydney, the New South Wales marriages index was my next request to Google. A search of that gave me the same result.

"Perhaps, Queensland…," I murmured, and typed in my request.

After a search of what I considered an appropriate date range, I was about to move on from Queensland, when I thought, 'one more period, just in case'. And there it was….

I had found an entry for the marriage of Darcy Henry Finchley to Mary Tremaine. Who else could it be? While I was convinced I had found the correct marriage, there was a problem with the date. It appeared to have occurred much, much later than I expected. And what about the bride? Who was she? I was almost prepared to stake my life on her having been the former Daphne Mary McDonald, who later became Daphne Mary Tremaine. A scan of my notes from my interview with Gladys Tremaine found the date when Gladys' mother was declared deceased. The suspicious index entry I had found was for a marriage that took place almost 12 months after the missing woman was declared deceased. Is Gladys aware of the marriage but 'forgot' to mention it, and more importantly, was she aware of it at the time it occurred? I will be having another chat with Gladys.

"Okay… So I think I've found the marriage, but what about this Finchley bloke's death?" I mused as my printer spat out the details of the marriage index entry.

Often, a copy of the death certificate is included in the probate paperwork, but there wasn't one in the file Kath sent me. Although a copy of the certificate is required before all the probate processes can begin, a copy isn't always included in the final probate file, and that appeared to be the case in this instance.

Damn! Both the Finchley marriage and his death are too recent to easily obtain copies of the certificates… except if I am a direct family member. Of course, I wasn't, but might I be able to engineer it to appear otherwise?

'Shouldn't be too hard…,' I told myself, and promptly set about planning how to do it. In the end, I decided that all that was needed was a little skullduggery and proceeded accordingly. After all, so many lies had been told along the way, one or two more shouldn't make any difference. Besides, as a researcher engaged by Gladys to write her mother's story and by Gabby to research her maternal family history, I was simply doing what I was engaged to do. Several minutes later, I submitted requests for both the marriage and death certificates, citing family history research as the reason for the requests. When no questions were forthcoming, I felt somewhat relieved.

"Right… Well, that deals with the Finchley side of things, but what about Mary Finchley?" I asked the universe.

Was this Mary Finchley none other than Daphne Mary McDonald/Tremaine/Finchley? If my suspicions were correct, she, too, should have died some time ago … but when and where? The other big question is about which surname she used after her marriage to Darcy. Did she change to Finchley or remain Tremaine? I began a new search of death indexes, checking all her known surnames. The thought that niggled me all through my searches of the indexes was whether any of the information provided by any of the certificates bore any resemblance to the truth. So far, that pair had shown scant regard for the truth, and it's probably not difficult to work out why.

After all, if assumptions are correct, the woman Finchley married supposedly disappeared and was declared deceased, yet here she was still alive years later. Unfortunately, if my assumption that 'Lois Parker was Daphne McDonald' is correct, it undermines the scenario I created regarding what happened back then. And it poses another huge question: *Why did Jane pay Darcy Wilson that second huge sum of money if it wasn't for him to arrange Lois Parker's 'disappearance'?*

Now that I think about that, I suppose, perhaps he did orchestrate her disappearance, but not in the manner that everyone believed at the time. Had Wilson and Parker developed something of a relationship while Jane employed her? Perhaps when Jane approached Wilson to help Parker disappear, Wilson worked out how he could boost his bank balance while continuing his relationship with Parker. If none of that is true, and Wilson didn't spirit Parker away somehow, then why did Jane pay him so much money, and what really happened? Two things remain clear: Jane paid Wilson a substantial sum of money, and a major search and coronial inquest was held following Parker's (or D M McDonald's) disappearance.

Another aspect of this subterfuge is whether the two of them were together from the moment she 'disappeared' or if she immediately fled to somewhere else and they linked up later. Somehow, I don't picture them waiting around separately until after Daphne McDonald was declared deceased. A strange but compelling thought occurred to me, and moments later, it had me out of the house and heading to the library.

"What year…?" I murmured as I stood in front of the shelves with the electoral rolls. It was an unlikely chance, but my excitement was increasing.

I second-guessed myself as I selected a roll for a local council election and carried it to a table. Although Kennedy's General Store was still trading at the time, and Darcy Wilson, the then owner, was living in the flat above the store, the election was held about halfway between when McDonald disappeared and when Kennedy's Store closed down. There was no real logic to my choice, but I told myself it was as good a time as any other. Initially, there were no surprises.

Darcy Wilson was registered as an elector, and his address was given as above the store. So far, so good. Now for the interesting part, but under what name should I search for her? After all the fuss and bother about her disappearance, I doubted she would be using her McDonald surname. So, what about her Lois Parker name? I struck out on that one. That left me with the Tremaine surname to try. As I flicked back through the roll, a rogue thought slammed in, almost stunning me: *Why would the woman, regardless of what name she was using, even bother to register as an elector, particularly if she was intent on staying 'disappeared'?*

My scrutiny of all the surnames beginning with T had me almost at the end of that alphabet section when it leapt out at me. There it was, the Tremaine surname. But it was for a Lois Tremaine, housekeeping, whose address was the same as that of Kennedy's Store. I read the entry several times before finally convincing myself it was the woman I was searching for. The different name threw me for a moment, but the fact that she bothered to register at all completely baffled me. A bit stunned, I remained seated at the table with the roll open in front of me.

Clear thinking returned, and I realised I had two courses of action to choose between. I could assume the couple had been together since her disappearance, or I could continue to search the electoral rolls for Lois Tremaine's first appearance in them. The latter option won, and I spent the next few minutes checking all the earlier rolls for elections held after her disappearance. Lois Tremaine's first appearance was at the next election about 12 months after her disappearance. I left the library still a bit dazed.

How brazen the pair had been amazed me all the way home. I took a coffee onto my back deck and spent some time pondering my discovery. Slowly, I realised that their actions were not so much brazen as necessary. If Tremaine were indeed a live-in housekeeper for Wilson in the flat above the Store, the community would have known of her and even seen her around the place. I'm sure they would have been circumspect and cautious about her being seen too often – or by anyone who might have recognised her from before her disappearance. How difficult was it to radically change your appearance in those days? I didn't have a clue, but I suspected the lady in question did a fine job of it.

While it was nothing more than guesswork, I assumed the couple moved away from the district as soon as the Store closed down. Did they continue their roles as employer and housekeeper, or did they pose as a married couple? The answer to that probably lay in the electoral rolls of wherever they next established their lives … But where was that? Indications were either Sydney or Brisbane. After some thought, I decided it was important, but it could wait until later. There were more interesting aspects of the couple's lives to investigate first. Despite that, as I drove home, I knew my genealogical researcher friend, Kath Manwaring, would receive another call in the near future. After all, she almost haunts the archives, and on one of her visits, she might check the Sydney area electoral rolls for me.

Later that evening, as I prepared a casserole for dinner, Diana Beatson came to mind. I had used Diana a few times over the years when I needed research for articles I was writing. She was the Brisbane equivalent of Kath Manwaring and spent her days in the Queensland State Archives.

With the casserole for dinner organised, I escaped to my home office to check my emails… And found myself hoping Warren didn't stay too long tonight. The various certificates I had ordered had arrived.

Chapter 25

I was out of bed much earlier than usual this morning. There was much to do, not the least of which was adding all the recently received information to my people's timelines and stories. Breakfast was no more than a formality that was over in a blink.

As I sat perched behind my desk in my home office, waiting for my computer to fire up, I idly wondered about Gladys Tremaine and how she might react to the story I was putting together about her mother. Regardless of her existing feelings, the picture of her mother created by my research is unlikely to improve her feelings about her. If I were more generous, I might suggest that being abandoned by her mother at such a young age probably resulted in a better life for the child. I had discovered no evidence of anything even vaguely maternal in Daphne Mary (MacDonald) Tremaine's make-up.

"It's all starting to come together … I think … But it is a slow, painful process," I thought aloud as I studied the timeline I initially created for Gabby's project.

Like the proverbial Topsy, the timeline had grown exponentially to include a 'branch line' containing the Daphne Mary McDonald information. If the two genealogists currently ferreting out information for me have any amount of success, it could be possible to close the investigation down within the next day or so. That still leaves the question of when to discuss her mother with Gladys Tremaine. I'm still not sure how much she really wants to know. She says she wants to know everything, but there's a hollow ring to it when she says it.

My phone demanded my attention. I checked the caller ID and hesitated. "God, that's spooky," I whispered, wondering how my thoughts could have flown to Gladys so quickly.

"Gladys, nice of you to call. Is everything all right? Is there something I can help you with?"

"Well, I think it might be more a case of me being able to help you. I know you're busy, but I've found something that I think might interest you."

"Sounds intriguing. What have you found?"

"That's still a bit of a mystery, I'm afraid, and it probably will remain that way until I get the thing open."

She had my full attention, but she wasn't making much sense. After several questions that failed to elicit anything worthwhile from her, my planned morning abandoned, I was on my way to Gladys' cottage. All the way, common sense kept telling me it was a waste of time and reminded me of all I could be doing at home this morning. How wrong could it be?

No time was wasted. As I marched up to her front door, she flung it open and waved me inside. I stopped a short distance inside and turned to face her.

"What has happened, Gladys?"

Did she look excited or frightened? Not knowing what to say, or not say, I allowed Gladys to control the conversation I hoped would be forthcoming.

"It started a couple of days ago when I noticed a couple of loose floorboards out the back there beyond the kitchen." She pointed to a small, closed-in area attached between the kitchen and the back door that might once have been used as a sleep-out. "Loose floorboards are dangerous for an old lady like me. It's easy enough for me to trip these days without loose floorboards."

"You're right, but I don't think you called to tell me you had loose floorboards. I think I see some new boards out there, so the problem appears to be fixed. Is there more to this story that I should know?"

"Of course… I wouldn't have called you about floorboards. I called a carpenter, and he dealt with them. I called you about what he and his team found when they ripped up the boards. He assessed the boards as needing replacement. His team arrived and removed the old boards. That's when we discovered it." She beamed at me when she finished speaking, until I said I had no idea what she was talking about.

"Come through. I'll show you." She led me through to the area of new boards and indicated a trapdoor set in the floor. "There wasn't a trapdoor there before. The whole area was covered with just long boards. When they ripped up the old boards, they discovered a small room underneath – a small cellar, I suppose you'd call it. It was empty… Well, it was empty, except for that," she said, pointing at a small metal object in the far corner.

"Is it some sort of metal trunk or small filing cabinet?" It was immediately apparent that it was old, had not been well-maintained, and was covered in dirt and other crud accumulated over time.

"A filing cabinet… The front of it is facing that way. The carpenter and his team brought it up out of the cellar. What a job that was. They cleaned the front off for me, but couldn't open it. It's probably locked, and I don't have a key."

"What do you think might be in it?" Gladys shook her head and shrugged. "Okay… Well, what do you know about it? Who put it there and when?"

"I didn't know there was a cellar, never mind a filing cabinet that's been down there for God knows how long. I think it's my mother's doing, but when or why she put it there, I don't know. All I know is that I'm curious about what's in it. Any ideas on how we might achieve that?"

A quick call to a locksmith friend of mine brought him and his offsider to the cottage. After asking the same questions as I had asked Gladys and receiving the same responses, he announced that, due to its condition, opening it could result in some damage. I was relieved when Gladys assured him she wasn't concerned about it being damaged. I wasn't too happy when he told Gladys and me to go and have a cup of tea while he and his offsider got to work.

After about an hour, a cup of tea, and more conversation about Gladys' childhood, I was relieved when he called Gladys to join them. Adopting appropriate decorum, I allowed Gladys to go first – and followed right on her heels. The two men stood, hands on hips, admiring their handiwork.

"There you are, Ma'am, all done. Now, is there anything else you'd like us to do before we go?" I followed Gladys around to the front of the cabinet and peered over her shoulder.

The cabinet was jammed full of paper. Unlike filing cabinets, it didn't comprise drawers with multiple hanging files. In this cabinet, folders, envelopes, and notebooks were stacked on top of one another in no particular order, filling every available space on its two shelves.

"It's more like a safe than a filing cabinet," I murmured as I gazed at its contents.

"Is it safe to remove all that?" Gladys asked. "Just look at the state of it. Are we likely to come down with some terminal disease if we touch it?" It was a good question and one that sent me dashing out to fetch masks and gloves from the box of equipment I keep in my car.

We spread a sheet over the dining room table before carrying bundle after bundle of material from the cabinet to the table. Although all the paper was old and some of it quite fragile, we managed to empty the cabinet without any major disasters. Then, as Gladys rattled around in the kitchen making us lunch, I sorted it all into piles of similar-looking material. We returned to the dining room after a hasty lunch, and the real treasure hunt began.

By the end of the day, we were both covered in grime and the crud of ages, but so many treasures had been discovered. Gladys was quite emotional as we sipped the day's final cup of tea. She had concentrated on letters and photos, learning a great deal and gaining a deeper understanding of her family, in particular, her parents' marriage. It was painful for her to have so many of the beliefs she had held fast to for so long completely shattered. Selfishly, I knew it had made my job easier when the time came to share what I had learned.

My interest was centred on the mountain of folders, but of particular interest were the envelopes that looked as though they might contain legal documents. Some did, some didn't. Some legal documents were found in the folders. The ones of particular interest were the contracts. They related to various aspects of Daphne Mary McDonald's life: purchasing the cottage, buying a vehicle, and publishing agreements with Tremaine Publishing House. Some documents related to events that occurred before she arrived in this town. While some were of little or no interest to me, others provided answers to many of the questions that haunted me from the start of Gabby's project. All of them exposed hitherto unknown facts about others' lives.

It was heady stuff that filled my mind long after I returned home. I'm sure Warren was relieved to go home that night to give his ears a rest after I'd talked nonstop from the moment he arrived. After he left, my night began in earnest. I had so much information, so many details, to incorporate into my story of not just Jane's pirated manuscripts, but also the lives of those so closely associated with those manuscripts, and with Jane herself.

A late start this morning, after a long but rewarding night, had me struggling to make any progress until I checked my emails. My genealogist friends had come good. Missing pieces of the puzzle were no longer missing. I now knew so much of the story, but the more you know, the more you realise how much you still don't know. Although I'd accepted that I'd never know it all, it was frustrating. Thanks to the cabinet the carpenters found at Gladys' house, many niggling questions were answered. I would now spend the next couple of days compiling a story for Gabby and Gladys.

Copies of contracts (such as they were) found in Gladys' filing cabinet confirmed some of my earliest assumptions. Such confirmation did not enhance my opinion of Jane Creighton or Darcy Wilson. Henry Finchley and Daphne Mary McDonald (in any of her versions) did not score well either.

After slaving away all day and asking Warren not to come tonight, I had managed to commit most of the story to paper. Yes, there would be quite a bit of tidying up to do, but who did what when (and in some cases, why) was now recorded in a way that made sense.

The story as it now stands:

More than a century ago, Henry Finchley, the founder of Ravenshead Estates, had a wandering eye that settled on his young, single scullery maid, Erin O'Malley. When she became pregnant, Henry 'bought' her a husband, the unmarried, much older Thomas Wilson, a longtime employee at Ravenshead. Wilson received a promotion and was given a cottage. The marriage was a disaster. The husband was abusive and cruel, and Erin lost the baby. Consumed by anger and guilt about the situation he had created, Henry arranged for Wilson to meet with a fatal 'accident'. His widow, Erin, continued to live in the cottage and work at Ravenshead. In 1912, more than a year after her husband's death, she gave birth to a son. The baby, named Darcy Wilson, was registered as illegitimate. He was brought back and lived with his mother at Ravenshead.

At that time, Henry's only legitimate child, Jane, was about 13 years old. Possibly as a result of recent events, Henry and his wife, Martha, were not on the best of terms, and he was not at all happy that his daughter, Jane, spent all day, every day, in her room with her governess, Miss Glover. Martha explained that Jane was a talented writer, and her governess was nurturing her writing talent. Henry, however, was having none of it. Jane should be in the office, learning how to run the place that she would one day inherit. He forbade Jane from any further writing, and Miss Glover was sent packing. All he managed to achieve, apart from domestic discord, was to force Jane to become a covert writer. She assiduously continued to write a daily journal, but developed a personal, cryptic style that prevented her journals from being read by anyone who found them.

In 1917, Henry Finchley died unexpectedly, leaving his entire estate to his only (legitimate) child, Jane Finchley, then aged about 18. At the time, Darcy Wilson was about five years old. He and his mother continued to live in the cottage at Ravenshead, and his mother, Erin, continued to work there as a domestic servant. Jane's inheritance came with provisos: Erin Wilson must be allowed to continue to work and live at Ravenshead; Young Darcy Wilson must be extended every assistance to achieve a sound education; any arrangements regarding Henry's wife, Martha's, future life were for Jane to arrange as she wished. Regarding the latter, it appears Jane allowed Martha to continue living in a small apartment attached to the main house at Ravenshead. She was paid a small annual allowance in addition to having free access to domestic servants.

Henry's solicitor, who had handled the probate, continued to assist Jane with the running of Ravenshead. George Creighton, who had managed the property for some years prior to Henry's death, was retained as manager. Over the years since his birth, Jane and the young Darcy Wilson had become close friends, and that relationship continued and strengthened after Henry's death.

The family always hoped, and had some loose arrangement in place with the owners of the neighbouring property, that Jane would marry their second son. Jane had other ideas. The problem disappeared when the young man in question didn't return from the war. Jane, confident in making her own decisions by then, chose to marry her manager, George Creighton, despite his being much older, and her mother considering him unsuitable.

Jane married George Creighton in 1925, and their only child, Amelia, was born in late 1927. Whether Jane's marriage had some unsettling impact on Darcy Wilson is unclear, but 12 months later, Darcy was involved with a bad crowd and in trouble with the law. He avoided jail time when the court was told Wilson had found gainful employment. Not long before the end of 1926, Jane entered into an agreement with Richard Louis Kennedy, the owner of Kennedy's General Store, to forego dividends on half of her small number of shares in the Store in return for Kennedy employing Darcy Wilson. At the start of January 1927, Wilson commenced duties as a storeman. He later progressed to the position of delivery driver, making deliveries to the various properties in the area.

In his capacity as Kennedy's delivery driver, he visited Ravenshead every fortnight to deliver supplies. Such visits always included morning tea with Jane. Their relationship continued and strengthened over the years, even after Darcy began helping to run the Store and was no longer a regular visitor to Ravenshead. From the time of his employment, Wilson no longer lived at Ravenshead, as the long daily commute rendered that impossible. He then resided at a boarding house in town. Erin Wilson continued to occupy the cottage on Ravenshead for some time after Darcy moved to town, but then left the property. Nothing further is known about her.

The Creightons did quite well for themselves. When times were hard during the early 1930s, they purchased additional portions of neighbouring properties when the owners found themselves in dire financial straits. By then, Henry Finchley's loyal solicitor, who had assisted Jane when she inherited Ravenshead, had passed away. When the Creightons began buying additional property, George insisted they use his solicitor, and as was the custom of the day, that solicitor would deal only with George, and not a woman… And as Jane would discover later, it was much to George's advantage.

History appears to have repeated itself when George developed an interest in a young widow residing in a cottage just across the fence on a neighbouring property. Details of how that situation progressed are unknown, but in 1934, when supposedly camping overnight with the fencing team to check their progress, George failed to return as expected. Two days later, his body was discovered. The subsequent coronial inquest determined that George had died an accidental death after he came off his horse. That's when life really turned sour for Jane.

She discovered that, by some doubtful process, all of the additional lands they had acquired were held solely in George's name. In addition, she discovered that ownership of all the original Ravenshead lands she had inherited had also been transferred to George. As George's will had left everything to his daughter, Amelia, Jane found herself a widow with nothing at age 35. Amelia put in place a similar arrangement for her mother, just as Jane had established one for her mother, Martha. The difference was that Jane continued to live in the big house, while Amelia took over the apartment.

A critical piece of evidence was not presented at the coronial inquest into George's death. If it had been, a verdict of accidental death would have been highly unlikely. Just days before George supposedly rode out to the fencing camp, but spent the night with his lady friend, Jane paid Darcy Wilson a significant sum of money. As soon as a verdict on George's death was issued, Darcy Wilson bought a half share in Kennedy's General Store. A document later found in hidden files confirmed the payment to Wilson had been *the amount agreed for specific services rendered to George Creighton.* At no time during his life had George Creighton had any significant involvement with Darcy Wilson.

With George gone and her daughter Amelia now running Ravenshead, Jane's time was unencumbered by concerns about the property or looking after her husband. Her writing flourished, and as her collection of handwritten manuscripts increased, she engaged the services of Miss Lois Parker as a typist to transcribe them. The arrangement appeared to have worked well until Jane attended a fete at one of the district's big houses. She was drawn to the wares on a temporarily unattended bookstall. While perusing one of the books, Jane discovered it was one of her manuscripts that had been pirated and published illegally. Further investigation of the books on the stall discovered several more of her manuscripts. Her only action at the time was to purchase copies of the pirated book. A couple of days later, she confronted Miss Parker about the pirated manuscripts and terminated Parker's employment.

Nothing more was heard of Miss Parker. However, at about the same time as Parker disappeared from the landscape, Daphne Mary McDonald, owner of a cottage in town, also disappeared. McDonald's car was eventually located abandoned in a neighbouring township, but no trace of the woman was ever found, despite an extensive and prolonged search. It was longer than the usual seven years before McDonald was declared deceased. At the time, no connection appears to have been established between McDonald, Parker, and the publisher of Jane's pirated manuscripts, Tremain Publishing House. In reality, McDonald and Parker were the same person, and McDonald was the estranged wife of Randolph Tremaine, the owner of Tremaine Publishing House. The Tremaines had one child, a daughter, Gladys Tremaine, who eventually inherited what remained of her father's estate as well as her mother's cottage here in town.

McDonald's disappearance (or Parker's if you prefer) officially remains an unsolved missing person case. That might be reasonable, except for a couple of things that happened. Just prior to sacking Miss Parker, Jane paid Darcy Wilson another substantial sum of money, which, a few days later, he used to buy the remaining half of Kennedy's General Store. Wilson then moved to live in the flat above the store. When the search for the missing D M McDonald failed to find any trace of the woman, an inquest handed down an open verdict. The consensus was that, by whatever means, McDonald was dead, but unless a body were discovered in the meantime, there would be a seven-year wait for her to be declared deceased.

About a month after she paid Wilson the second large sum of money, and the open verdict on McDonald's disappearance had been handed down, Jane noted in her diary *Got it right this time. No loose ends to worry us.*

Darcy Wilson, as the sole proprietor of Kennedy's General Store, continued to trade for some time, but development eventually reached the area. It brought with it larger firms offering a wider, more affordable range of goods, and eventually led to the closure of Kennedy's Store. The old store's building disappeared from the landscape, and so did Darcy Wilson… Records indicate that he employed a live-in housekeeper while residing in the flat above the store. That housekeeper appears on the electoral rolls as *Lois Tremaine.*

It appears Jane paid Darcy Wilson a considerable amount of money for something that never occurred. Either that, or the intended victim of the conspiracy joined the Living Dead and continued living her complicated life for many years.

Following the closure of Kennedy's General Store and Wilson's departure from the district, he changed his name. Perhaps out of a long-held resentment of his illegitimacy, he became Darcy Henry Finchley, with 'Henry Finchley' clearly a recognition of his paternity. Later, when domiciled in Brisbane, he married his former housekeeper, Lois Tremaine, who had now become *Mary* Tremaine. Upon his death, his wife, Mary, inherited his entire estate and became almost a millionaire.

The search continues to discover when and where Mary (Tremaine) Finchley died and who benefited from her death. For the moment, though, the first draft of the story is complete.

Now, how do I share the story with both Gabby and Gladys, as it is part of both of their family histories? I believe neither of them is prepared for what I have to tell them.

The End

Also by the Author

Revenge is not Enough
Harbour Plaza: built on dreams
On the Way to Istanbul
An Unsuitable House
A Land Too Far
Paradise Interrupted
Unwelcome Mail
By Any Other Name
House of Secrets
A Life of Tea and Sugar
A Life of Seizing Opportunities

About the Author

KAYLA DANOLI spent her early years traipsing around Australia and then Europe with her parents, and then completed her tertiary education in England before returning to Australia. There were a variety of jobs in various parts of Queensland before eventually making her way towards the coast. She now lives in a small coastal town on the Queensland coast where she works part-time on a charter vessel.

In the early days after settling in that small town, to fill in her spare time, both when at home and while on cruises, she started scribbling down her ideas for stories. These days, she writes whenever time permits. Her *Harbour Plaza* series, previously released in 2015 as monthly eBook episodes, was updated, extended and released in 2016 as the *Harbour Plaza: built on dreams* compilation. *Revenge is not Enough,* also released in 2016, was her first full-length novel.

Forbidden, Hidden, Betrayed is Kayla's twelfth novel and presents another family saga to explore.

Discover more about Kayla and her work by visiting

www.eaglemountbooks.com.au/kayla-danoli

or contact her at

admin@eaglemountbooks.com.au